HEART OF THE WOLF

ALSO BY ALICIA MONTGOMERY

THE TRUE MATES SERIES

Fated Mates

Blood Moon

Romancing the Alpha

Witch's Mate

Taming the Beast

Tempted by the Wolf

THE LONE WOLF DEFENDERS SERIES

Killian's Secret

Loving Quinn

All for Connor

THE TRUE MATES STANDALONE NOVELS

Holly Jolly Lycan Christmas

A Mate for Jackson: Bad Alpha Dads

TRUE MATES GENERATIONS

A Twist of Fate

Claiming the Alpha

Alpha Ascending

A Witch in Time

Highland Wolf

Daughter of the Dragon

Shadow Wolf

A Touch of Magic

Heart of the Wolf

THE BLACKSTONE MOUNTAIN SERIES

The Blackstone Dragon Heir

The Blackstone Bad Dragon

The Blackstone Bear

The Blackstone Wolf

The Blackstone Lion

The Blackstone She-Wolf

The Blackstone She-Bear

The Blackstone She-Dragon

HEART OF THE WOLF

TRUE MATES GENERATIONS BOOK 9

ALICIA MONTGOMERY

CHAPTER ONE

"WHAT'S A PRETTY THING LIKE YOU DOING IN A PLACE like this?"

Isabelle Anderson flipped her long, dark glossy locks over her shoulder as she turned around toward the source of the voice. *Oh God*, she thought with a matching mental eye roll.

The man grinning at her was cute, she supposed, but attractive men salivating over her was an everyday occurrence. She had barely walked past the bouncers, and it was starting already. She was not in the mood. Not tonight.

Ugh. Security *really* needed to be more careful of who they let in. Although Blood Moon was mostly a Lycan club, a couple of humans still tended to wander in, and there really was no reason to keep them out without outing themselves. The world outside didn't really know about the existence of wolf shifters living among them, and it had been that way for centuries.

Punishment from the Lycan High Council for revealing their secret was severe. *This guy's fashion sense and cloying cologne were a bigger crime,* she snickered to herself. His distinct lack of scent meant he was definitely human, according to her Lycan senses. Her she-wolf sneered at him, at the audacity that this human dared come near them.

"You'll have to try much harder than *that*," she said in a disinterested voice.

He looked taken aback, obviously thinking she would fall at his feet. *Not in that outfit*, she thought distastefully. Not even one classic piece. Did this guy even *live* in Manhattan? *Brooklyn*, she guessed. Or Queens. *Yikes*.

"Did I say, pretty?" the man said nervously. "I meant gorgeous. Like a goddess from heaven—"

She snorted. "You think I haven't heard that before?"

The guy made some sound of protest, but she ignored him and made her way to the bar. Thankfully, it wasn't crowded. It was early yet, not even dinnertime, so the club was sparse; usually, it was packed wall-to-wall with young, single, and attractive people, all bumping and grinding to the beat of the current popular dance tune.

As a rule, she didn't show up to any club before eleven. But tonight, her parents were hosting a dinner for some VIP and pressed her to come. *Another boring dinner party where boring people talked about politics or finance.* She hadn't yet decided if she was going, but since she lived in the same building as her parents, she ducked out early before they could nag her about it. Plus, she really could use a drink. Of course, as a Lycan, it took a lot of alcohol to get her drunk, but she did enjoy that short buzz after and feeling so grown up ordering a drink at a bar. Speaking of which ...

"Can I get a vodka martini?" she said to the bartender.

The bartender chuckled. "Slumming it tonight, Ms. Anderson?"

Her eyes narrowed. Definitely Lycan. Her wolf could sense it. But then again, most of the staff here were shifters. "Excuse me?" He knew who she was. *Of course he did.* She spent almost every weekend here, plus her father, Grant Anderson, owned this club, *and* he was also the Alpha of New York.

"Why aren't you in the VIP section?" He nodded at the cordoned off area at the other end of the dance floor. "You could be having drinks served to you like you usually do, instead of having to elbow your way to the bar like the rest of the unwashed masses."

How dare you, she wanted to scream. The employees here probably gossiped about her all the time. One word about his rudeness, and she could have him fired. But she really didn't have the energy tonight. "I didn't feel like it," she said with a shrug. "Can you make it a double? And hurry up, will you?" Her nostrils flared as she stared at him.

The humor left his expression. "Coming right up, Ms. Anderson."

With a disinterested sigh, she took her phone out of her purse. As usual, it was blowing up with notifications from across her social media platforms, probably comments from her last post before she left the house. She had taken a photo of her outfit for the evening, a short white bandeaux dress, white fur coat, five-inch white heels—all couture from head to toe, of course—and posted it online. But sadly, even the hundreds of likes and comments from her followers weren't enough to cheer her up. Swiping them away, she checked her inbox.

I'm almost there, read the last message from Maxine Muccino, her cousin and best friend, followed by a liberal amount of smiling and sweating emojis. Isabelle had texted Maxine an hour ago to "get your ass out of the house and meet me at Blood Moon."

"Yeah, right." While Isabelle loved Maxine with all her heart, her cousin was one of those people who texted that they were "around the corner" when really, they were just getting out of bed. Which meant she'd be alone for at least another hour.

A strange feeling washed over her, and the hairs on the back of neck prickled. It felt like someone was watching her. Which was weird because she was used to people looking at her, but this was different. Before she could figure out who was watching her, the sound of glass clinking on top of the bar caught her attention.

"Here you go." The bartender nodded at the cocktail glass in front of her.

"Thanks." She slid a bill at him. "Keep the change." Not bothering to wait for the guy to thank her, she walked away from the crowded bar. But where to go? Nowhere really. So, she stood at one of the empty cocktail tables at the edge of the dance floor, set her purse on the top, and sipped at her drink. *Maybe I should just go home.*

"Oh God." The thought of spending an evening by herself in her apartment made her knock back the rest of her drink in one gulp. *You're only twenty-one,* she reminded herself. She would rather die than be alone at home like some loser, just because she was heartbroken. *He's just a guy.* With a snap of her fingers, she could have any man on his knees, panting after her.

Okay, so maybe Zac Vrost wasn't just *any* guy. He was the perfect man—tall, blond, and hot—plus he was probably going to inherit a big chunk of the Vrost family fortune, not to mention his father was Beta of the New York clan.

They would have made a gorgeous couple—him, Nick and Cady Vrost's favorite golden boy, her, the darling youngest daughter of not one, but *two* Alphas. It should have been a match made in heaven.

At least it was, until Astrid Jonasson *ruined* it all.

How Zac could have picked that ... that ... fashion-challenged little nobody was beyond her. Astrid and her family didn't even rank high in the Lycan hierarchy nor were they long-standing members of the New York clan. She probably wouldn't know what bronzer was if it hit her in the head and constantly wore gross second-hand clothing from the Salvation Army.

Yet, Zac picked Astrid. It was like shopping at Zara instead of Prada, or vacationing in Daytona Beach instead of the Maldives, or, she thought with a shudder, drinking boxed wine instead of champagne.

And they had just gotten married two weeks ago. The thought made her wish she had got herself a second drink.

Of course, the only thing that soothed her ego at losing out to someone who probably couldn't even pronounce Christian Louboutin was the fact that Zac and Astrid were True Mates. It was something no one can deny. And when Maxine asked if she was depressed about losing Zac to Astrid, she laughed it off. "Well, fate intended them to be together. How could I possibly compete with that?"

That didn't mean it didn't hurt any less. Especially when she had her heart set on her own happy ever after with Zac. It had been so clear in her mind—he would work all day and go to meetings, and she could stay home and lunch with the ladies while focusing on her thriving social media modeling career. Maybe she'd start her own charity. Something with dogs or cats or other cute animals. And when she was ready, have a pup or two. *I would have looked so cute in maternity clothes and matching mommy-and-me outfits.* And once he or she was born, she could foist them off on the nanny, and she could work on getting her pre-pregnancy body back.

But now ...

I'm young, hot, and every man wants me, she reminded herself. She really needed to stop moping over Zac. He was too old for her anyway. And she was way too young and free to settle down.

Biting her lip, she marched toward the door. The cold blast of air as she stepped outside felt like a cool balm. As a Lycan, her body adjusted to the temperature easily, and while she didn't need to close her fur coat, she did it anyway out of reflex. She was always careful—as all Lycans were—to ensure none of the humans suspected that wolf shifters were living among them. Her father was especially cautious in protecting them from unwanted attention.

Unfortunately, that was what they had been clashing about recently—because how was she supposed to amass even more social media followers to advance her career when they wouldn't let her do any media interviews, photo shoots, or magazine covers?

Ugh. Maybe I won't go to that dinner after all. She checked her phone again. *Where the hell was Maxine?* If she had her driver, she could have sent him to fetch her. But unfortunately, the Lycan drivers and bodyguards assigned to her were loyal to her father, and then he could have easily tracked her down and demanded she attended that dinner.

Thus, she had to take a—*shudder*—cab here all by herself, and now, she'd have to take another one to leave. But the street was empty, and there was no taxi in sight. *Ugh, where are these cab drivers when you need them?*

Suddenly, that feeling from earlier in the club came back. It wasn't just the hair on the back of her neck that stood up, but also on her arms. Her wolf, too, went very still.

Pivoting on her heel, she turned around. Her breath caught in her throat when she realized someone really was watching her. A tall figure was casually leaning against the wall, hands in his pockets, looking straight at her. An unknown thrill pulsed down her spine as they locked gazes. Then her wolf did something unusual—it leaned its ears forward, front paws extending, then let out an excited yip.

Surprise flashed across the man's face for a brief second, meaning he sensed her wolf too. *Lycan,* then. But who was he?

As the daughter of the Alpha, she knew most of the Lycans in New York—those worth knowing anyway. But she would have definitely remembered meeting this man before.

His hair seemed to have all shades of brown and blond mixed together. Like most Lycans, he was tall and well-built, but his face—it was like the face of an angel, half-covered with a beard that wasn't overly thick, but enough to give him a dangerous, rough edge. Arrogantly, uncommonly handsome, pretty even. But there were definitely some bad boy vibes coming from him, judging from the two nose studs marring his almost perfect face and the tattoos curling out from his shirt that extended past his wrists, not to mention the well-scuffed riding boots, tight jeans, even tighter shirt, and the leather jacket he wore.

Wow, he wasn't even trying to pass for human in the middle of winter.

"Are you gonna stare at me all night, princess, or are you going to say hello?"

The deep, gravelly voice sent heat straight to her lower stomach, and her wolf yowled. She, however, did not appreciate his crassness. Angel? What was she thinking? Fallen angel, maybe. Lucifer himself, who clawed his way up from hell.

With a short, *harumpph*, she turned around and fished her phone out of her pocket. *I should have downloaded Uber before I left. Or had Maxine teach me how to use it.* Hopefully a cab would pass by soon, and she could be anywhere but here.

"Didn't anyone teach you it's rude to stare at people, then ignore them when they call you out?"

He'd moved so swiftly, she hadn't realized he was right behind her until she felt the warmth of his breath by her ear. She stiffened her spine and turned her head up at him. However, when she stared up into his eyes, all thought left her head.

His eyes—were they green or gold? She couldn't quite say. Maybe both. Gold in the center with large flecks of green. Her knees went weak, and for a second, he seemed taken aback again, but he composed himself quickly. Much quicker than she did because she stumbled backward.

A strong, muscled arm wrapped around her waist, pulling her up against him. An involuntary gasp escaped her mouth as she was pressed up against a warm, hard body. Though she was wearing her highest heels, her face was still at level with his chest. When she took in a deep breath, she got a whiff of his masculine scent—rain, musk, and leather. A shock went through her as an unfamiliar sensation coursed through her veins. She'd never felt anything like it before, but it was something she could only describe as hunger. But not for food.

"Let go of me." Unfortunately, she said it in a much breathier tone than she'd intended. "Please."

Gold-green eyes burned with challenge, but his grip loosened. "Whatever you want, princess."

She disentangled herself from him, but it didn't stop her heart from thudding wildly against her rib cage. Her wolf yowled unhappily at losing contact. *What the hell was going on?*

Straightening her shoulders and pulling her coat tighter around herself, she looked up at him. "I don't think I've seen you around here before. And I've met most of the New York and New Jersey Lycans." Usually, Lycans from one clan couldn't travel into another's without permission from the Alpha. But, since her mother was also the New Jersey Alpha, members of the two clans enjoyed free travel between territories.

He grabbed at the bottom of his shirt and pulled it up, exposing a set of defined abs. Her mouth went dry as a desert as she observed the taut, golden skin of his stomach, and the sprinkling of hair disappearing under the waistband of his jeans. A chuckle knocked her out of her daze, and she felt heat flood her cheeks.

A golden brow quirked up. "Had enough?"

The image of the wolf tattoo over his hip seared into her brain, and she spun around. So, he was a Lone Wolf. Lone Wolves were a special type of Lycan clan—or rather, they lacked a clan and territory. Most were nomadic, though some stayed put in neutral territory. They were, however, allowed to move within territories as long as they announced themselves should anyone ask them why they were in said territory or meet an Alpha.

"Sorry," he said scornfully. "You know, for getting my grubby Lone Wolf hands on ya."

Her heart clenched for whatever his situation was, but outrage bubbled within her. "Excuse me?" She whirled around to face him again. While admittedly, she could be particular about what she wore or where she went, she would never think less of anyone who had no control over what they were. "Do you think I'm one of those Lycans who look down on Lone Wolves? Just because I'm part of a clan doesn't mean I discriminate against those who aren't.

"There are many reasons someone might choose to go Lone Wolf, or more often than not, not have any choice at all, so I wouldn't be prejudiced against someone who might have gone through terrible circumstances. I'm sorry if you've had a bad experience with other clans, but you don't know New York, and *you don't know me.*"

He seemed taken aback. "Whoa, princess, don't get your panties in a bunch." He put his hands up in a defensive stance. "I didn't mean to get you all riled up."

Mist formed as she blew out a breath. She didn't mean to rant at him like that, but she hated it when people thought she was shallow and mean. Okay, she could be superficial sometimes, but she wasn't completely self-centered. Besides, one thing she hated was discrimination. Her own Grandpa Noah had been a Lone Wolf before he settled down with the Shenandoah clan, and he was the nicest person she knew.

"It's all right," she said with a toss of her hair. "What are you doing out here anyway?"

He shoved his hands in his pockets. "Saw you leaving. Wondered where you were off to."

So, he had been inside the club. Had he been checking her out since then? "Nowhere," she said glumly. "At least not until I can get a cab."

"It's colder than a well-digger's butt in January out here. Cabs are probably gonna be pretty scarce for a while," he drawled.

"Where are you from?" she asked. "Your accent ... southern?"

He shrugged. "From here and there. You know us Lone Wolves. Anyway, I should—"

"Give me a ride?" It was an impulse; one she couldn't stop. Nor was she sorry for asking him.

A blond brow lifted up. "Excuse me?"

"A ride."

The corners of his mouth curled up. "Are you sure you're old enough for my kind of ride, princess?"

Oh God. She didn't even realize ... ignoring the heat rising in her cheeks, she straightened her spine. "On your *bike*," she clarified. "And I'm twenty-one."

"How did you know I have one?" he challenged.

She pointed her chin down at his shoes. "My grandfather has the same kind of boots. He rides a Softail."

"Does he now?"

"So, are you just going to let me freeze here instead of offering me a ride home?" Oh God, what was she thinking, asking a total stranger for a ride? On his motorcycle? Did the bartender put more than vodka into that drink? Or was it that yummy masculine scent driving her wild and making her impulsive.

"You ain't exactly dressed for riding," he pointed out. As his gaze swept over her from head to toe, she felt like her body might spontaneously combust.

Oh dear.

Despite what most people thought of her, she wasn't exactly ... experienced. She'd made out with a couple of guys, maybe even had some of them feel her up, but the actual deed ... well, that was a whole other story. No one had ever felt right for her. Sure, she'd had a couple of puppy-love boyfriends back in high school, but long term wasn't her thing. "Collect and select," she'd always joked with Maxine. Besides, she couldn't even choose which shoes to match with her outfit, so how was she supposed to choose someone to sleep with for the first time?

But this man ... one look from him, and she was ready to explode. For the first time ever, she realized that what she was feeling was real, hot-blooded *lust*.

"I don't mind if you don't," she said, doing her best to disguise the tremor in her voice. "Of course, if you can't manage one female riding with you, then I suppose I could walk home."

His gaze pierced right into her, then the corners of his mouth turned up. "All right. Well, I can't let a poor, defenseless lady go home by herself." He motioned with his head to follow him, then started walking away from her. "Come on."

Oh, her she-wolf was practically panting after him. *Stop acting like some ... hussy,* she told it, though she followed the man anyway, teetering on her heels as she attempted to keep pace. Thank God he stopped about half a block away, right in front of a shiny black motorcycle parked on the street. Hopefully, he wouldn't ask her anything about bikes, because aside from Grandpa Noah's Harley, she had no frickin' clue about motorcycles.

He offered her a spare helmet after he put his on. "Here you go."

"Wait."

"What?" he asked impatiently.

"I don't even know your name."

His expression was pure exasperation, and he opened his mouth, then closed it quickly. "It's Ransom."

Ransom. It fit him so well, and she didn't know why. "I'm Isabelle."

He shoved the helmet into her hands. "Put it on, princess."

As she strapped the helmet to her head and secured the chin strap, she watched as Ransom swung a long leg over the bike and straddled it between his thighs. Despite the chill in the air, a bead of sweat formed between her breasts.

"Well, are you comin' or not?" he asked, head cocked to one side. "You're not chickening out on me, are ya?"

"No." She took two steps forward, trying to figure out how the hell she was going to get on that bike. *Should have thought this through, Isabelle,* she scolded herself. When he gave her an impatient glare, she shrugged and hiked her dress high up her thighs. She couldn't help but smile smugly as his eyes widened and nostrils flared, before turning away and bending his head down to check on something on his handlebars. *Ha.* While she wasn't experienced, she wasn't blind. She knew when someone wanted her.

Thankfully, she was able to swing her leg over the back of the bike and climb up on top, then settle behind him. She crossed her arms over her chest and drummed her fingers impatiently, waiting for him to go.

"Do you wanna fall off or what?" he asked without looking behind.

"Huh?"

"Grab on, princess."

"Grab on?"

"Yeah. To me."

"Right." Gingerly, she laid her palms on his broad back.

He snorted. "Not like that, princess." His hands grabbed hers and then wound her arms around his waist and pulled her forward. "Like this."

Electricity shot up her hand from where she touched him. Rather, where he was touching her because his hands were still wrapped over hers. His palms were so warm and rough, such a contrast to her own. He stiffened, then let go of her hands, relaxing as he gripped the handlebars. "Where do you live?"

Pressing her cheek against his back, she inhaled the scent from his well-worn leather jacket, which was mixed in with his own natural smell. "Have you been to New York before?"

"Can't say I have."

"How about I give you a tour first? Anywhere you've always wanted to see? The Empire State Building? Rockefeller Center? Times Square?"

"How about ... the Brooklyn Bridge?"

Her nose wrinkled. "The Brooklyn Bridge?"

"Yeah. Heard there was a park on the other side."

She smirked. "Only hipsters go to Brooklyn, and you don't seem like the hipster type to me."

He shrugged. "Just thought it would have a nice view of the city."

"Oh. I actually haven't been before. All right then. Let's go to the Brooklyn Bridge. Do you know how to get there?"

He nodded. "Hang on tight."

She did as he said and gripped him tighter as the bike roared to life and they sped on. Despite the freezing wind on the exposed bits of her skin, she wasn't cold, and it wasn't just her Lycan metabolism keeping her warm. Ransom had slipped her arms under his jacket and around his waist so she could feel every bump and muscle on his abdomen. Oh, how she wanted to run her fingers across them or maybe even slip her hand under his shirt to feel his bare skin.

Soon, they were crossing over the bridge. She held her breath, not because of the cold or how fast they were going, but because she'd never been out here at night. Or maybe she had, like when she was coming from or going to the airport, but it had always been in the back of a limo, and she never paid attention to what was outside.

But now, this moment ... everything seemed so much crisper and clearer as the frosty air prickled across her skin and woke up all her senses. The lights above them were lit up and reflected off the dark waters of the East River. If only she could find a way to bottle this moment and keep it forever.

As they finished crossing, the motorcycle turned right onto the off ramp before veering back toward the water. They slowed down when they reached a side street and stopped inside the park where they had a view of Manhattan. Ransom turned the engine off and engaged the kickstand.

"It's beautiful," she murmured as she got off the bike and straightened her dress. "I was born and raised here, but I don't think I've ever seen the city like this." All the tall buildings of Lower Manhattan were lit up, and the moon looked huge behind them.

"Gorgeous," he said.

The words made her shiver, and when she looked back, she realized he was looking at her. The blush on her cheeks made her turn away. Oh God, she was acting like some nerd. Ransom seemed so much more worldly compared to her. He was probably around Lucas's age, she guessed. Or Zac, who was a few months older than her brother. It seemed so ... exciting, being with an older man, and she had to act cooler or else he might think she was some dweeb.

"Do you want to have a closer look?" He nodded at the boardwalk.

"Sure."

They walked over, the silence enveloping them with each step. It was funny how she was so used to the noise of New York City that out here it was almost deafening. When they reached the boardwalk, Ransom planted his hands on the railing and looked straight ahead, his brows furrowing together.

"You look like you're deep in thought." She moved closer to him impulsively. "What are you thinking of?"

He turned to her. "Nothing you should know about."

"Oh?" She lifted a brow. "Why not?"

"Because it's inappropriate."

Now she was even more intrigued. Turning to him, she planted her hands on her hips. "Inappropriate for whom?"

"For princesses like you."

"Maybe I'm not what you think I am."

She thought he would ignore her or maybe even turn away, but to her surprise, he turned to face her and took a half step forward. His delicious scent filled her nostrils and drove her wolf crazy. Her heart pounded against her chest as he lifted his hand to caress her cheek. She barely had time to gasp when he bent his head and slotted his lips to hers.

This wasn't her first kiss, not by any means, but this felt like a first ... something. First time to feel like the whole world slowed down just for them. First time blood was pounding through her veins in excitement from the mere touch of his lips. First time she wanted anyone this bad.

His hand moved on her neck, digging his fingers through her hair to pull her head back, and at the same time, his tongue slid against her sealed lips to deepen the kiss. She didn't need more convincing as she opened her mouth, reveling in the taste and smell of him. His tongue touched the edge of her teeth, exploring as he pushed in deeper. His other hand, meanwhile, snaked around her waist and pulled, their bodies snapping together just right—a perfect fit.

The deep growl that rumbled from his chest made her press her thighs together as desire shot straight to her core. Her hand slid up to his chest, the wild thumping of his heart against his chest strangely satisfying. He shifted his hips, and when she felt a bulge brush against her stomach, she groaned and clung to him, her hands fisting around the thin fabric of his shirt. She arched against him, not knowing what she wanted, but only that she *needed* to be as close to him as possible.

His body froze against her, and he released her mouth, making her whimper pathetically at the loss. For a brief second, panic crossed his face, but then that cynical, handsome mask slid back into place. His hands dropped to his sides.

Her wolf whined and howled in protest, but she quickly recovered, smoothing her hands down her dress. *Act cool.* It would be mortifying to let him know how much the kiss shook her, especially now that he seemed totally unaffected. "That was nice," she said nonchalantly.

She expected him to react with outrage, like most guys when they realized they weren't getting farther than a kiss. To her surprise, the corner of his lips turned up. That smile, combined with the cynicism in his green-gold eyes was a devastating combination. "Sure. Nice." He shoved his hands in his pockets. "How about the ride home?"

A loud chime, followed by several successive ones, saved her the trouble of trying to find a witty reply. Grabbing her phone from her purse, she saw multiple messages on her notifications as Maxine was blowing up her phone.

I'm here!

Where are you??

The VIP tables are empty!

The bartender said you left! Where did you go??

Rolling her eyes, she tapped off a quick message to Maxine telling her to stay put. "That's my best friend. She's looking for me." She sighed. "I should get back to Blood Moon before she reports me missing or something. Can you give me a ride back there instead?"

He shrugged. "Sure."

They walked to his bike, and soon they were on the way back to Manhattan. She clung to him, not too tight, but she couldn't help but enjoy herself as she closed her eyes, pressed up against his strong back, her cheek resting on the buttery soft leather of his jacket.

It seemed impossible, this whole scenario. Never in a million years would she have thought that she would feel so attracted to someone in an instant—and someone like Ransom. He was magnetic, and all she wanted to do was be near him all the time. Her wolf, too, growled with pleasure.

A gasp escaped her mouth, and it was a good thing she was clinging so tight to him or else she would have fallen off. This instant attraction ... could it be possible that ...

The bike slowed down, and the engine sputtering to a stop interrupted her thoughts. She mentally shook her head, though her stomach flipped excitedly at the thoughts that had raced through her mind.

"We're here," he announced.

Reluctantly, she let go of him and hopped off the bike. "Aren't you coming in?" she asked when he didn't move.

He shook his head. "Not really my scene."

"But you had already been in there," she pointed out. "C'mon, I've got a table and bottle service."

He chuckled. "It's all right, princess, go ahead and meet your little friends. I'll be fine."

"But—" Her mouth snapped shut. Surely an older guy like him wouldn't want to be around some whiny, clingy girl. Her wolf scratched at her, not happy at the developing situation. *Cool your jets now.* "All right. Do you have a phone?"

"A what?"

"Cellphone. You know, a little device you carry around where you can call—"

"Yeah, I got one."

She held her hand out expectantly and raised a brow at him. His brows snapped together before realization hit him, and he handed her the device from his pocket. Tapping her number into the phone, she added herself as a contact on his phone, putting her name as "Isabelle Brooklyn Bridge" cheekily. "There," she said as she gave him back the phone. "Text me if you plan to stick around New York."

"Don't you want my number?" he asked.

She grinned at him before turning on her heel and sashayed toward the entrance. Oh no, she didn't text guys first. They texted *her*. And if her suspicions were true, then she wouldn't have to wait too long for him to contact her.

Despite her she-wolf's protests and whines, she managed to get back inside Blood Moon past the line of people waiting to get inside. Her cousin was already by the entrance, waiting for her.

"Isabelle!" Maxine's shriek was loud enough to pierce the music filling the club. "Where have you been?"

Her body practically vibrated with excitement. "Oh, Maxine, you'll never believe it ..."

CHAPTER TWO

WHAT THE FUCK AM I DOING?

It was a question Ransom had asked himself repeatedly for the last sixteen hours as he rode continuously from Kentucky, stopping only for gas and food. Now, as he stopped in New Jersey for a quick break, he could see the Manhattan skyline across the Hudson, a sight he hadn't seen in six months. So close, yet so far.

Manhattan. Home of the New York clan.

Growing up, even the thought of *those people* was enough to put him on edge. They were the ones to blame for where he was now. Or rather, *who* he was. And to think he'd never stepped foot in their territory until six months ago. Never wanted to.

But, for things to progress and move forward, it was a necessary evil. There was a plan in place, set in motion long ago.

A plan to get back at those who committed the atrocities that had forced him into this life.

A plan for revenge.

I should turn around.

His inner wolf, however, did not agree with that plan. It urged him to keep going, snapping at him each time he stopped or started to doubt himself.

"All right, all right," he groused. "We're here. You can stop yammering."

The animal had been relentless over the last six months, ripping up at him. Restless. Uncontrollable. Sometimes inconsolable. Pops had definitely noticed that something was not right. "What the hell has gotten your wolf all riled up?" he had asked one day. Ransom had merely shrugged him off because how was he supposed to explain that nothing seemed right or normal anymore, not since he'd met *her*. Isabelle Brooklyn Bridge.

He could barely count the number of times he'd stared at that name in his phone, finger hovering over the screen, wondering if he should message or call her. At night, he'd close his eyes, imagining her soft, curvy body against his, her delicious sweet and spicy scent—honey and cardamom—tickling his senses, or those gorgeous mismatched blue and green eyes.

And those sweet, soft lips. Lips that made him hungry for more. The moment they locked gazes and he looked into her eyes, he knew he was in trouble. That's why when she walked back into the club and away from him, he vowed to never contact her. But that didn't help at all.

She was not part of the plan. He had to forget her.

Distance and time did nothing to quell his need for her. If anything, not being able to see, feel, or touch her made his hunger grow exponentially. And his damned wolf hadn't been making it easy. Every spare thought in his mind was of her, and the wolf would keep reminding him of Isabelle's scent or the feel of her against him. He couldn't even find a substitute because even the thought of touching another female made his wolf furious. Not that he'd had a lot of female company anyway. It had been an embarrassingly long time since he'd slept with anyone, even before he met her. The plan was the focus. There could be no distractions.

He really needed to forget about her. Besides, she was one of *them*. If she ever found out the real reason he had been in New York, surely, she'd report him to her Alpha.

His teeth ground together. *Grant Anderson.* Alpha of New York and another name he could never forget.

Remember why we're here, he told his wolf.

The plan. It was set in motion long ago. He had a role to play in this game. And failure would not be tolerated. He couldn't be distracted. Not now.

It had been hard keeping everything from Pops and the rest of the Savage Wolves Motorcycle Club. Pops had been good to him; treated him like his own flesh and blood, taken him and his mother in when no one else would. If Pops hadn't married his mother, his life would have been different. He would have taken a darker path, where the worst of Lone Wolves went. But Pops had turned everything around. Put him on the right path, shown him that there was another way. The MC had become his life, his anchor, and a better life someone like him could have.

That's why lying to Pops had made his stomach tie up in knots. He had responsibilities back home as Vice President, but he asked Pops for a week's break, and the old man had happily agreed if that's what he thought he needed to get his head back on straight.

There was no way he could tell Pops the truth. Not about the plan. He just wouldn't understand so it was better to keep him in the dark.

Isabelle Brooklyn Bridge was not part of the plan. No, she was a distraction. One he couldn't afford this late in the game. But he never thought he'd be knocked off his feet by a petite, little thing with curves that made him weep and a face that haunted his dreams. The moment he saw her enter Blood Moon, he knew he had to have her.

He had called her princess because that's what she seemed like—a spoiled, beautiful princess dressed up in frivolous designer clothes with no substance. But she'd surprised him—knocked him off his feet if he was honest with himself—with her little speech about Lone Wolves. And kissing her had been a mistake. Because now, he couldn't stop thinking of her taste and scent.

But I have to.

For his own sake. For his family. For *revenge.*

Stick to the plan.

That was the only reason he was here in New York. Shaking his head and ignoring his wolf's pleas, he revved up the engine on his bike and continued on his journey.

Six months ago, he'd been here on a reconnaissance mission. His unique status as a Lone Wolf made it easy for him to travel into the territory. The initial information he had about the clan was outdated, older than him probably, so he had to make sure they were still correct. He'd staked out all the important places. Fenrir Corporation on Madison Avenue. Creed Security downtown. The Enclave. Muccino's. And of course, Blood Moon. That had been his last stop on his three-day trip, and he had been ready to pack up and go home. That was when he met her.

His wolf growled at him, as it did whenever he thought of her. *Forget it, pal.* They were not going to seek her out. Besides, he hadn't seen or talked to her since that night. She'd probably forgotten about him, and though that was probably for the best, it still made something in his chest ache.

This trip was another scouting mission. *Get the info, wait for the call, pass it on to his contact.* That was all.

When he'd last been in New York, it was in the middle of a winter and everything was calm and quiet. Now, on this late summer evening, the city seemed more alive and bustling. People hung out on their stoops, walked along the sidewalks, or sat outside at chairs and tables restaurants had set out. Eventually, he made his way to Midtown to a nondescript motel where he'd stayed previously. It wasn't the Ritz, but they took cash and asked no questions, not to mention, their garage was safe. After parking his bike, he made his way to the lobby and paid the dour-looking front desk clerk before heading to his room and dumping his bag. Then, after a quick change of clothes, he headed out and walked a few blocks to where Blood Moon was located. However, instead of heading in toward the front door, he walked to the alley that led to the rear of the building.

His enhanced sight easily adjusted to the darkness, and he grabbed an empty box lying on its side by the front of the alley. Picking it up, he hoisted it on his shoulders then walked farther inside. Two employees on their smoke break ignored him as he slipped into the rear entrance of the club, using the box to block his face from the other employees. The front security where the burly bouncers stood guard had been harder to get past the last time he was here, but the security from the back was nonexistent. It would be easy enough to get inside from there.

When he got past the kitchen, he tossed the box aside and headed into the main club area. *Easy as taking candy from a baby.* The dance floor buzzed with energy as a pulsing dance tune boomed from the speakers, the bass making the floor vibrate. Lights throbbed, bathing the club-goers in brilliant splashes of color as they gyrated on the floor. Ransom ignored everything going on, instead, glanced around trying to recall where the emergency exits were and how many security guards were on duty during—

Every single hair on the back of his neck and arms stood on end as he felt a strange, pulsing sensation behind his eyes. His inner wolf went very still, then began to make a ruckus, as if trying to catch his attention. Turning his head, his gaze landed on one of the cordoned-off VIP tables along the sides of the dance floor. A blur of white came into focus, and his heart slammed into his sternum.

Isabelle.

She was like a beacon in the darkness. Time slowed and everything else melted away—the club, the music, the dancers—as all his focus went to her. She was standing up and seemed to be trying to get past the other people seated at her table, nudging her way out of the booth when one of them snaked a hand around her waist and pulled her onto his lap, making her laugh and slap him playfully on the shoulder as she struggled to stand.

His inner wolf roared in rage. Ransom saw red. Red everywhere as his stomach twisted in knots at the sight of some other male with his hands around her. It was the one torturous thought he never fully allowed to form in his mind—that all this time, she could have been with any man she chose. His hands curled into tight fists at his sides as he closed his eyes, trying to calm himself and his wolf down. To tamp down the urge to tear that male—and anyone else who touched her—in half.

But it was no use. When he opened his eyes again, he saw she had made her way around the velvet ropes. He didn't even realize he was following her until he was halfway across the dance floor, ignoring the protests of the dancers he bumped into and shoved aside as he strode toward her. She ducked into an unmarked corridor, and he followed her down the dimly-lit hallway, his long strides helping him catch up to her.

Suddenly, she whirled around, her bi-colored eyes flashing with anger, fists raised. "Why the hell are you following—" She went slack-jawed, and her nostrils flared. "You." Her arms dropped to her sides. "What are you doing here?"

She was so fucking beautiful, he couldn't breathe. The first time he saw those eyes—one green, one blue—he thought they weren't real. Hell, he didn't think she was real either. Even now, with her glossy hair falling around her shoulders in waves, curves wrapped up tight in another all-white outfit, she looked like an avenging angel.

"What?" Irritation laced her voice as she placed a hand on her hip. "Did you forget to speak *and* how to use a phone?"

"You're mad that I never called," he managed to say despite the air still trapped in his lungs.

"Mad?" She flipped her hair and gave a little laugh. "Please. That was six months ago. Ancient history."

The edge to her voice gave him some hope. Despite her protest, she *was* pissed. Which was better than her being indifferent. "Who was that guy?"

"What guy?"

Cornering her against the wall, he slammed his palms behind her, making her start. "That. Guy. At your table."

Despite her initial fright, she squared her shoulders and looked him straight in the eyes. "Which one? There were so many of them—"

"The one who touched you," he growled through gritted teeth. How the hell was he the one losing control in this situation? "Are you his?" His wolf howled in protest.

"His *what?*"

She looked so damn calm he wanted to ... to ... "His woman. Was that your boyfriend? Lover? Any of them?"

"I don't know, maybe they're all my lovers—" She gasped when he gripped her arms. "Ransom—"

"So, they share you like some party favor—"

"Fuck off!" Underestimating her strength, he staggered back when she shook his grip off and shoved him back against the opposite wall, his head banging on concrete. "Asshole! I don't hear from you for months, and you think you can come here to *my clan's* territory and start slut-shaming me?" Her finger poked at his chest. "Let me tell *you* something, mister! I don't belong to anyone. I can sleep with a dozen guys if I want to. And no one shares me, *I* share me!"

She was right of course. Despite the rage burning up inside him, he knew it. He had his chance with her months ago, and all he had to do was pick up the damned phone. She could have been his. He swallowed the lump in his throat. "I'm sorry. For ... for what I said earlier." It left a burning, bitter taste in his mouth, but he had no right to judge her. "I should—" His heart stopped for a second when she laid her hands on his chest, and her sweet scent tickled his senses. "What are you doing?"

"Ransom," she sighed. "Why didn't you call? Didn't you want me?"

"Princess." She could have cut him with a hundred knives and it would have hurt less that having her think that. "I did. I do." God, how he wanted her.

Her hands slid up to his shoulders, and she pressed her body against his. "Me too," she confessed.

"We shouldn't. I'm too old for you." And he didn't want to hurt her. There was a plan that had been set in motion long ago. Even before she was born. And if she ever found out ...

"I don't care." Her fingers dug into his shoulders, and her breasts rubbed against his chest. "I didn't think I would ever see you again."

Fuck. A man could only hold out for so long. *One more kiss,* he told himself. One kiss and then he'd leave her alone.

Her eyes widened when he gripped her waist and lowered his head to plant his mouth on hers. Every nerve ending in his body lit up at the contact, and his lips moved urgently, kissing her as if his life depended on it, her sweet scent driving him mad. Flipping their positions around, he caged her body up against the wall, his mouth coaxing hers open, and his tongue swept inside. A moan escaped her throat as he rubbed his raging erection against her.

She broke away from him, her breathing ragged. "Ransom ... why ..."

Why indeed. He didn't know. He didn't care. "I want your mouth," he demanded. She wiggled, as if trying to get away from him, but his grip held her firmly in place. "So sweet. Give it to me. Just one more."

She let out a cry before he captured her mouth again. *Just one touch.* One touch, and he would leave her alone.

Her sweet little body surged up against him and as his hips held her lower half in place, he moved his hand up her torso, slipping underneath her tight blouse to cup her breast. She moaned into his mouth as he brushed a nipple to hardness, then whimpered when he pressed up against her.

"Ransom, we can't," she said, pulling her mouth from his. When she turned her head, he went for her neck, his lips moving over the soft skin, his tongue licking where her pulse thrummed madly. "Not here. Do you ... have a place where we can be alone?"

"It's close by," he murmured against her sweet-smelling skin, making blood rush out from his brain to his groin. He was angry with himself that he had let her slip away before, that she may have turned to other men in the past couple of months to take care of her needs. That was his fault. But tonight, she was *his*.

"We can take this exit." She nodded at the other end of the hallway. "There's a door that leads to the opposite street."

He followed her out, the next few minutes going by in a blur. His blood pumped hot in his veins as he took her hand, dragging her along the streets to his hotel. Shame crept into his gut at the shabbiness of the place. Isabelle was probably used to more luxurious surroundings. She would probably change her mind, he thought bitterly as they entered the elevator. He led her to his room, opened the door and let her go inside first, waiting with baited breath for her to protest at the threadbare carpet, the worn furniture, the faded covers on the too-small bed. But when he looked at her, she didn't say anything or wrinkle her nose at the surroundings. Instead, she took a step toward him and reached for the hem of his shirt. He helped her take it off, tossing the shirt to the side before grabbing her for another kiss.

She gasped against his lips when he hauled her up, carrying her over to the bed before depositing her on top. As she kicked her heels off, he undressed quickly, stripping his boots and pants off. Her pupils blew up with desire as she stared at his chest and torso, though she looked away and swallowed audibly by the time her gaze reached the waistband of his briefs. Kneeling on the bed, he crawled over her, covering her body with his as he bent his head to kiss her lips before moving lower, trailing his mouth along her neck. His fingers tugged impatiently at her top—though it was separate from her skirt, it was so tight he couldn't pull it over her breasts. When he finally realized it was held together with tiny buttons along the front, he grabbed the fabric and tore it down the middle, freeing her breasts.

She let out a shocked squeak, and when she tried to pull the blouse back together, he pulled her hands away.

"No," he said, his gaze soaking up the sight of her naked skin. "God, you're so beautiful, Isabelle." Her olive skin seemed to glow against the torn fabric of her top, her generous breasts heaved as she panted. Bending his head down, he took one nipple into his mouth, suckling on the already hard nub and teasing it with his tongue.

As she moaned and dug her fingers into his shoulders, he used one hand to caress her legs, moving higher to part her knees and slip his hand under her skirt. Gently, he pushed her thighs apart. As his mouth worked on her breasts, her body relaxed, and he moved his hand higher, caressing her over her silky panties. She whimpered when his fingers pushed the fabric aside to touch her bare, wet lips, her arousal mixing in with her natural scent. Slowly, he pushed a finger inside her, a groan escaping his mouth as he felt her tight, slick pussy grip his finger.

Lifting his head, he looked at her. Isabelle's head was thrown back in pleasure, and he watched in awe as her face twisted, and her pretty mouth parted as he worked his finger inside her. Her hips lifted up off the mattress, her pussy drawing more of his finger inside her. Lust tore him up from the inside, and he wanted more. Wanted to taste her. So he moved lower, pushing her skirt up to her waist, yanked her flimsy panties off her, and buried his face between her legs.

"Ransom!" she squealed. "Oh God! You can't ..."

Fuck, she was delicious. He couldn't get enough of her. He lapped at her sweet little pussy, tongue scooping up every bit of her cream. His fingers found her clit, and he rubbed the tight little bud until she was lifting her hips up. He pushed her back down and switched his finger with his mouth so he could slicken her while he slipped a digit into her tightness. She screamed as her thighs clamped around him, her body shaking as her orgasm hit her hard and fast.

He needed her. Needed to be inside her now. As her body sank down on the mattress, he discarded his briefs then kneeled above her. She would be his now. Tonight. Nothing else would matter.

Her mouth parted and drew in a quick breath as he gripped himself in his hand. Though her cheeks tinted with pink adorably, she didn't turn away as he stroked his cock; in fact, she almost seemed fascinated. Pushing her thighs apart, he covered her body with his.

"You're so goddamn beautiful, Isabelle," he whispered in her ear, making her shiver. He began to kiss her neck, enjoying her little sighs of pleasure as the scent of her arousal made the air around him thick. He reached down and wrapped one of her legs around his hip, then slipped a hand under her bottom to raise her up as he lined the tip of his cock against her. She held her breath as he pushed in slowly. Fuck, she was tight and hot. He gritted his teeth, concentrating so hard on trying not to come right then and there like some teenaged boy that he didn't notice how her entire body tensed. He pushed in, getting about halfway inside her when he felt the slightest resistance. The scent of salt filled the air, and his heart stopped when the realization hit him.

"Isabelle?" He went still then hoisted himself up on his elbows to look down at her. Streaks of tears tracked down her cheeks as her lips pursed tight, and her pretty face was twisted in pain. *Fuck.* "You're a ... you've never ..."

She shook her head, her eyes pleading at him. "Don't be mad, please!"

"Darlin'," he began as he brushed the tears from her face. "I'm not mad. I just—" He tried to withdraw her leg wrapped tight around him. "We should—"

"No, don't stop," she urged. "I want this. Want you. Please."

Holy fucking hell, she was begging him to take her virginity. It was wrong. So wrong. It shouldn't be him. But goddammit, there was a primal feeling inside him that urged him, that relished the thought that she would only know him. He blew out a breath, then gathered her into his arms. He could hear and feel her heart pounding against his chest. "I'm sorry I have to hurt you."

"You won't—"

He silenced her protest with his mouth, coaxing her lips open so he could taste her again, then shifted his weight and pushed all the way inside her. She sobbed against his mouth, the sound of her cry making his chest twist in knots.

"Shh ... it's going to be okay," he soothed, then kissed her again, wishing he could really take her pain away. He held her tight, burying his face in her neck, breathing in her scent and listening to her heartbeat.

A few seconds passed before her body relaxed. "I think ... I'm good."

"I don't want to hurt you."

"You won't." She looked up at him as her palms caressed his cheeks, her eyes trusting. "I want you, Ransom. Please make love to me."

A growl rattled from his chest, and he sucked in a deep breath as he withdrew from her. She sighed, as he moved forward again. He reached down to her clit, circling it with his fingers until her hips were arching forward. His cock pressed deeper, stretching her, her tight passage giving way and becoming slicker as she relaxed. He cuddled her, kissed her as tenderly as he could manage as her body lost its resistance. His hands moved under her, to lift up her hips as he moved carefully. "Are you—"

"Yes," she whimpered. "Oh yes." And her arms wrapped around his neck, lifting her head up to kiss at his throat.

He grabbed her ass firmly. "Isabelle ... Isabelle ..." He moved faster, each time opening her up more. Her hips met his every thrust, as he continued to rut into her, her body gripping him so tight he thought he would pass out. "I can't ..." He closed his eyes tight, gritting his teeth as he groaned and felt his cock throb inside her. He held on, waited for the shuddering of her body to peak and die down before he pushed in one last time, filling her with his hot seed as his own orgasm ripped through his body, draining him.

Their breaths matched as they slowed down. He tried to pull away but she kept her hold on him. So he rolled them to their sides, their bodies still joined together. She sighed and rested her head against his chest, and he closed his eyes and sighed.

They must have dozed off because his eyes flew open when he heard an unfamiliar ringing sound. Isabelle, too, sat up and disentangled herself from him. "Sorry! That's my phone."

She scrambled off the bed and got to her feet, pushing her skirt down from around her waist as she grabbed her purse. Taking the phone out of her bag, she glanced at the screen and then tapped on it.

"That was my cousin. She was wondering where I went. I only told her I was going to the bathroom," she chuckled. "I should go back to Blood Moon."

His instincts screamed to tell her not to go, as did his wolf. He was about to protest when his own phone began buzzing across the side table. It was a message from an unknown number.

Urban Diner. 3rd Avenue. Midnight.

He didn't need a second guess to know who that was

from. *Get the info, wait for the call, pass it on to his contact.* He had to remind himself that was the only reason he was here. The time on his phone told him he had thirty minutes to make it to that meeting.

"I can't believe you tore my top. That was Armani couture." Isabelle glanced around, then picked up his T-shirt and slipped it on, tucking the hem into her skirt. "This'll have to do, I guess, though I don't know how I'll explain it to Maxine," she said with a chuckle.

Rolling off the bed, he hopped into his jeans and put on a fresh shirt from his bag. "I'll walk you back," he offered.

They strode out of the room and the hotel in strangely comfortable silence. All he wanted to do was drag her back to bed and keep her there all night long. But he couldn't miss this meeting, and she wanted to go back to her friends. *And those guys at her table.* His teeth ground together, thinking of them. It was obvious she hadn't been with any of them, but what about now? What if—

"We're here," she announced as they stopped across the street from Blood Moon. "Why don't you join us inside?"

"I can't," he said. "I shouldn't."

"You're overthinking this." Her mismatched eyes sparkled as she smiled up at him. "Look, you don't have to do anything you don't want to. But don't think that—"

God, she was so beautiful. He couldn't help himself and he pulled her into his arms and kissed her until the air in his lungs expired.

She blinked and sighed, then lay her head on his chest. "Will you call me?"

No. "Sure." He couldn't. Too much had passed between them. If he was smart, he'd pass on the intelligence to his contact and then leave New York and Isabelle Brooklyn Bridge and never look back.

Pulling away, she dropped her arms to her sides. "I'll be waiting for that call." She turned on her heel and headed back to the club.

You'll be waiting a long time, princess. Of course, he wouldn't call her. *Delete her number,* he told himself. Isabelle was not for him. Sure, she'd be mad, but she'd get over it. She was young and had the rest of her life ahead of her. She would meet someone more her style, better suited to her, someone who could give her everything she wanted. She didn't deserve a rough, jaded Lone Wolf biker like him. The only reason he came here was for revenge.

It took all his strength to turn away, but he managed to do it. Jogging back to the hotel parking garage, he got on his bike and headed downtown. He made it to the meeting point with two minutes to spare, though, when he entered the dingy diner, there was only one customer inside. The figure sat in the farthest booth in the corner, his back to the door, his head obscured by a dark hat. Ransom knew this had to be his contact, even though he'd never met any of them in the flesh. He strode toward the man in the hat and slipped into the opposite seat.

"I got your message," he said.

The man raised his head slightly, though his eyes and face were obscured by dark glasses and the brim of the hat. He wore a dark trench coat, and the only bit of skin Ransom could see were his pale hands clasped together on the tabletop. "And what can you tell me about Blood Moon?"

He rattled off his observations, about the weakness in the security in the back. Before he left with Isabelle, he did notice

a few other things—about how many employees were
working and the amount of people inside. "Is that all?" he
asked when he finished.

"Possibly." The man stood up. "But ... don't leave New
York yet. Seeing as you're able to slip into places my
colleagues and I cannot, I anticipate that we will have need of
you."

"Need of me? What are you planning? Why Blood
Moon?"

"Why do you think?"

Realization hit Ransom like a ton of bricks. "You're
planning some kind of attack, aren't you?"

The man didn't answer.

"That's not part of the plan. It's not just Lycans in there.
People could get hurt." He slammed his fist on the
countertop. "You said we were going to get back at Grant
Anderson!"

The man remained unruffled. "We will hit the Alpha of
New York where it will hurt the most—by getting rid of his
subjects. What do you care about these people? You don't
know any of them. Your people are safe, far away from here."
His thin lips pulled back. "Don't tell me you're getting cold
feet now."

He gritted his teeth. "I'm not."

"Then let me and my colleagues take care of everything.
And be ready when we call on you."

That last part sounded like a threat, and Ransom held his
breath, waited for the man to walk away, and expelled it only
when he was gone.

A dreaded feeling formed in the pit of his stomach. This
was what he'd wanted for what seemed like forever. Grant

Anderson was going to pay for what he did. The thought had been ingrained in him his whole life.

But he never thought he would meet Isabelle. She, obviously, was a regular at Blood Moon. What if she was there and they attacked—

Goddammit! No, he could not let her get hurt. He would have to make sure she wasn't at Blood Moon tomorrow. He quickly grabbed his phone from his pocket and opened his contacts, not even hesitating as he typed out a message to her.

I know I said I would call, but I couldn't wait until morning, so how about a text?

To his surprise, the reply came back right away. *A text is nice too.* There was a pause as dots appeared on the screen, indicating she was still typing another message. *I can't stop thinking about tonight.*

His stomach flip-flopped. Now he couldn't either. Couldn't stop thinking of her lips, her scent, her body. *How about you come by tomorrow? Around eight p.m.*

Should we meet at Blood Moon first?

"No!" He said it so loud, the lone waitress dozing in the corner started. Clearing his throat, he said, "Ma'am, can I get a cup of coffee?" He turned back to his phone and typed out a message.

Let's skip Blood Moon for tomorrow. Just come over.

All right. Winky face emoji. *I'm off to bed. Didn't want to stay at the club longer.*

Sweet dreams, princess.

With a deep sigh he put the phone back into his pocket and raked his hands down his face. For tomorrow at least, he'd keep her away from danger.

Ransom told himself he was doing this to protect Isabelle, to keep her away from Blood Moon and the danger that may befall her there. That he was keeping her distracted and safe. But a week later, no attack had happened, and he hadn't heard from his contact, but he continued to bring her back to his hotel room and keep her occupied—and satisfied—until she was too tired to leave until just before dawn, long after the club had closed.

"Oh God!" Her body shuddered as she rode him, her thighs around his hips, generous tits bouncing up and down. Reaching up, he grabbed a handful, pinching her nipples just the way she liked them. She growled, a sound that he loved to hear from her lips, especially when he was inside her and she was ready to come.

"Fight it, princess," he ordered. "Don't come yet."

"I can't! You—Ungh!" she whined when he slapped her ass playfully. In retaliation, she scratched her fingernails down his chest, leaving red marks in its wake.

God, she was perfect. She made up for her inexperience with her enthusiasm, surprising even him with her voracious sexual appetite and adventurousness. And he loved making her come, watching her fall apart, feeling her squeeze him as her body was overcome with pleasure.

"That's it," he urged as she continued to move her hips, gripping his cock tight inside her. "Come, darlin'. Come for me."

She squealed and moved her hips harder, her body shuddering, back bowing back as she slowed down. He rolled her over, slamming hard into her, fucking into her with all his might, all the while holding onto his own pleasure as he wrung out another orgasm from her. When she was pleading and crying, he finally let go, grunting like an animal as his cock exploded inside her, filling her up with his come. Aftershocks rocked his body, but he didn't release her. He held on tighter, as if she was going to disappear.

"Ransom," she rasped as she gently pushed him back. "Oh God."

"Hmmm ..." He licked at her neck, ignoring her protests as he took a whiff of her sweet and spicy scent.

"Oh." She practically melted against him. It was her weakness, having her neck kissed and licked. "Ransom ..."

He loved hearing his name on her lips and so he continued to nibble at her collarbone, moving lower—

"Ransom, I can't breathe," she moaned. "And I'm all sweaty and gross."

"Not gross," he said, but lifted himself off her. Grabbing the towel he kept on the headboard, he gave her a quick rubdown before he wiped the sweat from himself, then lay down next to her.

Isabelle sighed and then tried to roll off the bed, but he reached for her hand and pulled her back to bed. She didn't protest and allowed him to roll her over. "Don't," he said. "Just stay here with me tonight." *Or forever.*

"You know I can't," she said. "And I'm not sleeping on that bed."

A twinge of shame plucked at his chest. Isabelle was obviously classy and well-to-do, and he wished he could afford a better place than this dingy hotel. She deserved better. Had he known that night had been her first time, he would have at least moved to a place that didn't have cockroaches scattering across the floor in the middle of the night. "I know you're used to better—"

"Stop that!" She patted him on the chest. "It doesn't matter to me. But this bed is tiny, and you're huge; I'd have to sleep on top of you for both of us to fit here."

"I have no problem with that."

She laughed and then pulled his head down for a kiss. "You'd roll over and crush me," she said. "I bet you're one of those guys who splay all over the bed."

"And I bet you're one of those girls who hog the covers," he shot back playfully. "Why don't we find out?" In truth, he'd been wanting to know what it would feel like to wake up with her in his arms. There was just something not right about her leaving every night. His inner wolf agreed. It was strange really; his wolf was always indifferent to all the women he'd been with before. Isabelle was the exception, and his inner animal was crazy about her. Hell, if he was honest, he was crazy about her.

"You know I can't." She sighed and got off the bed, then began to pick up her discarded clothing. "My cousin's covering for me, but only if I go home." Hopping into her panties, she did a little shake that made her tits jiggle, and his cock went half hard. "Ransom, are you listening to me?"

"Huh?" He smiled at her. "Sorry, got distracted," he said with a nod at her chest.

She smiled wryly at him, then slipped her dress over her head. "Anyway, Maxine's a worrywart, and if I don't video chat with her from my apartment, she'll freak out. But don't worry," she gave him a quick peck. "She knows that if anyone asks, I've been with her every night. She pinky-promised, so she'll cover for me, even with my dad."

"Your dad?"

She nodded. "Mm-hmm. My dad can be overprotective, but that's because I'm the youngest, and he still thinks I'm a baby. And he was the Alpha of New York until my brother took over a few months ago, but he's cool, even with Lone Wolves."

Alpha of New York.

His vision went briefly red.

Grant Anderson.

Her father was the Alpha of New York.

Grant Anderson.

"Ransom?" A small frown pleated between her eyebrows. "Are you okay?"

"I ..." He shut his mouth quickly, unsure of what to say. His stomach filled with dread as he swung his legs over the side of the bed and rubbed his face. *No, it couldn't be.* His entire body went numb and a cold feeling ran through his veins like ice. He didn't even notice her sit beside him and wrap her arms around his waist as she kissed his neck.

"Ransom? Are you mad at me or something?"

"Mad?" His throat felt dry and scratchy. "No, princess, I'm not." He wasn't mad at her. He was mad at himself. Why didn't he ask about her last name or family? He should have, but he was too busy listening to his dick.

"Then why does it feel like you're pulling away from me?"

"I'm not." He pulled her hands away. "You're right. You should go before your cousin freaks out." *And tells your father we've been sleeping together.* Realization crept up on him: He'd been fucking Grant Anderson's daughter. *Fuck me!* This was not going to end well.

"Oh. Okay." She shrank back from him, a look of hurt flashing across her face before she turned and got up to walk toward the door.

Goddammit if that didn't make him feel like a piece of shit. This whole thing made him feel like the biggest piece of shit ever. "Isabelle—"

The door slammed loudly as she exited the room. "Fuck! Fuck, fuck, fuck!" He buried his face in his hands. God, he wanted to tear the room apart. His wolf, too, pressed at his skin, wanting to shred him from the inside. That pain would have been preferable to the ache in his chest.

A buzzing sound from the bedside table made him start. "Goddammit!" he shouted as he glanced over and saw "unknown number" flashing on the screen. Grabbing the phone, he threw it across the room and got to his feet.

I have to leave. His gut was telling him this wasn't going to end well. The best thing to do was get out while he could.

He threw his empty duffel on the bed and flung open all the drawers as he began to stuff the clothes into the bag. Swiping his keys from the dresser, he grabbed the duffel and dashed to the door, yanking it open. His heart stopped when he realized there was someone on the other side. "Isabelle?"

"I didn't want to leave like that. Ransom, I want you to know—" Her bi-colored gaze dropped to the duffel bag. "Are you leaving?"

He swallowed hard. "Yes."

"Were you even going to tell me?"

Unsure what to say, he remained quiet.

Anger flashed across her face. "Just like that? You're going to leave New York without even telling me?"

Yes, he was. It was for her own good. And so was what he

was about to do. "I don't know what you want me to say, Isabelle. This was just fun for both of us." The look on her face made him want to tear his own heart out because surely that would have hurt less. "It was your chance to slum it with a nobody Lone Wolf like me before you went back to your castle, princess. Sleeping with me could be your good deed for the year."

Her jaw dropped. "Do you honestly think that's what this is about?"

"Then what is it about? Why are you keeping me a secret from your friends? Was the fucking not good enough for you? Or was it too good which was why you kept coming back like a bitch in heat?"

She flinched at his words. "You don't know me if you think that way."

"That's the problem, princess," he spat. "I don't know you at all." He huffed. "But since you're here, why don't we have one last fuck before I—"

"Go to hell, Ransom!" A glitter of tears was trapped between her thick, dark lashes. "Go to fucking hell and never come back!"

Every muscle in his body froze as he watched her bolt down the hallway. His wolf was growling at him, wanting him to chase after her. *No.* This was for the best. He shouldn't have gotten involved with her in the first place. She was Grant Anderson's daughter. The man who ruined his life. The man he wanted to see dead.

Shaking his head, he slammed the door behind him and made his way to the garage. After securing his duffel, he started the engine and drove out into the street heading uptown, not caring if he was breaking speed laws.

Though he tried to focus on driving, his mind kept wandering to Isabelle. The look of hurt on her beautiful face was something he could never forget, and the stabbing pain in his chest only grew exponentially. He was so focused on the pain he didn't realize there was a figure in the middle of the street blocking his way until it was too late. With a loud curse, he jerked the handlebars and the bike skidded and threw him off. He tumbled head over feet into the grass and smashed into a brick wall.

"What the fuck?" Groaning, he got to his feet, bracing himself against the wall. He planted his palms on the edge and blinked to get his vision into focus. Light scattered like diamonds across the wide body of water before him, and farther out, he could see a ridge with buildings built along the edge. He had been on Riverside Drive when he skidded off, which means this was the Hudson River.

"Ransom."

Ice flooded his veins at the sound of the voice. Slowly, he turned around. Sure enough, it was the man from the diner. Even out here in the dark, he was still dressed in his hat, sunglasses, and trench coat. "What do you want?"

The man's nostrils flared. "I told you to be ready when I called you. Instead, you ignore my calls, and now you're running away."

"Find someone else to be your errand boy," he spat. "I changed my mind."

"Changed your mind?" the man said incredulously. "Have you forgotten the bargain that was struck? The plan that's been set into motion?"

How could he forget. "It's not worth it." The words left a bitter taste in his mouth, but it was true. Revenge was one thing, but he couldn't allow anyone else to get hurt. Especially not Isabelle. "We'll find another way."

"Ha!" The man laughed cruelly. "You think you can just turn your back on our agreement like that? I don't think so." His lips turned up into a malevolent smile. "Do you think I don't know what you've been doing? And *who* you've been doing it with?"

Rage flared in his chest, but he tamped it down. "I'm sure I don't know what you're talking about. Now if you'll excuse me—"

"The plan has changed," he declared. "I want you to bring me Grant Anderson's daughter."

Fuck! "I don't know what—"

"Don't take me for a fool, Ransom!" he warned. "You'll do as I say."

Now he was mad. Did this man not know what he could to him? What his animal was capable of? "No one tells me what to do."

"You're going to take the girl and bring her to me ... or else I'll have to take someone else. Your pretty little sister would make a good substitute I bet. Or how about your mother? She—"

"Fuck you!" he roared. "Touch a hair on their heads and I'll—"

"Bring me Grant Anderson's daughter now!" the man bellowed. "Or I'll—"

Ransom barely felt his wolf reach for the surface, but by then, it was too late. His animal was filled with hate and rage for this insignificant creature who dared to threaten anyone under his protection. It lunged for the man, who screamed as gigantic claws raked down his face and shoulder. The wolf rolled away, then turned back for a second attack.

The man got to his feet, cursing as he clutched at his face. "You'll never get away with this you filthy animal!" Blood ran from between his pale fingers. "When my colleagues find out that you've betrayed us, they'll kill you and every last one of your family!"

The wolf howled and reared back, then sprang forward. The animal was quick, but it didn't see the man take something out of his pocket and toss it at them. Something hit the wolf's snout then exploded in a flash of light. Pain shot straight into its brain. However, massive limbs managed to stretch out and found its target, claws ripping into flesh and bone as a blood-curdling scream tore through the quiet evening. The wolf tumbled forward, its paws clinging to its victim as they both hurtled over the wall and fell down, the waters of the Hudson River swallowing them up.

They're safe. Ransom's thoughts began to muddle as water filled his lungs and his vision turned dark. *Isabelle. Silke. Joanie.* This sacrifice was worth it if it meant they would live.

CHAPTER THREE

PRESENT TIME ...

Isabelle started as her phone's alarm woke her up from her dreamless sleep. "Oh God!" Outside, it was already light. Turning off the alarm, she got up from where she had fallen asleep on the couch and stretched her arms out.

Must have fallen asleep right after the call from Sofia. Last night had been the big battle between the Lycans and their enemies, the mages. Having had no combat training whatsoever, Isabelle had no choice but to stay at home. However, she stayed up until past midnight, waiting for news. Finally, at just before two o'clock in the morning, Sofia had called her and relayed the news that everything was fine and that no one was killed, though there were some injuries. Exhaustion had taken over and she closed her eyes, then she must have fallen asleep right there on the couch.

Pulling on her robe, she made her way toward the nursery. As she ambled toward the cribs at the far end, she breathed a sigh of relief as she looked in and saw both Evan and Kier were still fast asleep. She sank down on the rocker in the corner.

Everyone was safe, she told herself. Still, tears burned in her throat at the memory of last night when her sister had dropped off her son. "Isabelle," Julianna had said. "If anything happens to me and Duncan, will you take care of Kier?"

"What?" The words had shocked her. "Julianna, nothing will happen—"

"*Promise me.*"

But they were safe. They all were. She leaned back and closed her eyes, placing her hand over her chest as all the tension and worry she'd been holding in began to ease away. If anything had happened to Julianna or Duncan, she didn't know what she would do. The two of them had been her rock, her support since she found out she was pregnant with Evan. They'd been there through everything—even flying back from one of their missions when she was about to give birth. Julianna was always there to kick her in the butt when she was feeling sorry for herself, and Duncan never failed to make her laugh. When Julianna wanted to go back to Scotland to give birth, Isabelle had gone with them, bringing one-month-old Evan with her so she could be there when Kier arrived.

A sharp cry caught her attention. *Evan.* She knew every cry and sound he made. As she got up, a second voice joined her son's, and she smiled to herself. Kier, on the other hand, didn't seem appreciative of being woken up as a fierce frown marred his cute little face.

"All right, my loves," she cooed as she reached the two cribs set together side by side. Evan had already sat up and propped himself in the corner. "How about breakfast?"

She picked up Evan first and then Kier. Despite being

the youngest, Julianna and Duncan's son was longer and chubbier than Evan or his older cousins. Good thing she was a Lycan, otherwise Isabelle wouldn't have been able to pick up both boys.

After cleaning them up, she set the two pups into their highchairs and prepared their food, taking turns to feed each boy equal amounts of the mashed bananas and cereal she prepared. Watching the two boys made her smile. Though they had identical mismatched eyes—a trait from her mother's side of the family—they looked so different. Kier had gotten Duncan's smile and his mother's nose. While Evan ...

She swallowed hard, trying not to think of *him*. But it was so difficult, even after two years. Her traitorous little heart clenched when her mind strayed. She couldn't even bring herself to think of his name.

Her she-wolf yowled sadly. During the weeks after he left, it had been inconsolable. Of course it was—he was their True Mate after all. She had suspected it the first time, but since he never called her, she thought she had been wrong. However, it wasn't until she realized she was pregnant two months after he left the second time that she confirmed it.

While the signs had been there—how her wolf reacted to him and that his scent was unusually pleasant to her—the only way to really know if a couple was True Mates was if the female got pregnant the first time they had sex. Then, once the female was pregnant, she became invulnerable to any harm. It had been too late when she found out. He had left her—tossed her aside like she was nothing.

"Stop it," she said through gritted teeth. That was the past. Over and done with. She had Evan to think of now. He was the love of her life—the only thing in the world that mattered now.

Truthfully, she would have never guessed this is how her life would have ended up—nor that she would be so happy being a single mom to Evan and working in her family's restaurant. Her life before Evan seemed like a million years ago, and the person she was then was a mere memory. Sure, there were times when it was difficult and she longed for the days when the only problem she had was that her favorite boutique had run out of the must-have shoes of the season, but she wouldn't trade her son for all the shoes and clothes in the world.

"What the—Evan!" A splatter of banana hit her in the chest. Looking at her son, he grinned at her, raising the spoon triumphantly. Somehow, he had gotten his hands on it and had tossed a spoonful of his breakfast at her. "Oh, baby. What am I gonna do with you?" She put her hands on her hips and tried to look serious, but the two boys laughing and giggling made her heart melt. "I—"

A ringing sound interrupted her and she fished her phone from the pocket of her robe. The caller ID flashed her brother-in-law's name, so she didn't hesitate answering it.

"Duncan? Is everything all right?" Fear caught in her throat. "Did something happen? Is Jules okay?"

"Hush, lassie, I'll tell you about Julianna in a bit," came the soothing brogue from Duncan MacDougal. "But first, I wanted to check on you and the wee ones."

"I just fed them breakfast."

"Good. Thank you for watching over Kier, Isabelle."

"I wish I could have done more."

"You did good, lassie," Duncan assured her. "Knowing

that Kier was in good hands while we were fighting put us both at ease. Thank you so much, Isabelle."

"Of course, you know I'd do anything for you and Jules."

"Aye, and I'm grateful to you."

Glancing over at the boys, she saw they seemed to be entertaining themselves, so she turned around and whispered into the phone. "But what about Julianna? How is she?"

"She's doin' fine now, but it was pretty bad. A fireball got her, and she passed out from the pain."

Her chest contracted. "Oh no! Please tell me she's okay now. Is she conscious?"

"Awake, yes, but if it's not too much trouble, could you come down to the Medical Wing and cheer her up? You don't have to bring the boys, especially as both of them can be a handful."

"Not any trouble at all. I'll find someone who can watch them while I run down there."

"Thanks, Isabelle, you're a gem."

Putting her phone away, she turned to the boys. "C'mon. Let's get cleaned up and see if Aunty Sofia and Alessandro can watch you."

After cleaning the boys up and changing her own clothes, she strapped Evan into his stroller and carried Kier in her arms, and rolled them out the door. Her apartment was only a few floors below her brother and sister-in-law's penthouse, which had actually been her childhood home when her father had been Alpha. It was actually convenient whenever Sofia had needed someone to look after Alessandro while she was at work, though now with Isabelle's job at the restaurant, they had found other arrangements. But since today was unusual and her usual babysitter might not be ready to accept both pups, Sofia would be the best option. Thankfully, Sofia didn't mind having them drop in unexpectedly and happily took in both boys so Isabelle could visit Julianna at the medical wing.

The medical wing was on the far end of The Enclave, the compound on the Upper West Side that housed most of the Lycan of New York and their families. She herself had been born there, and so had Evan. She entered the facility, waving hello to Janet, the receptionist, who manned the front door. She guessed that Julianna would probably be in the recovery ward upstairs, so made her way to the third floor.

Peeking through the doorway of the recovery ward, she saw Julianna lying down on one of the beds, and she gasped. It was difficult seeing her strong, no-nonsense sister in a hospital bed. Growing up, she was the tough one, and now ...

"Jules! Oh, my God, Jules," she cried as she burst through the door. "Duncan told me what happened, are you all right?" She hugged Julianna. "I thought—"

"Oh, for crying out loud," Julianna mumbled. "I'm fine. I'm a Lycan, remember? I may not have True Mate healing powers, but I'll be fine in a couple of days."

"The fireball burned a chunk of flesh off her left arm," Duncan said through gritted teeth. "She fainted from the pain."

"And they patched me up, but this thing"—she nodded at the bandage on her arm—"itches like the dickens. And don't even get me started on what generating new skin feels like."

"Thanks for watching over Kier," Duncan said to Isabelle, mentioning their infant son.

"Oh, no worries, he's fine. Whenever he cries, I just give

him some food and he's good to go." She chuckled. "No wonder he's so chubby."

"He's not chubby," Duncan said indignantly. "He's—"

"Husky," Julianna and Isabelle quipped at the same, then they both burst out into giggles. "Anyway," Isabelle continued. "He and Evan are with Sofia now since I wanted to come see you." She suddenly realized they weren't exactly alone, and she felt a little foolish for her earlier outburst. "Oh hey, Sabrina! Cross!" Cross Jonasson was a member of the New York clan and a powerful hybrid—half Lycan wolf, half warlock—who had recently been reunited with his mate after years of separation. She had met Sabrina when Cross asked the clan to keep her safe. According to what Sofia had told her, it turned out Sabrina had one of the artifacts the mages were looking for, which was why they had to hide her. "Are you guys okay? Were you injured too?"

"No, we're good," Sabrina said. "But my dad was here, and we're taking him home."

"Oh?" Isabelle walked toward them, but as she got closer, her gaze dropped to the figure on the bed in front of the couple. "Is that—"

No.

It couldn't be.

Her wolf scrambled to attention, ears lifting up.

Oh God. It wasn't possible!

But it was Ransom on the bed. Not only did she recognize his face, but also the exposed bit of the wolf tattoo on his hip. His chest was covered in bandages, and his skin had a pale gray pallor. Her wolf yowled, seeing him in such a state.

"Isabelle?" Sabrina cocked her head to the side. "Are you all right?"

I have to get out of here! "I'm ... fine!" she said nervously, her hands waving in the air. "I just remembered something I have to—"

"No ..." A low moan escaped from Ransom's lips, and the familiar timbre of his voice made her heart palpitate.

"I should go see to Evan." Every drop of blood drained from her face. Before anyone could say anything, she dashed toward the exit.

Her heartbeat didn't slow down even as she left the building; in fact, it only went faster and thumped harder against her ribcage. How was he in New York? What was he doing in the medical wing inside The Enclave of all places?

It didn't matter. No, his presence didn't matter at all. The only thing that did was Evan. She had to keep him safe and away from Ransom.

All this time, she had kept the secret of Evan's father safe, and it would stay that way. If anyone found out ... or if Ransom himself did, who knows what would happen?

She wouldn't think of that possibility. Couldn't think of it. Because there was no way she was going to let that happen.

CHAPTER FOUR

THAT VOICE.

That scent ... honey and cardamom ...

It called to Ransom and his wolf. Pulled them out of the darkness.

As he struggled for consciousness, he let out a groan. His throat felt parched, and there was a searing pain coming from his left shoulder.

But he swam on. Out of the darkness. It felt like he'd been treading for hours. Days maybe. He didn't know why; he just knew he had to pull himself out of this.

"Argh!" He reached out and sat up. Vision blurred. Ringing in his ears. Scratchy fabric around his chest. Shaking his head, he blinked several times and rubbed his eyes.

"Easy there. Don't try to move too much."

His wolf sensed the presence of another Lycan. Did he know that voice? Or that accent? Irish? Definitely not American. He attempted to open his mouth, but only noises came out and his throat burned. Sniffing the air, he couldn't smell it any more. Couldn't smell *her*.

"I—" His vision began to focus. The air was antiseptic, like in a hospital. Wiggling his legs, he realized he was on a bed, so he swung his legs over the side.

"I don't think that's a good idea. Take it easy, there. D'you want me to call the doctor?"

The haziness was starting to fade away. He'd heard that voice. At the briefings. It all became clear now. He was in New York, had come here to help fight the mages. They had a big team, but he'd heard the man with the accent talking a couple of times.

Lifting his head up, Ransom found himself staring into bright green eyes. "No, I'm fine," he rasped. "Just ... thirsty. And hungry."

"Do you want one of my cheeseburgers?" someone offered cheerfully. "I can spare three ... maybe two."

Turning to the source of the voice, his chest tightened when his gaze crashed with mismatched green and blue eyes. For a moment, he wanted to leap out of the bed and go to her. But his wolf knew what his eyes did not—this was someone else. The eyes and dark hair were the same, but it wasn't *her*. The woman who haunted his dreams for the last two years. "I ... thank you." He took the glass of water next to his bed and took a long gulp, then looked to the man with the bright green eyes. "We won, right?"

"Aye," he nodded. "Thanks to you, my friend. By the way, we didn't have time to get acquainted yesterday. I'm Duncan MacDougal."

He took the offered hand. "Ransom."

"And this," he jerked a thumb behind him, to the woman in the other hospital bed, "is my wife, Julianna."

"Hey!" she greeted with a wave. "Nice to see you up."

"Uh, yeah." He turned away, unable to look at those eyes. He knew who she was, of course. After what happened two years ago, he'd looked up Grant Anderson and his family. Though there was very little public information about them, he recognized the eyes that all his children inherited from their mother. If he'd only done his due diligence earlier, he would have recognized it. And maybe he would have stopped this whole thing.

He scrubbed a hand down his face. *I should have stayed home.* But Cross Jonasson had come to him, asking for help. *Everyone in my clan ... they could die.*

Had he asked over two years ago, Ransom would not have given two fucks over what could happen to New York. It could have sunk into the ocean for all he cared.

But then ...

"You sure you don't want a cheeseburger?" Julianna waved the half-eaten burger in her hand. "They're good."

"I'm fine." He scratched at the bandages. The skin underneath was knitting itself back together, and the itching was driving him crazy.

The knock on the door caught everyone's attention, and a tall figure entered the room. "Hello," Cross Jonasson greeted as his eyes locked with Ransom's. "Glad to see you're up."

"You're a sight for sore eyes," he said. "And I'm not talking about you, Jonasson." He was, after all, the reason Ransom was injured in the first place. And the reason he didn't die in the watery depths of the Hudson River. He nodded at the woman who came up behind Cross. "You all right, Sabrina?"

She smiled at him, her violet eyes sparkling. "I am now. Thank you for what you did last night."

"Yeah, well, Silke will kill me if I let anything happen to you." A couple of days ago, Cross had asked him to keep Sabrina safe back in Kentucky. He had agreed, though mostly it was because his sister Silke had taken a liking to Sabrina.

She chuckled. "I'm glad. Thank you."

"Where have you guys been?" Julianna asked. "Did you get your dad home safe?"

"Yes, he's home now." Sabrina's cheeks pinked. "And also ..." She raised her hand up, showing off a sparkly ring on her finger. "We got engaged."

"Holy shit!" Julianna cried. "Congratulations!"

Ransom saw something on Cross's face that he had never seen before: genuine happiness. "Congrats, man." He had heard the other man refer to Sabrina as his True Mate, though Ransom wasn't sure what that meant exactly. He'd only heard rumors about such things.

"Thank you." Cross gave him a strange look. "Maybe you'll be next."

"Yeah, right." Ransom pushed himself off the bed, his bare feet landing on the cold concreted floor. "Is there someplace we can talk? I need you to fill me in on what happened and make sure Silke and everyone back home knows I'm okay."

"I've taken care of that," Cross said. "We stopped by on the way back here." The hybrid, after all, could travel long distances in seconds. "I need to talk to you too."

"Why don't you go to the waiting room outside?" Sabrina suggested. "I'll stay here and keep Julianna and Duncan company."

Ransom waved off the hand Cross offered and followed

him outside to the empty waiting room. "So, what happened last night?"

"You mean after you decided to make yourself into a human pin cushion?" Cross asked with a lifted brow. "If you didn't jump in and the mage hadn't stabbed you with the dagger, he would have gotten away with all three artifacts. Thank you for saving us."

He was, of course, talking about the dagger of Magus Aurelius, one of the three artifacts the mages were trying to get their hands on in order to rule the world. A bitter taste formed on his tongue. What would Cross do if he knew the *whole* truth of why he agreed to come here in the first place? "Didn't have much choice."

"Still you saved—"

"What happened with my guys?" he said, quickly changing the subject. "Are Hawk and Snake good?"

"Yeah," Cross said. "They're back at GI headquarters. I told them I'd give them a lift back to Kentucky any time they're ready."

"We're ready," Ransom declared. "I need to get back." *Now*. Before he did something stupid.

"Sure, but there's something I need to tell you." Cross lowered his voice. "The Alpha asked to meet you."

He ground his teeth together. "What for?"

"Well I'm sure he's thankful for what you did," Cross said. "You did save all of us."

"I didn't do it for him." But he couldn't say why he did it at all. "I don't need his thanks. I just need to go home."

"You should hear him out. He wants to take you to dinner."

As if that would ever make up for anything. "Why?"

Cross's face turned gloomy. "What you saw last night? That's not even a fraction of what could happen if the mages succeed in what I think they're planning. This isn't just about New York or the clans. Every single Lycan out there will be in danger. And Lucas wants to talk about how we can all work together and—"

"No." Absolutely not. The sooner he got out of New York, the better. "Look, we're already even after you fished me out of the Hudson, right? Actually, I believe *you* owe me one now."

"You still haven't told me why you were floating, half-dead in the river."

And he never would. "Is there a phone I can use? I should call Silke."

Cross's shoulders sank in defeat and fished his phone out from his pocket. "I just got this, but you can have it. I can get another one."

"Thanks."

"If you change your mind—"

"I'll know where to find you."

The hybrid gave him a curt nod. "I'll go back inside and give you some privacy."

Ransom waited until the other man disappeared through the door before dialing the number he knew by heart. It rang three times before the person on the other line picked up.

"It's me."

There was a huff. "So, you survived. When are you heading back?"

"Soon," he said.

"Is he dead?"

"Who?" he asked.

"You *know* who."

"Grant Anderson wasn't even there," he groused. "And I told you, he's not the Alpha anymore."

"Who cares? He still has to pay." There was a pause. "Tell me what happened."

Ransom ran through the events of yesterday and the night before, including what Cross had said. "Don't worry, I'm leaving soon."

Another pause. "Wait. Don't go yet."

"*Wait?*" he said incredulously. "You didn't want me coming here in the first place."

"I know. But maybe we can use this to our advantage."

"Our advan—what the fuck are you saying? I thought we decided after the last time I was in New York we were going to forget about this whole revenge thing."

"No, *you* decided that. Don't be ungrateful. After what I did to cover up for what you did? Our *friends* aren't as forgiving as you think. They haven't forgotten us. And if they find out the truth, you know what could happen."

Fuck. He assumed their *friends* had forgotten about that little incident in the Hudson. Apparently not, and it was time to pay the price. "Why won't you tell me who they are? I can take care of them—"

A laugh cut him off. "Stop acting like an overconfident pup. You don't know what they're capable of. And it's better you don't know." There was a pause. "Now, are you going to do as I say or not?"

"Fine. What do you want me to do?"

"This is your chance. Our chance. Build their trust. Let them think you're allies. Do what it takes. I'll take care of the rest. And then, when there's an opening, we'll destroy Grant Anderson."

The pit in his stomach grew. But what choice did he have? Those men ... their "friends" ... they could do so much more harm. "All right. I'll take care of it."

"See that you do." The line went dead.

He scrubbed a hand down his face. *This wasn't supposed to happen.* After surviving the incident in the Hudson and the aftermath, he thought that was the end of the plan. It seemed all his life had been devoted to destroying Grant Anderson, that he thought he would miss having the idea of revenge from fueling his reason for existing.

But he should have known. The plan hadn't been tossed away; it had only been delayed.

What to do now? He wasn't sure. This was his chance to redeem himself, to realize the plan that had been set into motion long ago. But truthfully, he wasn't sure anymore if he could pull the trigger.

With a last huff, he strode back into the recovery ward where Cross and Sabrina were standing beside Julianna's bed. All conversation stopped, and four pairs of eyes looked at him.

He cleared his throat. "I've changed my mind." The words were difficult to get out. "When does your Alpha want to talk?"

CHAPTER FIVE

"Watch what you're doing, *pendejo!*"

"That motherfucker's hot!"

"*Hay tomates?*"

"Get it yourself!"

Isabelle grinned to herself as she entered the kitchen of Muccino's. It was chaotic, loud, hot—and she loved every minute of it.

The restaurant was the Manhattan branch of her mother's family's business back in New Jersey and currently run by her cousin, Gio Muccino, who had taken over from his father. Uncle Dante had retired fully a few months ago. A couple of months ago, the manager and the hostess had quit at the same time, so her mother, Frankie, had to take over. Finding herself with nothing to do except stay at home with Evan, Isabelle volunteered to help, and so she took over the hostess duties. Frankie wanted to go back into retirement, so eventually Isabelle had slid into the role of hostess and manager, much like her mother had when she was younger.

"Hey, watch your mouths, *cabrons!*" Alejandro Garcia,

the sous-chef, called out when he spotted Isabelle. "There's a lady present!"

"Lady?" Gio asked, winking at Isabelle. "What lady? I don't see a lady around here."

Isabelle crossed her arms over her chest. "The only ladies I'm seeing are the grandmas in here," she shot back. "*Madre de dio! Is this a fucking quilting bee at the senior's home? I thought you were all supposed to be the best damned cooks in New York? You're all gonna wind up in the weeds tonight if you keep this up."

Everyone in the kitchen laughed and hooted, then headed back to their stations. A few months ago, when she started, everyone in the restaurant hazed her, being the newbie. Of course, she knew that a lot of them, especially the waitstaff, were probably getting back at her because of the shabby way she had treated them when she dined here. She had cried almost every day during the first week, but one day, Gio had taken her aside and explained what restaurant culture is like. "It's high pressure in there," he had said, "and sometimes the staff just needs to blow off steam. Unfortunately, you're the newest one around here so that makes you a target. Don't let them get to you and push back when you need to, okay? You're a Muccino, for God's sake. The kitchen is in your blood."

Honestly, she had wanted to quit, but Gio was right. And so, she developed a thick skin, a spine, and a mouth as foul as any of the line cooks and they had begun to back off. Then one day, a particularly nasty Wall Street big shot type had been harassing one of the servers and started making a scene in the dining room. Isabelle had backed the poor girl, threw the asshole out, and banned him. That had solidified all the staff's respect for her, and she learned that day that above all else, employees needed to know they had a manager who had their back.

"Looking good tonight, Bella." Alejandro smiled at her, his handsome face beaming. "But then again, you always do."

"Flattery will get you nowhere, Garcia. Get back to work," Isabelle retorted with a roll of her eyes, but she couldn't help the giddy fluttering of butterflies in her stomach. Alejandro had been one of the few people who had been kind to her when she first arrived. Lately, though, things had gotten, well, cozy between them to say the least. They had been spending their breaks together, drinking coffee in the back room, chatting mostly about his childhood in Puerto Rico or about Evan.

She'd seen the gleam of interest in his eyes, and knew that she only had to say the word, and he would ask her out. Frankly, she would be a fool not to date him; Alejandro was handsome and charming, everyone at the restaurant loved him because he was hardworking and kind, and he didn't mind that she was a single mom. In fact, the few times she'd brought Evan around, he had seem genuinely interested in him, even playing with him and making him laugh.

Still, there was just something about it that didn't sit right with her. Her wolf, too, did not appreciate the presence of the human male sniffing around them.

"Should I meet you in the back when it's time for my break?" he asked, a hopeful expression on his face.

"Sure," she said. Checking the time on her watch, she let out a deep sigh. "Dinner rush is about to begin. I'll see you later."

On weeknights like this when they mostly had the

business dinner crowd, Isabelle worked at the hostess stand. She found that she loved this part more—being in the front of house, chatting with regulars, greeting newcomers, and making sure everyone was happy, rather than boring, backroom managerial stuff.

The dining room was full tonight, and she was quite happy that all their reservations had shown up, and they had a healthy amount of walk-ins too. She was walking back to the hostess' station after seating one of their regulars when she saw a familiar face waiting.

"Lucas!" She jumped at him and embraced him in her excitement. He hadn't been at the battle with the mages, but he'd been directing their forces. According to Sofia, it pained him not to be out there, but it was too risky because the mages had tried time and time again to kidnap him. Being the child of two Alphas who were also True Mates gave his blood special properties that made the artifacts more powerful. "I didn't know you were coming for dinner."

Lucas hugged her back heartily. "It was a last-minute thing. Is the chef's table free?"

"Of course," she nodded. "I'll let Gio know. How many —" Her lungs squeezed tight as she saw the man behind Lucas, standing next to Cross.

What the hell was he doing *here*?

Gold-green eyes bore into her for a second, then flickered away disinterestedly. She flinched inwardly at the dismissal, so she decided she too could play that game. To pretend that she didn't know him. "Just the three of you then?" she asked brightly.

"Yes. By the way, this is—"

"Gio will want to know right away, so I'll do that right

now. You know the way." She spun on her heels and walked away from them. It was a miracle she made her legs work, seeing as her knees were like jelly.

The heat and noise of the kitchen was a welcome respite, and she told Gio about Lucas's arrival and that he had two guests, then made a beeline for the dining room. Before she left, Alejandro caught her gaze as he stood at the pasta station. He sent her a concerned look and cocked his head, in a silent question that seemed to ask if she was okay. She flashed him a tight smile and then ducked out of the kitchen. To her relief, there was no sign of Lucas or Ransom.

She leaned against the nearest wall and took a deep breath. Seeing Ransom that morning as he was sleeping had been nerve-racking, but now to have him up close was too damned much.

Control yourself.

This was no big deal, right? He didn't seem to be affected by her at all. Meanwhile, her inner wolf—and all her female instincts—stood at attention in his presence. Had she forgotten how magnetic he was? And how handsome he looked? His hair was a little longer and his beard thicker, but that didn't seem to lessen his appeal. *Lucifer himself, crawled up from hell*, she recalled thinking the first time she saw him. And—goddammit—even in his usual T-shirt and jeans, he still looked hot, and her body craved for his touch. Memories flashed in her head—of him on top of her. Or behind her. Or—

"You okay, Isabelle?" Mina, one of the senior servers, asked as she stopped by.

"Yeah, I'm fine." She smoothed her palms down her white blouse and black skirt, wishing that she'd put on something fancier like she usually did on weekends. "I'm just a little tired."

"Evan still keeping you up?" Her face was filled with concern. "I know a couple tricks to help him sleep through the night. I've had three kids, and I trained 'em all from an early age," she said with a chuckle.

"I'd like that, thanks," she replied. "Maybe later after shift."

"You betcha," she said before walking away.

After another deep, clearing breath, she walked back through the dining room, stopping by a couple of the tables to make sure everyone was all right, taking her time to hear compliments and trying to solve any complaints. She kept herself busy, though couldn't help glancing toward the hallway that led to the private chef's dining table in the back, expecting ... something to happen. But what, she didn't know.

"James," she beckoned one of the servers over. "I don't think we're going to have any more walk-ins, but could you watch my station please while I take a break?"

When the young man nodded, she headed straight for the break room, which was in the same hallway that led to the chef's table but thankfully, veered off to the left.

As she turned into the small hallway to the back room, she heard footsteps behind her. *Probably Alejandro.*

"Did you bring the espresso and biscotti? I think there were two left in the tin," she asked him as she pushed the door open to the break room, then turned to him. "If Gio catches you—"

But it wasn't Alejandro who had followed her, and the shock at seeing who it was had her jumping out of her skin.

Ransom.

The intensity of his golden-green eyes slammed into her full force, making her stagger backward until she bumped into one of the break room tables. "You're not supposed to be here," she managed to say, barely controlling the quiver in her voice.

He continued to stare at her, his expression unreadable. His gaze pinned her to the spot, making it hard to move. Or breathe. "I wasn't expecting to find you here."

"That makes two of us," she huffed.

"I didn't know you worked here. Or that you worked at all."

Her nostrils flared. "What do you want?"

He took a step forward, and the room seemed even smaller. "I ... I just wanted to make sure you were okay."

She ignored the way the warmth of his body and his delicious scent called to her. Oh no, she wasn't going to give him the satisfaction of rattling her. "Me? Of course I'm fine." She gave a nonchalant shrug but crossed her arms over her chest. "What makes you think I'm not okay?"

"Isabelle—"

"I found out where Gio was hiding the biscotti and—" Alejandro stood by the doorway, stopping short as his gaze moved from Ransom to Isabelle. "What's going on here?"

"Nothing." Isabelle pushed herself away from the table and circled around Ransom. "My brother's guest got lost on the way to the bathroom."

Alejandro didn't look like he was buying it, but knew better than to make a scene with a customer. "Sir, you should really be careful of where you go," he said in a cool voice. "Why don't I show you where the facilities are?"

"That won't be necessary." Ransom stretched out to full

height and straightened his shoulders. Alejandro was over six feet, but Ransom was taller and wider. "I was just having a chat with—"

"Thank you for the snacks." Isabelle snatched the espresso cup from Alejandro's hand and one of the cherry chocolate biscotti.

"Bella," Alejandro lowered his voice and placed himself between Ransom and her, then wrapped his free hand on her arm. "Did he come in here after you?"

A growl rippled from behind him. "Get the hell away from her."

Alejandro's face turned dark. "Who the hell do you think—"

"Ransom, I was wondering where you were."

Three pairs of eyes turned to the tall figure in the doorway. Cross stood there, his blue-green eyes darting from Isabelle to Ransom, then to Alejandro. "Looks like my friend got a little lost." Striding forward, he caught Ransom's arm. "Bathroom's the other way."

Ransom yanked his arm away, then turned to Isabelle. Before he could say anything, a warning gaze from Cross made him step back. He then motioned to the door. "Lead the way."

"Nice seeing you, Isabelle," Cross said as he herded Ransom out of the door.

Her lungs collapsed as air rushed out of her chest. It had been bad enough that Ransom was there, but Cross ... Would he tell him about Evan? Her hands shook so bad the dark liquid in the tiny cup she held sloshed to the side.

Alejandro took the espresso cup from her gently.

"Isabelle, what's the matter? What did that guy do to you? Do you want me to tell Gio—"

"No!" She protested and grabbed his wrist. "It's fine. He was lost, that's all." She forced a laugh. "Thanks for getting the biscotti and risking Gio's wrath."

"Anything for you." A smile spread across his lips. "I only have ten minutes left on my break."

"Then let's not waste it."

They sat down on the chairs and as Alejandro started a story about his pet puppy when he was kid back in San Juan, she nodded along. But truthfully, she was only half listening. She tugged at the collar of her blouse, trying to cool down the heat that was spreading through her body. Damn Ransom and his effect on her. She reminded herself that it was only lust and that it was because she'd never been with anyone else except him. Since Evan was born, there wasn't any time for dating.

But why was he here? And what was he talking about with Lucas? She glanced at the clock surreptitiously. Hopefully Lucas would finish his dinner soon and they would leave the restaurant. And Ransom could get out of New York and go back to wherever the hell he'd come from and never come back.

CHAPTER SIX

RANSOM FORCED HIMSELF TO FOLLOW CROSS OUT OF the break room, even as his feet felt like lead. His inner wolf wasn't making it easy for him either, snapping its teeth and ripping his claws at him from the inside. *What the hell do you want?*

The wolf growled.

Of course, he already knew what the animal wanted.

Isabelle Anderson. When he first came into the restaurant, he didn't recognize her as she stood by the hostess' station, dressed simply in a white blouse, black skirt, and sensible shoes. But his wolf knew in an instant, suddenly perking up as it sensed her. The moment he looked into those bi-colored eyes, he knew why his animal was acting weird.

It had been a shock to his system, seeing her after all this time. It was a possibility that he risked coming here, but working as a hostess at a restaurant was the last place he'd expected to see her again. Nor did he expect the deep, clawing need to be near her, touch her, hold her, and breathe in her scent. There she was, three feet away, but he couldn't do any of those things. Not when Cross and the Alpha—her brother—were there too. So he kept quiet, while battling the maelstrom raging inside him.

"Are you all right, Ransom?"

He didn't turn away from Cross and instead, looked him straight in the eyes. "Yeah, I'm fine. Got a little lost, as you said."

There was an expression that crossed the other man's face briefly that said he didn't buy that excuse. Did Cross know something? Did he suspect that he and Isabelle had been ... whatever they were? It seemed impossible that he didn't say a word all this time, and not even right after he fished him out of the Hudson.

"We should go back. Your Alpha is waiting." He began to walk toward the private dining room, clenching his fists at his sides. It had been difficult, trying to control himself as he met the son of the man he had hated all his life. Lucas Anderson was practically a copy of his father, save for the blue and green eyes. He wanted to hate the son, too, despite his innocence. But then again, he realized Lucas couldn't be blamed for his father's sins, no more than Ransom could. The thought made his stomach clench.

What was he doing here? He should have packed up and gone home. Fuck the plan. Fuck New York.

"Everything okay?" Lucas asked. "Cross went to get you when you didn't come back."

"Yeah, just got a little lost." He sat back down on the seat across from the Alpha, and Cross took the chair beside him. "Now, why don't we get back to business?"

Lucas's expression turned serious. "All right, I'm all for not wasting time. Let's start with the mages."

Ransom found himself unable to concentrate since they sat down to eat. All he could think about was Isabelle, which was why he excused himself so he could go back to the dining room. It was just his luck that he saw her going to the break room and couldn't stop himself from following her. Why he did it, he didn't know. There was this urge to be alone with her, and he knew this might be his only chance.

She had looked even more incredible, more beautiful than he remembered. Even in her simple uniform, she was more gorgeous than any woman he'd known. There was something else about her too ... something different that he couldn't quite put his finger on. And the fact that she was working here stoked his curiosity all the more. What the hell happened to the vivacious fashionista who loved to get all dressed up and take selfies?

"Ransom?"

Cross's voice jolted him out of his thoughts. "Yes. The mages. You were saying?"

Lucas cleared his throat. "As you know, the mages want the three artifacts of Magus Aurelius. They have the necklace and the ring but we have the dagger, thanks to you. Cross thinks he knows what they plan to do with it."

"As we found out, the ring has the power of death and life. Literally." He further explained how the ring had killed Sabrina when she was an infant and brought her back to life. "I think they mean to bring Magus Aurelius back to life. But without a body, they can only do it with powerful blood. Double Alpha blood."

"Double what?" Ransom asked.

"Lucas and his sister are Alphas and also the children of two Alphas, who are also True Mates," Cross began.

Ransom frowned. "True Mates ... that's a real thing?"

Cross's expression became inscrutable, and Lucas continued. "Yes. My parents were True Mates, and both Alphas. It's unprecedented, for sure, but we've seen the effect of my blood in particular when it was used with the dagger, as it allowed Cross to travel through time."

"You're shitting me," Ransom exclaimed.

"I'll explain later," Cross said. "But for now, we need to make sure they don't get the dagger and don't get Lucas's or Adrianna's blood."

"But we want to end this once and for all." There was a determined expression on Lucas's face. "It's been difficult tracking them down. We crush one stronghold, and another two pop up. They also have some powerful people on their side, witches and warlocks they've turned to their cause and a couple of billionaires who fund them. Mostly we've been waiting for them to attack us, and react, but this time we want to be ready."

"We're finalizing a plan," Cross said. "And we need all the help we can get."

Ransom crossed his arms over his chest and leaned back. "I'm no Alpha. I may be president of the Savage Wolves, but that means I protect my guys, not send them out on suicide missions. I don't want part of a fight that could get my guys killed." Every single member of the Savage Wolves had been through hell and clawed their way back to some semblance of a normal life. He was not going to throw that all away.

"This fight isn't limited to New York or just those with clans," Lucas said. "The mages want every single one of us dead. While you think you're safe now, you won't be in the future. Cross told me the mages attacked you a couple days ago when they were trying to get to Sabrina."

He ground his teeth together. That had been too close, and he was still wondering how the mages even managed to find them. If Logan hadn't mauled them all, who knows what would have happened? "All right, so what do you want?"

"Fight with us," Lucas said. "But even if you don't, you could still help keep our most vulnerable safe."

"I told them about your property in Kentucky," Cross said.

"My sister's property," he corrected. "It ain't mine to give. And she runs a business on part of it." The Seven Peaks Mountain Lodge and Cabins were Silke's pride and joy, which she had inherited from her mother.

"We're not asking for you to give it to us, but we want to know if you'd consider making it into a shelter for our pups, the elderly, the humans that are part of the clan," Lucas said.

Only two Lycans could produce a Lycan offspring, and thus anyone of their kind who mated with a human produced fully human children, much like Silke, his sister, or to be more technical, his stepsister. Silke's mother was human, and she had died when Silke was a baby. Not long after that, Pops had met Joanie and they got married.

"We'll offer protection, of course," Cross said. "We have witch and warlock allies who can come and put magical barriers around the entire property. Plus, we will alert the clans nearby, and they'll come to help as well if things go bad."

Ransom huffed. "It's Silke's decision, you ask her." The truth was, Silke was a bleeding heart, and all Cross would have to say is "protect the children and elderly," and his sister would open up her arms and take in as many people as she could.

"What about your wolves?"

"They're not mine, I'm not their Alpha. They're Lone Wolves, they can decide for themselves."

"And you?" Lucas's mismatched gaze bore into him. "Would you help us out?"

Build their trust. Let them think you're allies. Do what it takes. I'll take care of the rest. And then when there's an opening, we'll destroy Grant Anderson. He huffed. "I suppose."

"Great," Lucas held his hand out. "On behalf of my clan, thank you."

Don't thank me yet. But he shook the Alpha's hand anyway.

"Why don't you stay for a couple of days, and we can talk some more. You can also see what we're doing here and how we can include you in our plans. I'll take care of whatever you need." Lucas stood up. "I need to get back home, but Cross knows what to do. If you'd like to stay and have more food, please help yourself."

Ransom stood up too. "No, I think I'd rather get on with it." He looked at Cross. "Can I hitch a ride back to Kentucky?" If he was going to stay in New York, he would need a couple of things.

"Of course." Cross got up as well and held out his hand. "As you said, we should get on with it."

———

There were certainly a lot of advantages to having someone like Cross around. In a couple of hours, Ransom had taken two trips to Kentucky and back to New York. He had a few things to settle back at home, including letting Silke and the other Savage Wolves know about Lucas's proposal. Silke, of course, agreed to turn the property into a sanctuary if necessary. As for the rest of his guys, Ransom left it up to them if they wanted to volunteer to fight if things got tough.

"This is a decision you each have to make yourself, as Lone Wolf, not as a member of the MC," he had told them. "And I'll respect whatever you decide."

After that, Ransom packed up a few things he needed while he stayed in New York, including his bike, which Cross was happy to transport. It was after midnight by the time Cross left to go home, and although he knew he should probably hit the hay, he wasn't tired. That, and there was a niggling itch in his chest that wouldn't go away. And he knew there was only one way to scratch that itch, so he got on his bike and made his way to Lower Manhattan.

He arrived outside Muccino's just as the lights in the dining room turned off, which hopefully meant Isabelle hadn't left yet, if she was working here. Frankly, he was still confused why she was working at all. When he saw her last, she didn't seem to have a job as she spent most of her time shopping, getting dressed and made up, or playing with her phone. She was a billionaire's daughter, for God's sake. If she wanted to work, surely Grant Anderson could have found her a better gig elsewhere, working in an air-conditioned office with an assistant to pick up her morning lattes.

He saw a couple of employees leave through the front door, but not lock it. Good thing that asshole who had barged in on them was one of those employees. His wolf seethed at the thought of the human who had the balls to touch Isabelle like that. It wanted Ransom to follow him and rip his fucking hands off.

While it sounded like a very good idea, he tamped down the urge. That wasn't why he was here. Of course, between getting revenge on her father, and now getting mixed up with all this mage business, things were bound to get messy, and he should really leave her alone.

But there was just something he couldn't put his finger on … there was something there that wasn't quite right. Like a mystery that he needed to solve. What had happened to her?

His questions were about to be answered because the front door opened and she came out. Slinging her purse over her shoulder, she locked the door, gave it a test wiggle, then walked up to the edge of the sidewalk. She didn't notice him crossing the street as she was busy tapping on the screen of her phone.

"Do you need a ride home?"

Her shoulders tensed, and slowly, she looked up, her mismatched eyes going wide and her lips parting. It took her a second to compose herself as her mouth snapped shut. "No thank you," she said tightly. "I've called an Uber."

"You always loved riding." Her eyes flashed with outrage as she figured out his double-meaning, but he cocked his head back toward his parked motorcycle. "On my bike," he finished with a grin.

Her face went all red. "I'm not dressed for riding," she pointed out, glancing down at her skirt.

"That never stopped you before."

She let out an indignant sound as her hands fisted at her

sides. "Look, I spoke with Lucas after you left, and he told me who you were and what you're doing here. While my clan and I appreciate what you've done for us, I don't know what you expect me to say or do right now."

The direct approach was not something he expected, so he decided to do the same. "What happened to you, Isabelle? Why are you working here?"

"I—I don't know what you're talking about," she said. "Am I not allowed to have a job? Everyone has one."

"You didn't before," he pointed out. "Back then, you seemed pretty content at spending your trust fund. Fenrir Corporation ain't hurting, so I know this isn't about money. Now, tell me what happened." He frowned. "Why lower yourself and take a menial job like hostessing?"

If it were possible, she looked even angrier. "You have no right ..." She took a deep breath. "My ride's here," she stated, then sidestepped around him. "I hope I never see you, but in that tiny chance our paths ever cross again, don't you *ever* talk to me."

He watched her get into the nondescript sedan car that pulled up to the curb, not bothering to stop her. Instead, he jogged back to his bike, hopped on, and drove uptown, taking a few shortcuts and running a yellow light or two, just so he could make it to the Upper East Side before she did. He parked his bike by the entrance of The Enclave and waited. Sure enough, a few minutes later, Isabelle's Uber stopped right behind his bike.

As she stepped out of car, she glared at him. "What the hell are you doing? If I didn't make myself clear, I don't ever want to see or talk to you."

"You haven't answered my question." He walked toward her, reaching his hand out. "What's going on—"

"Don't!" She held her arms up. "Just leave me alone," she said before turning on her heel and fleeing toward the entrance.

Nothing about this sat right with him. After what happened between them, he expected many different reactions from her—anger, cool indifference, or maybe even to laugh at him and pretend nothing was wrong. But, for a moment, he saw fear on her face, and that really made him even more suspicious. So, he chased after her, dashing through the door and followed her into the lobby.

"Isabelle!"

She whirled around, her face a mask of indignation and fury. "What are you—Johnny!" she barked at the young man sitting behind the concierge desk. "Call security! Tell them that someone is trying to breach The Enclave."

The wide-eyed young man shot to his feet and swallowed. "I-I'm sorry Ms. Anderson, I can't do that."

Her hands planted on her hips and she glowered at him. "What do you mean?"

Johnny eyed Ransom and then his gaze slid back to Isabelle. "He's a guest here, ma'am. The Alpha himself came down here and introduced him to the door staff."

Slowly, her head turned from the young man to Ransom. "What is he saying?"

"Lucas invited me to stay for a few days so we can iron out details on our alliance," he said smugly. "And housed me in a guest suite in South Cluster."

Blood drained from her face. "Tha-that can't be ... you're joking."

"Do I look like I'm joking, princess?"

Her nostrils flared. "Fine," she harrumphed. "But I'm w-warning you. Stay away from me!" Spinning on her heel, she headed toward the door at the end of the hallway, slamming it behind her.

Ransom knew he had pushed her buttons enough for one night. But that didn't mean he was giving up. *Oh no.* There was something up with Isabelle, and his instincts and his wolf were screaming at him to find out what it was. And he would not stop until he did.

CHAPTER SEVEN

THE MOMENT SHE OPENED HER EYES, A PIT OF DREAD formed in Isabelle's stomach. Glancing at her clock, she realized her alarm wasn't going off for another ten minutes. *Not like I got much sleep anyway.* If only she could stay in bed. *Forever.* If only last night had been a dream. But it wasn't. Ransom really was here in New York, and he was staying in The Enclave, a few buildings away from her and Evan.

Dragging herself out of bed, she quickly got through her morning routine, refusing to look at her reflection in the mirror because she didn't need to see how big the bags under her eyes were. After getting dressed, she headed to the nursery where Evan was already up, babbling to himself.

"Good morning, sweetheart," she cooed as she picked him up. Evan was such a happy baby, always smiling and laughing, though he did have his moods. Whenever he frowned, he reminded her so much of Ransom—he also had a little line that formed between his eyebrows. The dread in her stomach grew as she wondered if anyone would begin to see the similarities between them, now that Ransom was around.

He's only here for a few days, she reminded herself. *No one will notice if you don't act suspiciously.*

The truth was, she'd never expected to see Ransom ever again. After he left that night, she had been a mess. That whole week with him had been like a dream, and there had been an element of excitement, sneaking around with him. She was living in the moment, but certainly didn't expect him to just leave like that.

He started acting weird when she mentioned her family, and she'd been hurt by his dismissiveness that she walked out. As she was leaving, however, she realized that maybe he was miffed that she was sneaking around with him and that she was ashamed of him. It had filled her with hope—maybe this wasn't just a fling. Maybe it was something more, that he wanted more. So, she rushed back to tell him she was willing to give things a try.

And that was when she saw him with his bags, and things turned to shit. He wasn't some golden-hearted bad boy. No, he was just another asshole.

Evan fussed as she held him in her arms, and she realized that she had been standing there, staring into space. "I'm sorry, baby." She kissed his temple. "Let's get you breakfast."

After changing his diaper, she carried him to the kitchen and placed him in his high chair. As she prepared his breakfast, her phone buzzed in her pocket. "Hello?"

"Hey, Isabelle. It's me." It was Sofia. "Just checking in. Are we good for today?"

She cursed inwardly. How could she have forgotten? Yesterday afternoon, Sofia had called and said she had to go into the station early today. Her job as a detective for the NYPD meant that she was on call, especially when she had a large load of active cases. So, she asked Isabelle if she could watch Alessandro and Kier until their regular babysitter came at ten, when Isabelle left for work. "Don't worry, I'll be upstairs by seven to pick up Alessandro and Kier as soon as I'm done feeding Evan."

"That's great. Actually, we have a slight change of plans. When John found out you'd be watching all three kids this morning, he offered to come up here and give you a hand."

"Oh, that would be very helpful. Thank you!"

After she finished feeding Evan and getting him dressed, she made her way to the penthouse apartment. She rang the doorbell, and a few seconds later, a familiar face opened the door. "Oh! Hey, Jared."

"Good morning, Isabelle." The older Lycan gave her a kind smile. Jared Patrick had been her father's personal assistant, and now served as the head executive assistant for the entire Fenrir Corporation. Dressed in his usual dark suit, his white hair combed neatly, he was obviously dressed to go into the office today. "It's lovely to see you."

"Yeah, it's been a while. What are you doing here?" She entered the penthouse as he stepped aside to let her in. "Sofia told me that John was going to be here, but not you."

"John told me that you guys were watching all three pups this morning," Jared explained. "So I thought I'd join you before I head to work."

John Patrick, Jared's husband, had been a member of the Lycan Security Force and served as bodyguard to Isabelle's family for years. He had retired a while back, though now he was Alessandro and Evan's regular babysitter whenever Sofia and Isabelle were both at work. John was very loving and kind, and had a lot of experience with pups since he and Jared had adopted and raised three kids of their own.

"Well, it's nice to see you," Isabelle said. "I hardly do since you work all the time."

"That's what I keep saying." John Patrick walked up to them, carrying Kier. He slipped his free arm around Jared's shoulder and pulled him close. "See? Even Isabelle thinks you work too hard, honey."

Jared smiled at him wryly. "You know I would drive you crazy if I stayed home all the time."

John laughed heartily. "You're right. Besides, who would pay for my expensive hobbies?"

"Oh, thank God you're all here!" Sofia rushed into the room, hairbrush in one hand, while holding Alessandro to her hip. "I'm running a bit behind. Thank you," she said to Jared as he took the baby from her. "I'll be out in a sec!" She rushed back to the bedroom.

"Hello, Alessandro," Jared greeted. "How are you today?"

Alessandro's lower lip quivered, then he let out a cry. Jared looked taken aback and tried to calm him down.

"Let's switch." Isabelle handed Evan to Jared and took Alessandro. "There, there, now. Aunty Isabelle is here. Sorry," she said to Jared. "Alessandro's picky about who holds him."

"That's all right." Jared nuzzled Evan's cheek. "Our youngest was the same. Wouldn't let anyone but me or John hold her."

"How *is* Layla?" Isabelle asked. "John said she finished her training. How is she liking being part of the Lycan Security Team?"

They chatted about Layla and their sons for a few more minutes until Sofia came out, all ready and dressed for work. "Thanks again so much." She kissed Alessandro on the cheek. "Be good, sweetie. I'll see you soon. You know where to call me," she said to John.

"Yes, Lupa," he said. "Don't worry, I'll take care of them. Go catch some criminals and keep the streets of New York clean, okay?"

She laughed. "Will do!" With one last wave, Sofia left the penthouse.

"Now," John began. "I think these kids have been cooped up indoors for too long. So, I was thinking we can go to the playground so they can have some fresh air and sunshine." He motioned to the picnic basket by the door. "You don't have to leave for work yet, do you Isabelle? Why don't you join us? Jared's playing hooky for the morning." He winked at his husband.

"I only told the Alpha I'd be delayed by an hour," Jared replied, but smiled warmly at John. "So I can at least enjoy some coffee."

"That sounds good," Isabelle said. "I have an hour or so before I have to get ready." It would be nice to be outside, now that the weather was mild.

They all left the apartment and soon were on their way to The Enclave's playground, located right in the middle of the compound. Isabelle had played here herself with Julianna when they were little, often in the morning like this with their mother watching over them before she went to work at Muccino's. Usually it was busy on weekends or afternoons, but this morning, they had it all to themselves.

John handed Kier to Jared, then took a checkered blanket

from the basket and laid it on the ground. They all sat on the blanket as John took out coffee and pastries for the adults, and some kid-friendly snacks for the pups.

"This is a good look on you, Isabelle," John commented as she fed Kier bits of cereal. Alessandro stayed on her lap while Evan sat on the blanket in front of Jared. The older Lycan was trying—unsuccessfully—not to let the boy's sticky hands leave marks on his otherwise immaculate suit jacket.

"Hmm?" She glanced up at him. "What do you mean?"

"I think he means you're doing a good job as a mom," Jared clarified as he finally wrangled Evan and wiped down his sugary fingers. "I happen to think so too."

"Oh." She blushed in embarrassment at their compliments. "I'm just doing the best I can."

"You were meant for this, Isabelle," John added. "I, uh, had my doubts when Jared told me about you being pregnant." Jared shot him a warning look and then shot an apologetic grin at her. "But I always knew you were going to turn out great."

Isabelle laughed. "I was a brat, and you know it."

"But you have a big heart," John said. "Always have."

"And that's why you were always my favorite, John," she said. "And—" Suddenly, she felt all the hairs on the back of her neck stand on end. Her wolf sniffed the air as a passing breeze wafted by, and they both caught a familiar scent.

"Oh, hello," John greeted to someone behind Isabelle. "Are you new to The Enclave?"

Slowly, she looked behind her. Not that she needed to see who it was.

Ransom stood there; eyebrows snapped together. "I just moved in. Hello, Isabelle."

She swallowed as her mouth went dry at the sound of his low, raspy voice. It didn't help that he looked damned sexy in his usual attire of jeans and a T-shirt. The fabric of his shirt stretched across his broad chest enticingly, and covered the tattoos that she knew covered most of his upper torso. Quickly, she turned her head back to Jared and John, who looked at each other with strange expressions on their faces.

"Aren't you going to introduce us to your friend, Isabelle?" Jared asked.

It took her another second to recover. "This is Ransom," she grumbled. "Lucas's guest from out of town. Ransom, this is John and Jared Patrick."

"And this is Alessandro, Evan, and Kier," Jared introduced, motioning to each of the pups. "We're all volunteering as babysitters this morning."

"Why don't you join us, Mr. Ransom?" John said. "I have more coffee if you like."

"It's Ransom. Just Ransom, and I don't—"

"Please, sit," Jared urged and motioned to the empty spot on the blanket next to Isabelle.

Oh, please no. But her wolf had the opposite reaction, practically begging him to come nearer. When she felt the blanket tug and shift as he sat down beside her, her heart pounded in her chest like a drum. She tried not to look at Evan. Her wolf, on the other hand, yipped happily at Ransom's presence.

"You're a guest of the Alpha's?" Jared's eyes narrowed at him. "We must have met before at Fenrir, right? You seem familiar. Please do forgive me if I can't quite remember."

Her stomach dropped. *Oh God, please don't let Jared realize it!*

"No, I don't think so. I just came here two days ago." He quickly told the two men about how Cross had recruited him to help with the fight and Lucas inviting him to stay. "Usually when I'm out in Kentucky, I wake up early and sit on my porch or walk around. I was missing nature, and I saw this little patch of green, and I thought I'd come out here and get some air." He glanced disinterestedly at the children. "I guess you guys had the same idea too."

"The pups have been cooped up inside because of this nasty mage business," John said. "I thought it was a good idea to bring them out. Fresh air and sunshine are good for them."

Ransom frowned. "Are they all yours?"

John chuckled and shook his head. "Oh, no."

"Ours are all grown and flown the coop, I'm afraid," Jared said, smiling warmly at John. "But John's always been the mother hen type, so he watches the pups while their moms are at work."

"Moms?"

Ransom's question made Isabelle's heart stop. *Oh God.*

"I think it's pretty obvious who these kids belong to," John said. "Look at those eyes."

"Ah."

Isabelle waited for the other shoe to drop, but seconds of uncomfortable silence ticked by, and he didn't say anything else. She released a breath she didn't realize she was holding.

"So how do you know our Isabelle?" This time, John eyed Ransom with suspicion, his tone very much fatherly.

"Lucas brought him to Muccino's last night," she said quickly. "I was working the hostess station."

"And so, you saw her out here and thought you'd come over and say hello," John stated.

"Yeah," Ransom answered. "Anything wrong with that?"

Jared and John looked at each other again—and Isabelle recognized that silent communication that often happened between spouses. Did they realize anything?

"Not at all," John said. "Especially since you helped with the fight. Thank you for that."

"John fought at the Battle of Norway," Jared said. "He was very brave."

John laughed. "I was scared shitless and injured so bad, I thought I wouldn't make it. The Alpha, I mean the former Alpha—that's Isabelle's dad—saved my life."

She sensed Ransom tense beside her, and she sensed a trickle of anger from him. What was going on?

His jaw clenched. "Battle of Norway?"

Jared looked taken aback. "You don't know about the Battle of Norway?"

He shook his head.

"Ransom is a Lone Wolf," Isabelle explained, then turned back to Ransom. "You were probably around Lucas and Adrianna's age when that took place, so you wouldn't have remembered unless you learned it from your father or mother or someone else told you about it."

"About thirty years ago, when the mages first appeared, the final battle with them was fought in a small village in Norway," Jared began. "They kidnapped Sebastian Creed, Meredith, as well as Zac Vrost, who was a pup back then. Anyway, that was when we defeated Stefan, the old master mage and his forces."

Alessandro began to wiggle in Isabelle's arms as he planted his feet on the ground and attempted to stand up. "Ma! Ma!" he babbled.

Jared chuckled. "Oh Alessandro, Aunty Isabelle isn't your mama. She's E—"

"Look at the time!" Isabelle scrambled to her feet so fast, she nearly knocked Alessandro over. Thankfully she caught him in time, though he seemed to enjoy it and giggled as she settled him down on the blanket. "Be a good boy, Alessandro." She glanced over at the two other boys, her heart thrumming wildly in her chest. "Evan ... Kier ... be nice to John and Jared ... I'll see you both later."

Her wolf protested, wanting to stay, to be near Ransom. However, she paid it no mind and scampered from the picnic blanket, then turned toward the direction of her building. *Calm down*, she told herself, though she picked up her pace. Her stomach tied up in knots. *Almost there.* When her building came into sight, her anxiety levels dropped.

"Isabelle! Isabelle!"

She pretended not to hear him and dashed straight through the door and into the building. Her finger jabbed at the elevator call button, and she thanked God profusely when the doors opened. By the time they closed, her heart was pounding so loudly she couldn't hear anything else.

Slumping against the cool metal wall, she placed a hand over her chest. *That had been too close.* It had pained her not to kiss Evan goodbye, but she didn't have a choice.

Her knees were practically jelly by the time the elevator reached her floor. *He's just here for a few days*, she reminded herself as she made her way to her apartment. *He'll leave soon.*

Once again, her wolf made its displeasure known, growling at her. *Shut up!* Didn't it remember what it was like when Ransom left? How it felt to have been abandoned by their True Mate, the pain that they carried around? All those tears they wasted ... that feeling of despair for days after ... only the knowledge that they carried a pup pulled them through the depression.

Her she-wolf yowled woefully. "See?" she said. "We don't want to go through that when he leaves us again." And he *would* leave again.

She bit her lip, forced down the wave of tears threatening to spill over and swallowed it all. No, she wasn't going to cry for him anymore. He was the one who walked away and had his phone disconnected. Nor did he try to contact her, even to see how she was doing.

"He abandoned all of us. You, me, and Evan." she told her wolf bitterly. No way was she going to let him see Evan. Evan was *her* son. She birthed him and cared for him. He was hers alone, as far as she was concerned.

CHAPTER EIGHT

WHAT THE HELL DID I DO?

Ransom shook his head as he watched Isabelle bolt into the building. He tried calling after her again as she didn't hear him the first time. *Or pretended not to.*

It stuck in his craw, how she was avoiding him still. Sure, things hadn't ended the right way between them, but he left for her own good, even if she didn't know it. After he'd recovered from the fall in the Hudson, he'd wanted to go back to her so many times. To see her again. But it wasn't right. He told himself he couldn't, because she was the daughter of his enemy. The man he wanted to crush like a bug under his heel.

And now?

Well things had gotten worse.

But still, he couldn't leave her alone. Something spooked her, for some reason. Did she sense that her father's name had put him on edge?

He had to forget about her. His wolf let out a guttural

sound. It didn't want to leave Isabelle. It wanted to be near her, wanted him to touch her and feel her again.

Turning on his heel, he headed back to the South Cluster garage where he'd parked his bike. He felt his phone buzz in his vest pocket but ignored it. He knew who that was. Who had been calling him since last night. Unfortunately, he had no answers. There was really no update on the situation—hell, he didn't even know where Grant Anderson was at the moment.

For now, he had to focus on what he could do. Cross wanted to take him to the Guardian Initiative headquarters so he could meet with the team and figure out how they could work together. He offered to transport him there, but Ransom declined. Traveling using magic, though convenient, still didn't sit well with him. Besides that's why he'd brought his bike back, so he could move around without relying on anyone else.

Though he'd been inside the headquarters of GI, he didn't actually know where it was since Cross had transported him in and out of the building. The hybrid gave him the cross street where they were supposed to meet so Cross could show him the way. *Don't know why he couldn't just give me the address.*

Soon, he found himself on the right street, and slowed his bike to a stop as he approached an alley hidden between two large buildings.

"What the fuck?" There wasn't anything here that seemed like the headquarters he'd been to. Was he at the right place?

"Oh good, you're here."

Ransom was so used to Cross's powers that he wasn't

surprised he just popped out of nowhere. "I wasn't sure this was the place," he said. "I don't see any door or entrance."

Cross nodded at the brick wall at the end of the alley. "It's over there."

"Where?"

"The wall," he said. "Just drive through."

"Is it going to open up like in some James Bond movie?" He scrubbed his hand down his face when Cross smiled at him mysteriously. "You've got to be kidding me. I'll survive the crash, but my bike won't. If it ends up in pieces—"

"I'll get you a new one," he said wryly. "Now, go ahead and drive in, and I'll meet you inside." With a last wave, Cross disappeared.

Ransom gritted his teeth and revved his bike, then headed straight for the end of the alley. Holding his breath, he sped up and then braced himself, waiting for the impact. But, much to his relief, he went straight through the wall, into a long, well-lit tunnel. He continued on, until finally he reached a large space, like the inside of a warehouse. Cross waited for him at the other end, arms crossed over his chest.

"That smile you've got on your face is as big as the Brooklyn Bridge, I'm almost tempted to wipe it off with my fists," Ransom noted. "Where the hell are we?"

"In the Brooklyn Bridge."

"No, really, where are we?"

Cross laughed. "Like I said. *In* the Brooklyn Bridge. One of the towers over the water, to be exact."

"Motherfucker." He parked his bike in one of the empty spots, then hopped off and strode over to Cross. "All right. Let's get this show on the road."

Cross led him to the waiting elevator in the lobby just

behind them, then pressed the button for the top floor. He recognized the office where Cross had first brought him to a few days ago, remembering thinking to himself that it looked more like the offices of a Fortune 500 company than secret headquarters of an anti-mage task force.

"Mika and Dad are already waiting for us," Cross said as he nodded to the corner office.

Ransom followed the hybrid as they crossed the room, and he knocked on the door. They entered as someone from inside called them in.

"Mika, Dad," Cross began. "This is Ransom. Ransom, this is Daric, my father, and Mika Westbrooke. They're co-heads of the Guardian Initiative."

Ransom recognized the two people inside the office from the other day. The tall man standing behind the desk was obviously Cross's father—they were practically twins, except Daric was older. The woman seated behind the desk, on the other hand, had led the meeting and the team.

"Welcome," Daric greeted warmly. "Nice to finally be introduced to you, Ransom. I've heard so much about you from Cross."

"Thanks for coming on board," Mika added.

"Yeah," he said with a shrug. "Let's skip the small talk and get on with business. "

Mika raised a dark brow. "The Alpha told me you prefer to get to the point. I like it. I don't like bullshit either. So, let's go on a tour first, and then we can talk some more about how we can work together."

As she got up from behind the desk, Ransom noticed something he didn't realize before—her stomach protruded out in front of her. Mika was obviously *very* pregnant.

"Something the matter?" Mika asked, foot tapping on the floor. "Yes, I'm pregnant. Do you have a problem with that?" she finished before he could say anything.

"Uh ..." He didn't know what to say exactly. "No problem at all. Ma'am." Though he and Mika were probably the same age, he suddenly felt like a kid being chastised by his teacher. "Just ... concerned."

Her gaze narrowed into slits. "About *what*?"

Daric cleared his throat. "Ransom, you needn't worry about Mika's safety. She is carrying her True Mate's child."

What was it with these people and supposed True Mates?

"Dad, Mika," Cross began. "I'm afraid Ransom doesn't know anything about True Mates." He turned to Ransom. "When a female is pregnant with her True Mate's child, she is invincible. Nothing can harm her."

"They're also especially fertile," Daric said. "As you know, it's very difficult for Lycan to reproduce, but not with True Mates. Their first coupling always produces a Lycan— or in my case, a hybrid—pup. Why, Cross himself was conceived when his mother and I—"

"Let's not talk about my conception, Dad." Cross covered his face with his hands, though that wasn't effective to hide the redness flushing his skin.

Ransom shrugged. "I didn't mean to offend you, Mika," he said. "I had no idea ... or any idea really." It seemed his entire world had flipped around in the last few days. Mages and magic babies? Who knew? He didn't really care much about babies, though it made sense now, thinking back to this morning. Isabelle did seem to have an abundance of nephews. Were they triplets? They seemed to be similar looking and all around the same age, except maybe that large chubby one.

"So, now that we're done discussing the birds and the bees," Mika said impatiently. "Should we get on with that tour?"

"Yes, ma'am."

He followed Mika out of the office as she started the tour, which lasted most of the morning and covered the entire headquarters. Ransom had to admit, the GI headquarters and their operations were impressive. What he thought was a boring, bureaucratic office was actually a well-oiled machine, with everyone working together, from the somewhat chaotic IT department to the well-disciplined combat division. He also met everyone in charge, including Cross's cousins, Lizzie Martin and Arch Jones, and was left starstruck when he was introduced to Cliff Forrest, former MMA Champion of the World. The guys back home would probably freak the fuck out when he told them Forrest was a Lycan.

"Now," Mika began as they concluded the tour back at her office. "Lucas, Daric, and I are still discussing a final plan to lure the mages out."

"And how would you do that?" Ransom asked.

Daric sighed. "I hate to say it, but the only way we can lure them out is with the dagger, or Lucas or Adrianna, or maybe all of them."

"But at the same time, we can't alert them to any trap." Mika rubbed her temples with her fingers. "And it's not like we can capture any of them when they attack the clans. It's like they're taunting us, but we still don't know why."

"Taunting you?" Ransom asked. "What do you mean?"

"For the past year or so, the mages have grown in their

numbers and powers," Daric began. "They've also been attacking many of the clans around the world. Yet, there seems to be no rhyme or reason or pattern."

"They go to a clan's territory, attack them, but only cause damage and injury," Cross added. "They don't steal anything or kill anyone."

"Hmmm." Ransom scratched at his chin. "That's weird."

"Tell me about it," Mika said. "We've been trying to figure out what they want."

Infiltrating territories, but not doing anything ... "If I were them, I'd only risk doing that if A: I was confident I had the numbers to back me up and B: if I was trying get information," Ransom said. "Like trying out their defenses."

Mika, Daric, and Cross all looked at each other. "How could we have missed that?" Mika said incredulously.

Daric frowned. "We have been too focused on the artifacts and Lucas and Adrianna."

Cross gave him a funny look. "How'd you guess that?"

"Life as a Lone Wolf and bein' part of an MC isn't exactly a bed of roses." He swallowed down the memories threatening to surface. *Deflect,* he told himself. *Or they might figure out the truth.* "Pops said in the early days of the MC, before he settled down, it was like the Wild West. Lots of fights, wars, that kind of shit. He taught me a thing or two."

"Your father must have been a smart fellow and a strategic thinker." Daric's ocean-colored eyes—so much like Cross's—seemed to bore into him. "It seems to have benefited from an outsider's perspective. Thank you, Ransom."

"It was just a thought," he said nonchalantly. "Don't mean it's true."

"Still, it's a good start, and it'll help us figure a couple of things out," Mika said.

"We should definitely plan for this," Daric said. "I should be off for now. The former Alpha asked to see me."

Ransom's ears perked up. "Former Alpha?"

"Yes, Lucas's father." The warlock looked at him strangely, eyes narrowed. "Anyway, he's been at home in Italy, but he wanted to come back to New York to help out. He asked that I bring him and his wife back to New York right away."

So, Grant Anderson would soon be in New York. Useful information, but he filed that knowledge away for now.

"Will I see you and Sabrina tonight for dinner?" Daric asked Cross.

"I'm afraid not, Dad," he replied. "I promised Dee I'd bring Sabrina over for dinner."

"That's fine, I'll see you tomorrow then. Give Dee and His Majesty my regards."

"I will, Dad," Cross said before Daric disappeared.

"I have stuff I need to do," Mika said. "And it's almost lunch, and Delacroix's going to burst in at any moment to feed me," she said with a sigh.

"We'll be on our way then, Mika." Cross stood up and so Ransom followed him. "Did you need a ride anywhere? Perhaps a quick trip home in case you forget anything?" he asked when they left Mika's office. "I need to leave soon, but I can make a trip if you need me."

"Nah." He waved the other man away. "If you don't mind, I do have a few things I need to take care of, but just here in the city."

"I'll let you know next time we need to meet with the Alpha or Mika again," Cross said. "And Ransom?"

"Yeah?"

"Thanks ... for everything."

"Well, I ain't doing this for you."

Cross looked at him with an inscrutable expression on his face. "Who are you doing it for?"

Fuck if he knew. "Tell Sabrina I said hi," he said evasively.

"Speaking of Sabrina ..." Cross opened his mouth then seemed to hesitate.

"What about Sabrina?"

"Nothing." Cross shook his head. "I mean, she says hi too."

Ransom frowned. "Did she say—" But Cross disappeared before he could finish his sentence. What the heck was Cross about to say? He knew something was up, and it didn't sit right in his stomach.

An insistent vibration from his pocket made him sigh impatiently. It was the call he'd been dreading, and he knew he needed to answer or else. "Yeah," he said into the receiver.

"You've been ignoring my calls."

"There was nothing to tell you last night. I didn't know where Gr—our target was located," he said.

"Last night? What about now."

"He's coming back to New York today. That's all I know."

There was a loud huff. "Keep me posted. And don't ignore my calls again."

The line went dead. "What, not even a kiss goodbye?" he said sarcastically. He shoved the phone back into his pocket and headed to the elevator. He jabbed at the call button and walked inside when the door opened. Two people—a timid-looking female with glasses and a stack of folders clutched to her chest, and a skinny young man who didn't look old enough to be here—were already inside.

God what a mess. Was he really going to go through with this revenge plan? It was the only way he could protect his family now. And what about Isabelle? She would hate him if she knew what he was planning.

His wolf snarled at the thought, and the two other passengers in the elevator started. The young man pressed up against the far wall and the female dropped her folders, sending papers flying everywhere.

"Sorry, Alpha!" she squeaked as she got down and began picking up the spilled documents.

"I ain't no Alpha," he growled, though that only made the woman nervous. With a sigh, he got down and helped her, handing her the papers by his feet.

His wolf didn't like the presence of the female, so it let out another warning yip, and the woman let out a yelp. "Damn thing," he spat.

The door opened to the training floor, and the two of them quickly scampered out. He berated his wolf. "See what you did?"

Maybe a ride would help clear his thoughts and calm his animal. Cross had said he could go anywhere in New York City, Upstate, and New Jersey, but not anywhere else like Connecticut. He ignored the irony of those words and got on his bike.

———

Ransom rode for what seemed like miles and miles and hours and hours, first heading out to New Jersey, as if he were headed west, back home. But he couldn't even make it past Uniontown. So he turned around and went east, to Long Island and up the coast, eventually parking his bike at a rest stop so he could walk up to the water.

He'd seen an ocean a few times in his life, but never the cold Atlantic waters. What would happen if he kept on riding? If he never stopped and made it all the way to Canada? Maybe he could live in Nova Scotia, or even Newfoundland, where no one knew him. Where no one knew his past, and he could make his own future. Or he could just jump into the freezing ocean. There would be no Cross to rescue him this time, so maybe he would die and never have to feel trapped like this. He would be free.

But his wolf, his own goddammed wolf, fought him. "Asshole," he growled back as its claws dug into him. "Stop! I'm not going to kill myself, you bastard!"

Grumbling to himself, he walked back to his bike and hopped on. But that didn't seem to quell his animal. He knew what it wanted. "Fine," he grunted as he started the engine. "I know where you want to go." Just once more, he told himself. Just one look, and then he'd leave her alone.

It was late by the time he arrived in Manhattan. He parked his bike a block away and decided to watch Muccino's from across the street, hidden in the shadows of an awning of a bookshop that had closed hours ago. The lights were still on, but he could see the number of diners were dwindling.

He remained there, watching as the restaurant emptied, the lights turned off, and the staff began to trickle out. Finally, the front door opened and Isabelle came out as usual and he held his breath. Tonight, she was dressed in a T-shirt, light jacket, black boots, and tight jeans that molded to her ass. As she locked the door and gave it a test wiggle, a bright red sports bike rolled out from the alley next to Muccino's and stopped in front of the restaurant.

Isabelle waved her hand at the driver as she walked toward him. Ransom recognized the driver as the guy from the other night—Mr. Tall, Dark, and Handsome Fuckface. He handed Isabelle a helmet, and she put it on and hopped on behind him.

His chest went all hot and tight. She didn't want to ride with him the other night, but she'd get behind this asshole on a *fucking crotch rocket?* Seething anger blazed through him, and his hands clenched into fists at his sides. When Isabelle wrapped her arms around Fuckface and cozied up to him, his wolf let out a savage snarl.

"I'm going to kill him," he muttered as he dashed to his bike. He had never been so glad for his enhanced speed as he was now, and soon he was able to catch up to them. While he did stay a good distance behind, he didn't lose them. It was like his primal hunting instinct allowed him to track them even though they were a tiny dot a few blocks ahead.

It was already late, and if they headed anywhere else other than The Enclave, he would catch up to them and rip Fuckface's head off and shove it up his ass. That tightness in his chest eased as they headed uptown and west. As they neared The Enclave, he slowed down and then stopped a block away.

Isabelle hopped off the bike and handed the helmet back to him. As she was about to turn away, he grabbed her hand and tugged her back. He leaned forward and whispered something in her ear that made her smile before she pulled away and headed inside.

A primal, potent fury burned through him. *That son of a bitch!* His wolf urged him to go after the other male. And Ransom was tempted, he really was. But he couldn't act on instinct like he did when he was younger. While he wanted to see that asshole roughed up, no way was he going to do more time in the slammer. That bastard wasn't worth it.

He told himself he was going to stay away from her, that this was getting too messy. God help him, he couldn't seem to stop himself from wanting to be near her. Not even after all this time. He was drawn to her, but it was more than that. There was a need inside him, to ward off anyone who dared try get near, and to make her truly his.

And maybe, he was done fighting himself.

CHAPTER NINE

"C'MON NOW, EVAN, ONE LAST BITE," SHE URGED AS SHE placed a spoonful of mashed peas in front of his lips. Eagerly, he opened his mouth and swallowed it all down. "Good boy. Now"—she put her hands on her hips—"maybe next time we can get more in you than on you?"

The entire front of his shirt—and hers—was stained with bits of green from his lunch. Evan somehow thought it was funny when he spit out the food and then flung it at her. "What am I going to do with you, young man?"

"Looks like he takes after his mom. I seem to remember you didn't like eating your greens either."

Whirling around at the sound of the familiar voice, she let out an excited yelp. "Papa!" She ran to him and jumped into his arms. His familiar scent—ocean salt spray—filled her with nostalgia and made her throat burn. "I'm sorry I didn't come see you last night when you arrived," she said as she pulled away. "I came home late from work."

Grant Anderson smiled down at her. The fine lines around his mouth and at the corners of his eyes and the silver at his temples were the only indication of his age. Despite having stepped down as Alpha, there was still that power and dominance that exuded from him. A lion in the winter of his days, but whose strength had yet to erode. "Hello sweetheart, it's nice to see you. And how's my goose?" he said, using his nickname for Evan.

Recognizing his grandfather, Evan waved excitedly at Grant, swaying from side to side. Isabelle immediately rushed over and picked him up before the highchair could tip over. "Are you happy to see Grandpa?" she cooed and walked over to Grant with Evan in her arms. "Mama messaged me this morning and said I can come in late because she's going to be at Muccino's while you're at Fenrir. So, what're you doing here?"

"I wanted to see you and Evan before I headed to the office. Hello, goosie goose." He took the baby from her arms and kissed him on the check, then tossed him in the air. Evan giggled uncontrollably, and Isabelle's heart stopped until her father caught him again. "I missed you so much. Did you miss me?"

Isabelle couldn't help but smile as she watched her father with her son. She could still remember his initial reaction when she told him she was pregnant. There was anger and displeasure for sure, and then the disappointment in his eyes afterwards. It was something she could never forget. Sure, she'd done many things to cause her father's displeasure at that point, but she'd never let him down like that.

It still pained her now that she couldn't live up to his expectations. However, he'd been the most attentive and loving grandfather anyone could ever ask for, and for that, she'd always be grateful.

"Sorry, to cut this short," she said as she took Evan from him. "I'm a bit behind, and now we both have to change." She glanced at Evan's stained shirt. "John's waiting for us. I think Kier and Alessandro are with him already."

"I know, I was just there to see the pups, and when John said you were running late, I thought I'd come and check if you needed some help," Grant explained.

"I'm good, Papa," she said. "But why don't you come with me while I change Evan, and then you can watch him while I get ready for work?"

"Sure, I can do that."

They went to the nursery, and Isabelle placed Evan on the changing table. "Can you hand me a fresh shirt from his closet, Papa?" She pulled off the soiled shirt from his little body and checked on his diaper. "At least *that's* clean, you little stinker," she joked.

Grant returned immediately with a new shirt. "Here you go, sweetheart."

"Thanks." She turned to her father and paused when she caught a strange look on his face. "What's wrong?"

He shook his head and smiled sheepishly. "Nothing. I mean ... I was just looking at you and wondering to myself, 'who is this person in front of me?'"

She chuckled. "What do you mean? I've always just been me, Papa."

"My Isabelle ..." He touched her cheek, then cradled her jaw. "We weren't expecting you, you know. Your mama thought we were done having pups, and then you came along. But you were such a ray of sunshine, my beautiful baby girl."

A lump formed in her throat, and she closed her eyes as

she rubbed her cheek against his palm. "I never told you how sorry I was, Papa." Her voice was barely a whisper, because she was afraid it would break if it was any louder. "I'm so sorry I disappointed you."

"Is that ... Oh, Isabelle." He stepped forward and pulled her to his side, planting a kiss on top of her head. She buried her face in his shirt as tears formed in her eyes. "When you were a teenager, everyone said I treated you like a child. And that I spoiled you too much by giving you everything you wanted. Maybe that's because I didn't want you to grow up—the way I watched Lucas, Adrianna, and Julianna grow up so fast and realized they didn't need me anymore. You were my baby girl, but I knew you would slip away from me eventually. I just wanted to hold onto you for a little longer."

"Oh, Papa," she sobbed. "I'll always be your girl."

"I know." He soothed a hand down her back. "I wasn't disappointed in you. You could never disappoint me. I was just shocked when you told me that you were pregnant. I'm your father, and I'll always think of you as my baby. And then when you told us it was your True Mate's baby and that he wasn't around ... I didn't want you to feel the same pain I did when your mom rejected me."

She looked up at him in surprise. "Mom rejected you?"

"She didn't want me initially, didn't think we fit together," he smiled sadly. "We didn't even know we were True Mates, even though both our wolves did. And then ... then there was a misunderstanding, and I thought I'd lost her forever. It was only for a few days, but the pain that put me through, I could barely take it. And I didn't want you going through the same thing."

"I thought I let you down," she confessed, "because I was irresponsible. A disappointment and shame to our name."

"Isabelle, look at him." He gestured to Evan with his head. "Is Evan something to be ashamed about? A disappointment?"

"I ... no."

"See? There's no reason you should feel that way. I've always been proud of you, and I have to say, I'm even prouder now of the woman you've become."

"Thank you, Papa." She sniffed and wiped at her cheeks. Even through her tears, she could see he was misty-eyed too. "Look at me, I'm a mess. I should get going or I'll be late."

"I'll watch over Evan, you go ahead, sweetheart."

As she got ready for work, she couldn't help but reflect on her father's words. Most everyone assumed that Evan's father was dead, but her parents and siblings knew that he was out there, and things just didn't work out between them. None of them understood—after all, everyone in their family was with their True Mate, so how could he not want to be with her? But she refused to say more, and they never pressed her. Yes, she was pretty depressed when Ransom left. She wouldn't get out of bed, wouldn't answer her phone. She stopped posting on her social media accounts and even drifted away from Maxine. But then, when she found out about the pregnancy, she picked herself up, because she knew she had to take responsibility.

Obviously, Ransom didn't feel the same pull she did. If it wasn't for the instant pregnancy and invulnerability, she would have doubted they were True Mates. He wouldn't have left like that. He knew exactly where she was and who she was, so he could have easily found her. But no, he didn't

even try to contact her after all this time. God knows what—
or who—he'd been doing all this time. The thought of
Ransom with other woman sent a twinge of uneasiness in her
chest.

"Sweetheart?" Papa called. "Are you ready?"

"I'll be out in a sec!" Grabbing her purse, she bounded
out to the living room. "Thanks so much, Papa." She kissed
him on the cheek. "Let's go drop him off at John's."

Since it was a Friday night, Isabelle put on a little more
makeup than usual, styled her glossy black hair into waves
around her shoulders, and put on a fancy outfit. It was a
white vintage dress with red flowers, and though it modestly
covered her, the silk clung to her body and showed off her
generous curves. Her mother wore a similar outfit, and she
had to admit, the two of them looking so alike did have quite a
striking effect.

Dinner was busy as usual, and there were a healthy
number of bookings, but they didn't need to turn away any
walk-ins yet. Frankie had just escorted another one of their
regulars to their table, so she busied herself checking on the
reservations list. Everything looked all right so far, and it
looked like another good night for them.

"Table for one, please."

"Just a moment, sir, I'll see—" Her heart jumped in her
throat as she stared up into familiar gold-green eyes. "*You.*"
Her wolf stood at attention, paws tapping eagerly as it
detected his presence.

Ransom's mouth slowly spread into a sensuous smile.

"Hello, Isabelle." His gaze lazily dropped to her lips, then to her bust, then lower still to the rest of her body. "I have to say, this is a good look on you."

His previous words the last time they spoke came back to her—about not working and spending her trust fund. *Asshole.* "What are you doing here?" she hissed. "Did you come to make fun of my job again? Pardon my French, but *fuck off.*"

He looked taken aback. "I'm sorry about that remark the other night," he said in a repentant tone. "But I was surprised. When we met, you weren't exactly—"

"What do you want?" No way was she going to talk about what happened in the past.

"Like I said, I want a table."

"We don't have any tables," she shot back. "We're full for the night."

A brow lifted as he glanced behind her. "You're telling me there's not one table available?"

"Yes."

"And what if I'm willing to wait?"

She crossed her arms under her chest. "You'd be waiting a very long time." *A hundred years, when I'm dead and turned to dust.*

"Isabelle, is everything all right?"

Her spine stiffened as she heard her mother come up from behind. "Everything's fine," she said curtly. "Nothing to worry about here."

Frankie turned to Ransom. "Good evening, sir, are you being helped tonight?"

"Actually—"

"Actually, he was just leaving." She stared daggers at him, hoping he would get the message.

Ransom, however, ignored her and turned to Frankie. "Good evening. You must be Isabelle's older sister," he drawled, charm dripping from his tone.

Her mother's lips twisted wryly. "My, aren't you ... something. Are you Isabelle's friend?"

"Yes," he said.

"No," she denied at the same time.

Frankie's eyes narrowed. "Have we met before? You look ... familiar."

"He has one of those faces," Isabelle said quickly. A bead of sweat formed at her temple. First it was Jared yesterday and now her mother. If Ransom stayed any longer, the entire tri-state area might see the resemblance between him and Evan.

"I came here the other night as a guest of the Alpha," he began. "And I enjoyed the food so much, I wanted to come back again. It's the best Italian food I've ever had."

She shot him a dirty look, but he didn't seem to care as her mother practically glowed at the compliment.

"You must be the Lone Wolf." Mama's voice lowered. "My son, that is, the Alpha, told me all about you last night. He said you saved everyone by allowing the mage to stab you with the dagger." She placed a hand on his arm. "You have my utmost gratitude. How can we ever repay you for what you did?"

"I don't need any payment, Mrs. Anderson," he said. "But a table would be nice."

"Of course," she said without hesitation. "You can have our best table. We just had a cancellation. But please, call me Frankie. And you are ...?"

"Ransom, Mrs.—I mean, Frankie." A smug smile spread

across his face. "I'm glad to hear you have a table for me. Isabelle told me that you were booked for the night, and there were none available."

"None available? Why would she say—" Dark brows that had been drawn into a frown suddenly rose as her eyes widened. Her head ping-ponged from Isabelle to Ransom and back to Isabelle again, then her lips pursed, as if she was trying to stop a smile from forming. "Let me show you to your table, Ransom." Grabbing a menu from the stand, she motioned for Ransom to go ahead of her. As she walked away, she swung her head back to Isabelle and gave her that 'we're-going-to-have-a-chat-when-I-come-back' look.

Oh, brother. She buried her face in her hands. Would it be immature if she just walked out and caught an Uber home? Something about Mama's expression made Isabelle uneasy. This night was probably about to get worse.

"Isabelle!"

Her mother's voice made her start, and she whipped around. "What?"

"Did you just try to send that young man away by telling him we were all booked up?" Her mother cocked her head to the side, hands planted on her hips.

"Uh ... it's not what you think."

Her mouth turned up at the corners. "Do you remember that story I told you kids a while back? About when your papa was pursuing me, and how he kept coming back to the restaurant, no matter how bad I treated him?"

"What are you talking about?" She glared at her mother, but the excited expression on her face made her freeze. Oh no. Oh *hell* no.

"Ransom's single and never been married," Frankie said. "And he says he likes kids."

"Mama!" How the hell had her mother learned all that in the thirty seconds it took to show Ransom to his table?

"Don't you think he's hot? And handsome? Those eyes ..." She actually looked *dreamy*. "He's got that bad boy look down."

"Argh! Mama, stop. You're embarrassing yourself."

"He *must* be interested in you," she reasoned. "Why else would he come back?"

Her mother's mental gymnastics deserved a gold medal in the Olympics. "Uh, because we're the best Italian restaurant in the city?" she pointed out. "And it's only this one time. He's going to leave soon." Which was still not soon enough.

"Why did you tell him we didn't have any tables? You shouldn't turn away business."

"He was being rude."

"He was perfectly polite to me." She tapped a finger on her chin. "What did he say to you that was rude?"

She searched for an answer that wouldn't reveal the truth to her mother, but couldn't find one. "It's just—"

"Isabelle." Her mother put her hands on her shoulders. "I'm not saying you should marry the man tomorrow. I know ... I know you've done so well for yourself, and Evan is your life, but it's not always going to be that way. What about when he turns eighteen and goes off to college? You'll need someone, too, and you're still young, and you can find a man—"

"Ever heard of feminism, Mama? I don't *need* a man." And she certainly didn't need a matchmaking mother. "Look, he's just not my type, okay?" God, if her parents ever found out the truth, how would they react? Well, she didn't want to dwell on that, because they would never know.

Frankie opened her mouth, but thankfully, the doors opened, and a large group arrived just in time.

Isabelle let out a long, relieved internal sigh. "Are you, Maitland, party of eight?" she asked the older man who stepped forward, who nodded back in answer. "Great, I have your table all set up."

The rest of the night passed without much incident, though Isabelle did what she could to avoid Ransom. Of course, as she led people to their tables or roamed around to check their guests and help the staff, she couldn't help but feel his eyes on her, but she ignored him, despite the fact that her wolf was urging her to look his way.

Finally, she did turn toward him, and what she saw made her blood pressure rise. Ransom smiled up at his server, Jocelyn, as she put down a plate of pasta on his table. The young server had been a thorn in Isabelle's side ever since she got here, because she was constantly late to her shift and insubordinate, not to mention, always improperly attired. Servers were supposed to wear black button up shirts, but she always left a few of hers unbuttoned because she claimed it made for better tips. It was a miracle her huge tits didn't fall right into the Spaghetti Vongole as she ground black pepper over the plate.

Huffing, she turned away, "I need a break, Ma," she said to Frankie and began walking to the back without waiting for her mother to respond.

Why should it bother her that he was flirting with Jocelyn? He'd been with lots of women before her and probably more since. The thought of that made her wolf want to rip all their faces off. And maybe deep down inside—way down deep—she wanted to do that too.

She stomped off, trying to figure out where to go so she could have ten minutes alone. Not the break room as anyone could walk in there at any moment. The manager's office was too far out in the back, and her mother or Gio could walk in there as well.

Ah.

The pantry. They were done taking in diners for the evening, and the kitchen should be starting to wind down which meant no one would come in there. Walking past the kitchen, she headed into the refrigerated room. The chilly air soothed her nerves somewhat, but she had a feeling she could soak in the Arctic Ocean for a week and still not get rid of the tight knot in her chest.

The door suddenly opened and she whirled around. Her wolf yipped in happiness even before her eyes adjusted to the dim light to figure out who it was. "What—you can't come in here!" she groused at Ransom. "This is employees—"

She found herself scuttling backward as he advanced without warning or slowing down, until her back hit a shelf full of dry ingredients. His large body crowded her in, and when the scent of rain, musk, and leather hit her nose, she had to lean back to support her weakened knees. "Please. Stop this." Her voice sounded so unsure, the wobble making her curse internally. "I don't know what you want from me."

His arms rose as he braced his palms on either side of her, caging her in. "Tell me you don't want me here." The rough quality of his voice abraded her deliciously, making her skin tingle. "Tell me you don't feel this too. Don't feel this clawing, aching need." Leaning down, he whispered so close to her ear that she could feel the warmth of his breath. "Tell me you haven't been thinking about those nights we spent together. Tell me all that, and I'll leave you alone."

She bit her lip, wanting to deny him. It would be so easy to give in to what he wanted. But she had Evan to think about. "Just go, Ransom. Please."

"No. Not until you say the words."

His dominance was so thick, she could feel it clouding the air around them. He caged her in further, and she could feel the heat emanating from his large muscled body despite the fact that he was barely touching her. Her wolf responded immediately, and so did her traitorous body as she felt her core flood with wetness.

His nostrils flared. "You don't want me to go."

"I do."

"Then say you don't want me. Tell me you don't feel like wanting to crawl out of your skin with need. Tell me that having me near but not touching me isn't the worst torture in the world."

How could he possibly describe the feelings so perfectly? Oh God, she wanted it—him—so bad. But she had to push him away. "I can't. I'm ... dating someone else. Alejandro." Not really, but he'd brought her home last night and asked her out, and she said yes. They were supposed to have drinks tonight after work.

Apparently, telling him she was spoken for had the opposite effect as he snarled and then pushed her against the shelves with his body. "You're mine, and no one touches what's mine!" His hand crept up to her throat, collaring it loosely. The dominant move made her tremble, but not with fear. Lust surged hot inside her, and her body went limp.

"I don't belong to you or anyone."

"Really?" he challenged. "Maybe you need a reminder."

The whimper that escaped her throat never made it out as his mouth swallowed it up and any other protest she could have made. Not that she had any. No, her traitorous body immediately responded, her breasts thrusting up against him, and her arms wound around his neck.

It was just so unfair that he could do this to her. That even though her brain reminded her that he'd walked away from her, she could still want him. It was that damned True Mate instinct.

His hands captured her wrists and placed them above her head, on the highest shelf she could reach. "Hang on, princess," he murmured against her mouth.

Hang on? What did he— "Oh!"

Ransom hooked his hands under her knees and pulled her up, the skirt of her dress hiking up to her hips. He wrapped her legs around his waist and slid forward, thrusting against her so she could feel the significant bulge under his jeans press against her panties before capturing her mouth again.

Her body seemed to work with muscle memory as she thrust her hips at him, the friction against her pussy sending shocks of pleasure throughout her body. His hands moved to her ass, holding her steady against him. The containers on the shelves shook, but neither of them noticed or cared. He pressed deeper, harder, while his mouth and tongue followed the same rhythm.

Their bodies moved frantically, using their instincts and

desire to set the pace. She shuddered as pleasure began building inside her. She pulled her mouth away from him, causing him to growl in protest, but he let out a groan when she clutched at his head to turn it so she could lick and nibble at his neck. His scent was most potent there, and she wanted to bathe in it, be covered in it.

When his erection hit her just right, she muffled the scream that threatened to escape her by biting at his shoulder. He tensed but didn't stop her, instead, encouraged her with filthy words and lewd suggestions that only made her burn hotter and bring her to the peak.

As her body shook with her impending orgasm, it only seemed to fuel him more. Tubs of flour and pasta dropped all around them, but neither noticed as he thrust against her harder, rubbing his bulge against the front of her panties, stroking her clit until she couldn't think of anything else but the orgasm razing her body. She clung to him, whimpering and sobbing as pleasure made her shake and shudder, until all strength left her body and she hung limply from his arms like a wrung-out towel.

Her brain was screaming at her, telling her she shouldn't have done this with him. But she just couldn't deny how much she wanted and enjoyed it. His arms loosened around her, and he bent his head to nuzzle at her neck.

"I've missed this," he said, inhaling. "Missed you. Isabelle—"

"Ransom," she choked out. "Please, we—"

"What the *fuck* is going on in here?"

"Who—Isabelle?"

Time seemed to slow as the words and the familiar voice

sank into her brain, then it sped up as she and Ransom pulled away from each other.

Gio Muccino stood at the doorway, hands on his hips, brow furrowed. Beside him was Frankie, jaw hanging open as she stared at the scene before her.

"This isn't what you think, Gio, Ma!" she shouted at her cousin and mother as she pushed the hem of her skirt down. Beside her, Ransom was adjusting the front of his jeans, though it did nothing to hide the evidence of his desire. Maybe later she could relish the thought of him having blue balls, but for now, she somehow had to save this situation.

"Oh, really?" Gio's mismatched green and blue eyes narrowed at her. "Care to tell me what it is I could possibly be not thinking, hmm?" When neither spoke, he rubbed his temples with his fingers. "Goddammit, people really need to stop fucking in my restaurant."

"Wait, people fuck in here a lot?" Ransom asked.

"It's a restaurant," Gio said with a shrug. "There's a lot of fucking going on in here. People think they're so original. I swear, someday, *I'm* gonna fuck where people least expect it."

Frankie seemed to finally have found her composure as her arms crossed under her chest, fingers drumming as she raised a brow at Isabelle. "Not your type, huh?"

Oh, good Lord, let the floor open up and swallow me whole! Taking a deep breath, she smoothed her hair down with her fingers. "Did you guys need something? How did you find us anyway?"

"I searched everywhere when you didn't come back, and I remember I used to come here, too, when I needed to cool down," her mother replied. "And Gio was on his way here."

"Did you need me for something?" Isabelle asked nonchalantly.

"I was looking for you because Lucas, Julianna, Duncan, and your father just arrived. We were going to have a late meal at the chef's table." She looked at Ransom. "Should we set out another place? Seems like the three courses you already had wasn't enough to sate your hunger."

"Mama—"

Thundering footsteps cut her off as Julianna dashed in through the door. "There you are! I've been looking all over for you."

"What's going on?" Frankie asked.

Her sister's hands were in tight fists at her sides, and her face was a mask of pure fury. "I just got a call from Sofia. The mages invaded The Enclave."

Frankie went visibly pale, and Isabelle felt her stomach drop. She silently prayed to any god who would listen. *Please no, not my son.* She caught Julianna's eyes and the distress Isabelle saw there told her what she didn't want to hear. *Evan.*

"The pups?" Her mother managed to say.

Her sister swallowed audibly. "Alessandro was already safe at home, but Kier and Evan were still at John's. They went straight to his apartment and took the two boys ... I'm going to tear those bastards apart with my bare hands," Julianna roared. The fury of her wolf was evident as her eyes glowed.

As a cry escaped Isabelle's mouth, Frankie embraced her. "Oh, baby, don't worry, we'll find them. We'll get them back."

But even her mother's comforting arms and words didn't stop the sick dread creeping into her stomach. This was every mother's worst nightmare, to have her child kidnapped. And she was living it.

Julianna snarled. "We'll get them back. I swear to you, Belle."

"What happened?" Frankie asked. "How could the mages have gotten into The Enclave? We have protections against the mages."

"I don't know the details yet." Julianna shook with fury. "But when I get my hands on them—"

"I want to help."

All eyes turned to Ransom. Isabelle had been so sick with worry for Evan she'd forgotten about him. The dread in her chest grew even more. "This is clan business," she said. "You don't have to get involved."

"Belle!" Julianna admonished. "We could use all the help we can get. We're talking about Kier and Evan here."

She bit her lip. "I—"

"We're wasting time," Ransom said. "The kidnappers could be long gone by now."

"Right," Julianna agreed. "Come on, Cross'll be here any minute. He'll take us to HQ and we can regroup."

Ransom glanced at Isabelle before he left, the look on his face inscrutable. But she couldn't think about him now. Her baby was in the hands of their enemies, and who knew what they were planning.

"Isabelle, honey, let's go home," Frankie said.

"But I want—"

"Your brother will send us news as soon as he can."

"Oh, Mama." *God, please,* she thought as she sobbed in her mother's arms. *Don't let them hurt my baby.*

CHAPTER TEN

RANSOM FOLLOWED JULIANNA AS THEY HEADED OUT OF the storage room, though he didn't want to leave Isabelle, not after what they did, and certainly not now while she was in such distress. His wolf didn't either, but it seemed to understand that they were going to help her.

Coming here tonight had been impulsive, but he figured this was the best place to see her, short of storming her front door. Following her when she left the dining room ... well he didn't know if that had been stupid or smart, but at least he confirmed one thing: Isabelle still wanted him. All the months and months of dreaming about her lips and her sweet little body ... none of it compared to the real thing. Her lips, her curves, her scent ... it was too bad they'd been interrupted.

She was angry and hurt, as she should be. He was the one who'd walked out on her, said all those terrible things to push her away. Sure, she didn't know he did it for her own good, and he would do it again to keep her safe. He would have died for her that night, too, and he nearly did. But he would make it up to her, and he would start by saving her beloved nephews.

"How long ago did they take the pups?" he asked Julianna.

"Not long. I went to find Isabelle and Mama as soon as we got the call."

The dining room was empty, save for Lucas, Duncan, and Cross. The two fathers looked like they could tear the room apart with their bare hands.

"We'll find them, darlin'," Duncan said to his wife. "I swear to you, we'll get them back."

"Ransom? What are you doing here?" Lucas asked, looking flabbergasted.

"He was in the pantry with Mom, Gio, and—" Julianna leaned forward and sniffed at him, then her eyes narrowed. "What *were* you doing in there?"

He cleared his throat. Isabelle's scent was probably all over him. "We don't have much time. The kidnappers could be long gone by now. We'll have to move now to get your sons back."

Julianna's nose wrinkled. "Sons? Evan isn't—"

Cross cleared his throat. "Ransom's right. The clock is ticking."

"What do we know?" Lucas said. "How did they infiltrate The Enclave?"

"I thought we had magical protections," Julianna said. "To keep out the mages. And that we extended that to a one-mile radius around the perimeter?"

"But not their human army. They used sheer brute-force," Cross said. "A bunch of them stormed the front entrance and killed the doorman. We can worry about the details later. Lizzie's working on tracking down their vehicle via traffic cams and CCTVs around the city."

"I can follow them on bike. It'll be faster, and we won't draw as much attention." Ransom offered. "I'm parked outside."

"I'll go with you, but I need to grab a couple of things from HQ," Cross said. "But I'll meet you out there in a second." With that, the hybrid disappeared.

"Thank you again, Ransom," Lucas said.

"Don't thank me yet," he said grimly before turning toward the door. But he was determined to get the pups back, because as long as he was alive, Isabelle would have no reason to feel sad ever again.

As promised, Cross was already outside standing by his bike. The hybrid tossed him something gold and shiny, which he caught in the air. It was a gold coin of some sort with a wolf's head stamped on the face. "What's this?"

"A medallion that will allow me to track you if we get separated, and if you hold it and call my name, I'll know you need me," he explained, then handed him something from the palm of his hand. "This is a communication device so we can keep in touch with HQ. Lizzie said they're about to enter the Bronx and heading north. FDR should be the quick way from here. Go as fast as you can. I can take care of any cops and traffic lights."

"Let's go." He slipped the coin in his pocket and the comm unit into his ear, then hopped on the bike, Cross right behind him. He revved the engine and sped off, heading uptown on FDR. Just as Cross promised, all the traffic lights they encountered turned green for them, and they made it through the highway in record time.

"What's the plan here?" he shouted as he veered toward the last exit that would take them into the Bronx. "Can't you just use your magic and poof yourself into their van?"

The device crackled in his ear. "... doesn't work that way." Cross's voice sounded strange coming from the tiny speaker. "I can't transport myself into a moving vehicle, too dangerous. I think the best thing to do is for you to bring us as close to them as possible and then I might be able to hop onto the roof if I time it right."

The speaker burst and Ransom cringed in pain as his sensitive hearing blew out. "... traffic at Yankee Stadium," came the feminine voice. "Yankees were playing the Red Sox tonight, and the game just finished. Idiots!" she clucked her tongue. "You can probably catch them there," came the feminine voice. "Two brown vans with Delaware license plates. I have a partial on one—ending in three seven nine six."

"Thanks, Lizzie," Cross said. "Take Third Avenue," he directed Ransom. "I'll show you a shortcut."

Ransom followed Cross's directions, zinging around the Bronx's side streets.

"They just got through the snarl at Jerome," Lizzie narrated. "Looks like they're headed north."

"Probably to Ninety-Five," Cross guessed. "Keep going. The on-ramp's just ahead."

He pushed his bike to its limit when he saw the entrance to the highway. Two dark-colored vans sticking close together merged a few cars ahead of them, and his senses tingled.

"That has to be them," Cross said. "See if you can get near enough so we can see the plates. But we can't let them know we're on to them yet."

Ransom passed a couple of cars to get closer to the van, but stayed a good distance back.

Cross leaned forward. "That's it," he confirmed. "Rear van matches the partial."

"It's too busy here," Ransom said. "We can't just have you popping up out of nowhere, plus, we'll cause an accident."

"Keep following them," he instructed. "And we'll wait for the right opportunity."

As Ransom kept a good distance behind, he heard Cross relaying to HQ what was happening and where they were. His father, who Ransom guessed had the same power as Cross, was on standby to transport himself and backup when they stopped.

The vans continued on until finally, they took an exit somewhere past New Rochelle.

"I know this area," Cross said as they followed the vehicles. "It's mostly country clubs and golf courses."

"We can split up," Ransom suggested. "You take the rear van, I'll run after the lead."

"Sounds like a plan," Cross said. "Just get me as close as you can, and I'll take care of the rest."

The road was dark and practically empty, and those guys would realize any second that they were being followed. Adrenaline began to course through his system, and Ransom revved the engine and caught up to the vans.

"Now!" Cross said before he disappeared from the back seat and then reappeared on top of the vans crouching low to keep himself from falling over. Nothing happened for a few seconds, then the van swayed to the side.

Ransom avoided the vehicle and passed it. The lead van had already sped away. Gritting his teeth, he pushed his motorcycle harder. The bulky van was no match for him; but he couldn't keep chasing them indefinitely. He needed to stop them, but one or both of the pups could be inside. If the van crashed or overturned, they might get hurt or worse, since neither had developed their shifter healing yet.

One of the doors opened, and something zinged over his shoulder, causing him to swerve. "Motherfuckers!" They were shooting at him. *Son of a bitch!* He slowed down and dropped back, far away enough so the humans wouldn't be able to shoot at him, but he could still track them.

What the fuck was he going to do now? Even if he forced the van off the road safely, there could be any number of men inside there with guns. He'd survive a gunshot or two, but if they pumped him full of bullets, that would be the end.

A loud screech rang out from up ahead, but the adrenaline in his system only made him push his bike harder. The van loomed up ahead as it was stopped in the middle of the road. *What was going on?* He hit the brakes and skidded to a stop on the shoulder.

The back of the van opened up, and armed men in combat gear poured out. From out of the dark shadows, three large wolves jumped out, startling the men and sending them into a panic.

Ransom felt his wolf push for the surface, and he let it take over as he hurtled toward the melee. Growls and snarls, punctured by human screams and shouts, were all around as he transformed fully into his wolf form. It lunged forward, smashing into the nearest human and tearing into its shoulder. Though the thick protective gear stopped the wolf's teeth from ripping the man's body in half, it still delivered a monumental amount of pain as evidenced by the man's screams of agony before he passed out.

Satisfied the man was no longer a threat, the wolf released him and looked around for its next victim. A bullet whizzed by, and the animal turned its head. One of the men was shooting blindly in the dark at anything that moved.

Idiot! Ransom screamed from inside his wolf's head.

His wolf lunged for the man immediately, stopping him from firing any more bullets. Its large maw went straight for the arm, and the bone snapped in two with an audible crack. The man screamed as they went down, the large wolf's body smothering him. Satisfied, the wolf rolled away.

The shouts of alarm earlier had died down, and mostly moans and cries of pain could be heard. Glancing around, Ransom saw the three wolves snarling and yapping as they corralled the remaining men who were still standing into a circle.

"I'll take care of them." Daric appeared next to the men and waved his hand. Chains and ropes appeared around their wrists, ankles, and torsos, forcing them all down on the ground.

The three wolves began to shift, so Ransom's wolf followed suit. As his limbs shortened and his fur receded, he glanced at the other Lycans. He recognized Cliff Forrest's massive body as he towered over everyone else, as well as Arch Jones's tall and lean form. The third man, however, was unfamiliar to him. He was shorter, but easily one of the bulkiest men Ransom had seen. He cursed in what sounded like French as he nursed the bullet wound in his shoulder.

"*Feet pue tan!* Mika's going to kill me," the man groused.

"Are you all right, Ransom?" Daric asked.

"Yeah," he said. "I—whoa!" Clothes suddenly appeared on his body as Daric waved his hand. "Thanks." He'd only seen Cross do that, so he was disoriented for a moment. "But how did you—"

"I was able to track you, thanks to the coin," he said. "We—"

A loud cry made them all freeze.

The pups!

Ransom was closest to the vehicle, so he dashed toward it, hopping inside. The back of the van was small, so he easily spotted the two children lying on the ground, both wailing and bawling in distress.

Having no experience with kids at all, Ransom didn't know what to do, so he crawled low and hefted them both into his arms.

Cross's head popped into the van. "Are they—oh good." He looked relieved as he saw the pups in Ransom's arms. "Need a hand?"

He handed Cross one of the pups, then carefully crawled out from the back of the van. As a cool night breeze blew by, he was struck by a strange scent. Cardamom, with just a hint of honey, mixed with rain and musk. His wolf immediately perked up and scratched at him.

The pup in his arms had stopped bawling, so he looked down. Mismatched eyes looked up at him curiously. A small hand reached up to touch his face, and he felt a strange stirring in his chest. "Hello, little one," he said, brushing the tears away from the child's face. "Don't worry. You're safe now." He didn't know why he said it, only that he *had* to say it.

Someone clearing their throat made him start. When he

turned his head, he saw Cross looking at him strangely. "What's wrong?"

"Nothing," he said quickly. "Dad and the others'll take care of cleanup. They'll take care of your bike too. Why don't I bring us and the pups back to The Enclave? I'm sure everyone will be happy to see them."

Seeing as the Guardian Initiative team seemed to have everything in hand, he nodded. Cross grabbed onto him and the child, then he closed his eyes as he felt that familiar feeling wrap around in him.

His feet landed on solid, carpeted ground, and when he opened his eyes, he found himself in an unfamiliar apartment. It was plush and tastefully decorated, but everything about it screamed luxury.

"Kier!" Julianna, who had been sitting on one of the leather couches, bounded up and dashed to Cross, taking the infant from his arms and peppered his little face with kisses. "Oh, my God, my baby." Tears streaked down her cheeks as she looked up at Cross. "Duncan? And Papa?"

"They're fine," Cross said. "They're both still back there, helping with the cleanup."

Julianna looked relieved. "Thank God."

Ransom frowned. Why wasn't Julianna as concerned for her other son? "Um, your other boy's fine too," he reminded her, nodding at the child in his arms.

"Oh!" Julianna exclaimed. "Yes, I'm so glad they're both fine. Isabelle will be so relieved. Mama and Sabrina are with her in the guest room now, trying to calm her down."

Isabelle?

"Thank you so much, Ransom, for rescuing the pups."

She squeezed his arm. "Let me take him so I can show —Isabelle!"

Slowly, Ransom turned around. Isabelle was rushing out of the hallway behind him when she suddenly stopped. Her eyes darted to the child in his arms, then to briefly meet Ransom's gaze before quickly looking away. The boy squirmed, his hands reaching out to Isabelle as he let out a squeal. Her face white as a sheet, she strode forward and took the child from him.

"Oh, Evan," she cried as she held the boy against her chest. "Evan, I'm so happy you're safe."

The ground seemed to shift under him as he staggered back. A pounding throb behind his eyes made the edges of his vision blur, and he suddenly found it hard to breathe. This pup ... was Isabelle's.

The room filled with more people. The Alpha. Lupa. Frankie Anderson. All of them talking at once, too loud. They were thanking him, hugging the children, asking for explanations. The cacophony around him was too much, and he wanted to scream at them to shut the hell up while he tried to think.

"You must be Ransom," somebody said all of a sudden. "Thank you for saving my grandchildren."

As if he wasn't feeling disoriented enough, the new presence in the room made the world shift again. He didn't need to know who this was. He'd seen his picture countless of times. Looked into those emerald green eyes on his screen for so long, it had burned into his brain. The pure, dominant power from him marked him as an Alpha, even if he wasn't technically a ruling one.

"I'm Grant Anderson." He extended his hand. "I'm honored to meet you."

He stared at the palm, unblinking. Finally, he was face-to-face with the man who was the cause of his misery. But it didn't matter as a single thought now occupied his brain. Isabelle and her *son*.

A movement from the corner of his eye caught his attention, the object of said thought creeping out of the front door.

"Sure," he murmured. "If you'll excuse me, I need to get going."

Grant looked taken aback, but didn't say anything as Ransom turned on his heel and walked away. He picked up his pace, worried that he wouldn't catch her on time. Just his luck, she was still standing in the hallway, pacing in front of the elevator.

"Come on, come on, come on," she muttered. "Why are you so slow—Ransom!" The blood drained from her face.

He stalked toward her, hands fisted at his sides. She resembled a scared rabbit, cornered by a predator.

"He's your son," he stated, his eyes never leaving Evan. The boy turned his head to look up at him curiously.

She nodded, but didn't say a word.

"How old is he?"

She expelled a breath. "Evan isn't any of your concern," she began. "I'm grateful for—"

"How. Old?" he growled.

Her bottom lip trembled. "Ten months."

The moment she took the child from his arms, he'd already started the calculations. He swallowed hard. "He's mine, isn't he?"

Her silence told him the answer.

"Goddammit!" He punched the wall with his fist. The pain felt good because then he could concentrate on it and not the emotions inside him. "Why ... why, Isabelle? Why have you been hiding him from me all this time?" His son. He had a son. *Evan.* And he'd held the boy just moments ago. Held his son in his arms. God, if he had known, he'd have ripped those men who took him into shreds! "Answer me. You owe me an explanation."

"I owe *you?*" she asked incredulously as fury crossed her face. "*You* walked out on me!"

Pain slashed in his chest as his wolf slashed its claws at him. "I didn't know you were—"

"*You* were the one who left," she spat. "You said it was just for fun. Even offered me one last fuck before you hightailed it out of town. Called me a bitch in—"

"I didn't mean it!" he roared and slammed his fist into the wall again, making her cringe. Evan wailed in distress, and she stepped back, turning his head away to soothe him while shooting him a dirty look.

His eyes widened. "I swear, Isabelle, I'm sorry." He swallowed audibly, feeling the blood drain from his face. "Don't look at me like that. I would never hurt you. Or Evan." He would rather die. And he nearly did, that night. But he couldn't tell her. Now he felt like a trapped animal, but it wasn't a cage that trapped him, but his lies. "I have rights," he said. "He's mine too."

"I was the one who carried him for nine months, who gave birth to him, clothed, fed, and changed him for the past ten months, all by myself," she pointed out.

"Your family doesn't know about me."

"Ha!" She rolled her eyes. "And what? You're going to tell them? Go ahead. Tell my father, tell my brother, and let's see what they have to say about you leaving me pregnant and alone."

Her words sliced through him like a sharp knife. "You should have told me about him."

"And how was I supposed to do that?" she asked. "And for your information, I did think you should know, so I tried calling your number, but it said it was disconnected. I figured that was your way of telling me you didn't want to hear from me again."

"I ..." He remembered smashing the burner phone against the wall of his hotel room because he didn't want that man to contact him anymore. *I'm the biggest piece of shit in the world.*

"Ransom!"

Whirling around, he saw Cross and Sabrina walking toward them. The hybrid looked at Isabelle and Evan, then back at Ransom, his ocean-colored eyes stormy.

"You knew," he stated.

"I ... we," he looked down at Sabrina, who shot Ransom a sympathetic look, "suspected."

"What?"

The elevator dinged and Isabelle scrambled inside. "Don't!" she warned.

His feet were frozen to the ground. While his wolf urged him to run after her and their pup, the rational part of him told him to stay. *We've hurt her enough.*

"Did she confirm it?" Sabrina asked.

He swallowed and nodded. "How did you guess?"

"I wasn't sure, but I saw the resemblance," she began.

"But now, looking at you and Evan side by side, I don't know how anyone didn't notice."

"I thought Sabrina was just seeing things." Cross scratched his chin. "But I saw it, when you were carrying him." He stepped forward. "You were with her, weren't you? Right before I fished you out of the Hudson."

Confessing everything now seemed like the right choice to allay his own guilt. But with everything that was happening, if anyone found out the truth, he'd never see Isabelle or Evan again. "Yes. I was with her."

"What happened?" Blue-green eyes looked at him suspiciously. "Who tried to kill you? Is that why you didn't come back to New York?"

"It's ... complicated. Look," he ran his hands through his hair, "I can't tell you what happened that night. Not yet. But things between me and Isabelle ... they were left unfinished."

"Just talk to her," Sabrina said. "And explain that you were hurt that night, which was why you couldn't come back."

He huffed. "I don't think that's going to help."

"She's your True Mate, isn't she?" Sabrina asked. "She'll want to take you back."

"My ... what?" Did he hear her right? "True Mate? Did she say anything?"

Sabrina frowned. "I just guessed it too. I mean, I assumed ..."

He looked at Cross, who shrugged. "We all just assumed the father of her baby was dead," the hybrid said. "But what does your wolf tell you?"

Closing his eyes, he took a deep breath. His wolf let out a longing yowl. *Mine.* "I need her back." And hopefully, solve this mess before it bit him in the ass. She could never find out the reason he came to New York in the first place. "But first, I need to apologize for walking out on her when I did."

"Let me talk to her," Sabrina said. "I haven't known her long, but she needs a friend right now."

"I ..." He supposed he could let Sabrina try. "Okay."

"I'll let you know if she's ready to talk," she said. "But, do you promise you'll respect her decision, whatever it is?"

There was no way in hell he was going to let her and Evan go. They were *his*. But, at the same time, the guilt was starting to eat him up inside. He'd left her alone, all this time, to have his pup. She did it all by herself, and here she was, stronger than ever.

"All right." What choice did he have? He knew what it was like to have grown up without his biological father. All his life, he'd cursed the man for not being there for him, for what he and his mother had endured ... he would have let Evan go through the same thing.

He didn't deserve him, or Isabelle. But he had to at least earn her forgiveness.

CHAPTER ELEVEN

By THE TIME ISABELLE GOT INTO HER APARTMENT, THE pain in her chest had become so intense she couldn't breathe. Having the truth laid out after all this time should have brought her some relief, but in reality, it made the dread she'd been carrying around grow heavier.

Evan fussed in her arms and grabbed a fistful of her shirt, jolting her out of her thoughts. "It's all right, baby," she soothed as she sat down on the couch. She was just glad he was too young to understand what was going on. If only she could shield him forever.

The look on Ransom's face when he realized that he had a son—it was unexpected. Of course, in the past year and a half, she'd wondered what his reaction would be if he ever found out. With the way he'd walked out on her so casually that night, she expected shock, maybe even denial. Or cool indifference. She imagined telling him that he didn't have to take any responsibility, and he'd just shrug and be fine with it.

But she never imagined the fierce anger. Or the complete

acceptance that Evan was his, not even questioning if there was another man who could have fathered him.

Her wolf whined sadly.

Stop it. Ransom was in shock, that was all. Maybe he would still walk away from them, just like he did that night.

The knock on the door made her start. Evan still in her arms, she stood up and padded to the door, sighing in relief when she saw Sabrina's face through the peephole. For a second, she thought Ransom had come after her. But then again, who knew what he was doing right now? Telling Lucas —or her father, that he was Evan's dad? Of course, if that was the case, then it would be her entire family banging on her door right now.

The sympathetic look on Sabrina's face when she opened the door told her everything she needed to know. "How did you figure it out?"

Sabrina smiled weakly. "Before I met you and Evan, I'd spent a few days in Kentucky, hiding out at Ransom's sister's place," she explained. "Then I saw Evan. The resemblance ... it's startling." She chuckled. "I'm an artist, it's a hazard of the job. May I come in?"

"Did he ask you to come here to talk to me?" she asked defensively.

"I volunteered," Sabrina said. "But only because I wanted to see how *you* were doing. And to see if there was anything I can do for you. We don't have to talk about Ransom if you don't want to."

Though she wanted to tell Sabrina to leave, Isabelle didn't have the heart, not when Sabrina had been through a lot herself *and* had been nothing but nice to her. When she heard about the pups being kidnapped, she came right away to The Enclave to offer her support.

"All right." She stepped aside to let her in. "I need to get Evan ready for bed."

"I don't mind," Sabrina said. "I'll help."

"Thanks."

Sabrina took Evan as Isabelle went to the bath to get it ready. She called out to Sabrina once she was satisfied with the water temperature and level in the tub. After taking off his dirty clothes, she bathed him, then left him in Sabrina's care as she went to prepare his bottle before heading back to the nursery. Evan was sitting on the changing table, laughing as Sabrina played peekaboo with him, seemingly having no idea of the danger he had been in earlier or the current upheaval happening now.

"He's such a happy baby," Sabrina commented. "Did you have trouble with him at all?"

"I think all newborns are difficult, and I had trouble adjusting." Sabrina had already dried Evan and wrapped him up in a towel, so she put on his diaper and PJs then sat on the rocker. She cradled him in one arm and fed him the bottle, rocking back and forth gently. "Before Evan came along, I was a party girl. I never thought I'd enjoy spending quiet nights alone at home."

"You do it so well, though," Sabrina remarked. "The mom thing." Her hand went to her own stomach. "I just hope I do half as good as you."

"Oh." She glanced down at Sabrina's hand. "So it's for sure now? You and Cross ...?"

"Yes," Sabrina confirmed. "He told me about True Mates and ... and I thought I didn't want to wait. But now ..." A look of uncertainty passed across her pretty face. "My mother died right after I was born, so I don't really know what it's like to have a mom. I was raised mostly by nannies, though my dad was there as much as he could be."

"You'll do great," Isabelle said. "I was a disaster at first. I didn't know how to do anything. I had help from Julianna and Mama, but other than that, I was on my own." Looking down at him, she remembered those first few days, the frustration and the lack of sleep. Yet she would do it all over again. "But it's all worth it."

"You're so brave doing it by yourself."

She shrugged. "I try not to think of it that way. I didn't have much of a choice." Tension hung in the air, and she knew what Sabrina wanted to talk about. "I know you're on his side with him being Cross's friend and all, but you don't know what it was like."

"I'm not on anyone's side, Isabelle," Sabrina said. "You were kind to me. I just want to be able to do the same for you. I'm here if you need to talk. And as for being Cross's friend, well, I guess you could say Cross is the closest thing Ransom can call a friend. But he's a good man, I've seen it."

"He left me," she said. "Just ... packed his bags and left. I wouldn't have even known if I didn't catch him in the act." The bitterness seeped into her veins. "When we met, it was explosive. We couldn't get enough of each other and ... and he'd been my first." *And only.* "But I didn't know anything else about him. Didn't even know he had a sister."

"Did you ask him about his family?"

Her head snapped up to meet her gaze. "Are you saying it's my fault?"

"No, no." She walked over to Isabelle and placed a hand on her arm. "I'm not. I'm sorry it came out that way."

Isabelle shifted Evan to her other arm and sighed. "I guess I didn't. We just ... we didn't talk a lot." Her cheeks went hot, thinking of that week with him. How much she craved his touch. "But then he tossed me aside. Accused me of being ashamed of him and ..." Her throat closed up at the memory. "I wasn't. I swear I wasn't. I was just caught up. You understand, right? With Cross. That feeling when you're with him."

"I do. I know what you mean. It's like nothing else matters and it's all perfect and ..." She wrung her hands together. "I shouldn't be telling you this ..."

Evan had finished his bottle, so she put it aside and placed him over her shoulder, then leaned forward. "Shouldn't be telling me what?"

Sabrina glanced around. "What I'm about to tell you is what Cross told me. About how he and Ransom met. Well, kind of met."

Isabelle wrinkled her nose. She had to admit, she was curious how they had known each other all this time, since as far as she knew, Ransom had never even been to New York until that night they met at Blood Moon. "What did he say?"

"It was about a year and a half ago. Cross said he was taking a walk in Riverside park one morning when he spotted someone floating in the water."

Isabelle gasped. "Ransom?"

"Yes," Sabrina said. "He was half dead. Cross managed to transport him out, but when he realized Ransom was a Lycan like him, he couldn't just take him to the hospital. Ransom still had his wallet on him, so he brought him back to Kentucky, to his sister."

Her breath caught in her chest. "What happened to him? Why did he end up in the Hudson?"

"Cross doesn't know to this day," Sabrina said. "But I think ... from what he just told us, I wonder if it has anything to do with you."

"Me? I didn't do that to him. After I left him at his hotel, I went home."

"Not literally," Sabrina said. "I mean ... could he have felt guilty?"

"And tried to kill himself?" She shook her head in denial. "I don't think so, he's not the type." Ransom was stronger than that. "It doesn't make sense."

Sabrina smiled at her sadly. "Unfortunately, the decisions men make don't always make sense. And sometimes they think they're doing what's best for us, without even asking how we feel about it."

If that was the same night he left, then it would make sense why he didn't call her back right away. Had he been attacked? He was a Lone Wolf, and there were some Lycans who didn't like their kind. Was he afraid of the blowback of them dating from her clan?

"Will you talk to him, Isabelle?" Sabrina asked. "Just listen to what he has to say. I know you don't owe him anything, but all he wants is a chance to say sorry."

"I ..." She felt conflicted. All this time, she'd hated him for leaving her. What if he did have a good reason for walking away from her? Her heart soared and her wolf yipped, but she quashed them both down. "I'll let him say his piece," she said. "But that's all."

Sabrina clapped her hands together. "Thank you, Isabelle. That's all he wants."

"Tell him to give me half an hour," she said. "I need to put Evan to bed."

As Sabrina left, Isabelle got up and finished burping Evan and then placed him in the crib. His eyes were heavy, and though he fought sleep, he eventually succumbed as she stroked his head and hummed a tune.

"I love you so much," she whispered. "More than you'll ever know." How was it that she fell in love with him even before meeting him? Evan was the only good thing to come out of this whole debacle. She supposed she would always be grateful to Ransom for that. *That's the only reason I'm willing to hear him out,* she told herself.

When his breathing evened and she was satisfied he was deeply asleep, she padded out to the living room. Just as she was about to sit on the couch, a knock made her freeze. *You can do this.* She took a deep breath and marched toward the entrance.

Slowly, she opened the door. Her pulse picked up at the sight of Ransom, still looking devastatingly handsome in his dirty T-shirt and jeans. Her wolf let out a slow, needy yowl. If she moved a little closer, she could probably scent him and—

"Can I come in?" he asked in that low, rough voice that never failed to make her skin tingle.

"Just say what you need to say," she said. "I've had a long day—we all have."

"I ..." He raked his fingers through his hair and clucked his tongue. "I'm sorry. For leaving that night. I didn't want to."

"Why did you then?" *And how the hell did you end up in the Hudson?*

"I can't ... I can't tell you right now."

"Why not?"

"Because!" He braced his hands on the doorframe. "Sorry ... you have to trust me."

She crossed her arms over her chest. "It doesn't matter now, I suppose. What's done is done."

"You're right." He sighed. "All this time I thought there was something the matter with you ... did your father cut you off when he found out you were pregnant? Is that why you're working?"

"Ha!" she threw up her hands. "Is that what you think? Listen here, I went to work for Muccino's because I wanted to. You men, always thinking that we need you to—"

"You have to forgive me."

The statement, plain and simple, arrested her. "What?"

"You have to forgive me, Isabelle."

He took a step forward, and even though she told him he couldn't come in, she backed up. "Ransom, you can't—"

"You have to forgive me!" The plea was urgent now. "Please."

"I ..." Her heart clenched in her chest. "For what? For walking out on me? For making me hate you with what you said? For not being here when Evan was born—"

"Yes. Yes. Yes." He dropped to his knees. "Please, Isabelle. You have to. Forgive me."

Shock made her take in a breath. "I— Ransom!"

His arms came around her, and he pressed his face to her stomach. "Please. Isabelle. God, I can't fucking stand it. That you were alone though all this. That I ... that I did this to you and hurt you."

Tears pooled in her eyes. "Stop, Ransom—"

"I don't deserve it," he rasped. "I don't deserve you or Evan. But please ... you *have* to forgive me."

The ache in his voice made her burst into tears. Why? Why did the idea of him suffering make her sad? She should be happy that he was in pain. That he could finally feel how she felt when he left.

But her heart—oh, her damned, foolish heart—wouldn't harden against him. She pried his hands away from her waist. Her knees weakened, and she dropped down to the floor with him. Cupping his jaw, she looked into the brilliant green-gold of his eyes. "I don't know, Ransom." The hurt was still there, buried in her chest. All she had to do was think back to that night, and the memories made it flare up again. "What you did—"

"Please. Isabelle ... I'll never hurt you again."

His scent, his dominant nature, his ... everything was too overwhelming that she didn't protest when his arms encircled her and he melded his mouth to hers. The desperation and hunger in his kiss made her melt, and God forgive her, she needed it. Wanted it. Want. Need. Want. Need. It was all clawing at her. And she couldn't—didn't want to—fight it any longer.

"Bedroom," she managed to gasp against his mouth. "Last door down the hallway."

All the blood seemed to rush out of her brain, and she felt dizzy as he swooped her up into his arms. He moved so fast and soon he placed her on her feet right at the entrance to her room. Pulling him in, she pushed the door gently behind her so it closed. "Soundproofed," she said. "I—oh!" He pulled her to him and crushed his mouth to hers.

They made their way to her bed, stripping off their clothing, reluctantly releasing each other's mouths as needed. By the time her knees hit the back of her bed, she was only in her underwear, and he was nearly naked. God, he was magnificent. She remembered the first time she saw him like that—all that glorious, golden, tattooed skin, the bulging muscles of his shoulders and arms, and that perfect six pack and the trail of hair that led down ...

As if sensing her thoughts, he pulled down his underwear and stood before her, fully naked, his stiff, jutting cock bobbing up and down.

Desire curled in her, wanting him so bad. She knew the orgasm from earlier in the evening wouldn't even compare to what it would be like when he was inside her. Reaching for him, she curled her fingers around his thick shaft and stroked him until he groaned and pulled her hand away. Pushing her down, he spread her knees and covered her with his body.

His masculine scent enveloped her, making a primal part in her growl with need. His weight on top of her was comforting, even as his mouth peppered kisses on her neck. He moved lower, trailing down her collarbone to her cleavage. A sudden shyness came over her, and she crossed her arms over her chest in instinct. Though her body was able to bounce back quickly after giving birth due to her Lycan nature, not every part of her was the same as before the pregnancy.

"Shh," he soothed when she protested at him pulling her hands away. "You're beautiful."

As if to prove a point, he leaned back and pulled the

straps of her bra down and looked at her with awe. His large hands cupped her breasts gently, moving down to her stomach, over the last of the stretch marks that hadn't faded. There was a gleam in his eyes—something she couldn't name and didn't want to.

He leaned down again, to nuzzle at the space between her breasts, before moving to take her left nipple into his mouth. The wet heat sent pleasure zinging straight to her core. One hand trailed down to the front of her now-damp panties. She cried out when his fingers yanked the fabric aside and traced her naked, wet lips before sinking a finger inside. God, it had been too long ...

"Isabelle ..." he hummed against her breast.

She pushed her hips up at him, taking more of his finger inside her, clenching around him. When he withdrew his hand, she whimpered in protest. However, he released her nipple and began to move down, spreading her legs wider to accommodate him. Looking down, she met his green-gold gaze just as he was descending between her thighs.

"Oh!"

He growled against her when she closed her eyes. When he didn't move any further, she opened them and glanced down at him. It was like he was telling her not to turn away as he pressed his mouth to her.

She gasped as she felt his tongue graze her, but she didn't tear her eyes away. He feasted on her, licking and sucking at her most intimate part. It was dirty and depraved, and she loved it. Pleasure built up inside her, and the moment his tongue found her clit, she closed her eyes and lifted her hips up. His hands cupped her ass, bringing her closer to his mouth, tonguing her even harder as her body shook with her orgasm. Even as she felt the pleasure ebb away, he didn't stop but continued to lick and suck at her until her body gave him what he wanted.

"Ransom," she moaned. "I need you."

He let out a pleased growl, the rattling in his chest making her core clench despite the two orgasms she'd already had. His body slid along hers, the rough hairs on his chest tickling her. Bracing himself on one elbow, he reached below, but his gaze never left hers. She wanted to close her eyes, but she couldn't, and instead, held his. When the blunt tip of his cock nudged at her, she sighed and relaxed her body. Slowly, he slid in. She accommodated him as best as she could, but it had been too long. A bead of sweat formed at his temple, and his face scrunched up as if he was struggling. Finally, he was all the way inside, seated in her fully.

His face softened before he leaned down to kiss her again. His mouth moved against her with aching need, coaxing her lips open as his hips began to move. Her legs wrapped around his waist, taking him deeper into her, meeting his thrusts. Pulling away from her, he buried his face in her neck, inhaling deep.

Her fingers scratched down his back as the sensations became too much. His deep, hard thrusts and the drag of his cock inside her were pushing her closer and closer to the edge until she cried out and dug her fingers into his skin. She thought she heard a pained groan, but the blood roaring in her ears muffled it. Her body shuddered with a mindless orgasm making her forget herself and everything around her until she could only concentrate on the moment she peaked.

He slowed down, and she relaxed. But he wasn't stopping. No, he leaned back onto his heels, hooked his hands under her knees, then lifted her torso and pulled her onto his cock, impaling her as she sank down on him. Grabbing onto his shoulders, she moved her hips to meet his upward thrusts and pressed her mouth to his. Their tongues and lips met in a tangle of desperate need. She could feel all the tension in his body, but he wouldn't stop. She cried out at a particularly hard thrust and clung to him.

"One more, princess," he groaned. "Come on my cock."

"Gahh!" Her body seized as it shook with another powerful orgasm. He drove her down to the bed, pinning her with his large frame until she could only feel the pressure of his weight on her. He finally joined her over the edge, grunting and groaning as his cock thrust into her one last time, filling her with his warm seed. His arms wound around her tight and then pulled her on top of him as he fell back. She landed on top of him with a soft thud, melting against his chest. Her pulse was racing, but eventually, it slowed to normal, and she rolled off him, burying her face in the cool sheets.

The mattress shifted as he moved behind her, his large arm slipping around her waist. She always felt so safe afterward when he would hold her like this. But now, there was a scratching in her brain, a voice telling her not to let her guard down, to build the walls around her heart before he had a chance to sneak in there again.

It nagged at her, and she decided she couldn't go through that again. Couldn't fall for him only to have her heart crushed. And if she were being honest, she didn't tell him about Evan as soon as he came back, not because she was afraid for Evan, but for herself.

She wiggled away from him, but his grip tightened. "I ... I

have to go to the bathroom." His arm lifted away, and she scrambled off the bed and grabbed her robe. She dashed to the bathroom sink and cleaned herself up, dampening a washcloth to rub his scent and seed from her body. Tying the sash around her body tightly, she straightened her shoulders, determined to do what needed to be done.

Ransom was still on his back, eyes shut. As she drew nearer, one golden green orb opened, and his mouth curled up into a smile. "Come back to bed," he said huskily, curling his finger at her. "It's early yet. I might be down, but I'm a long way from out."

Her wolf and her body both reacted wanting to be near him, the memories of that week with him flooding her mind. He could go all night long, sometimes needing only a minute or two to recover. Heat crept into her cheeks, but she blew a breath out. "You should go," she said, trying to steady her voice.

"I said I'm not done yet, princess."

"Well, I am." She planted a foot down firmly. "Please. Leave."

He shot up quickly, rubbing his temple with his palm. "What the hell are you saying, Isabelle?"

"I'm s-s-saying you need to go." She had to do this now, before she lost the nerve. "You got what you wanted."

"What I wanted?" he roared, and in a second, he was in front of her, towering over her. "You don't know what I want, princess."

"All right, all right, I forgive you," she said. "Now we can move past all of this?"

"Move past all this?" He glowered, waving his hand. "And what's 'all of this'?"

She clenched her teeth. "*This*. We got this out of our system, and now we can move on."

"You think that's what it's about?"

"Isn't it?" she shot back.

He raked his fingers through his hair. "No, it's not. We're True Mates."

How the hell did he know? She supposed he figured it out when he realized they conceived Evan the first time. "So? That doesn't mean anything except we're biologically compatible." *That didn't stop you from walking out on me,* she added bitterly.

"You could be pregnant now."

"That's not guaranteed the second time around," she said. "My parents didn't have me until much later." Oh God, she was an idiot. Even though that was true, there was still the possibility. This couldn't happen again.

"Isabelle—"

"Look." She took a calming breath. "I know you have rights. Evan is your son, and I acknowledge that. We can talk about visitation and custody, but only if you leave *now*."

He opened his mouth and then closed it shut.

"Go." she pointed to the door. "*Please*."

Her wolf clawed at her in rage, tearing her insides to ribbons. But she couldn't give in, not again. Yes, they were True Mates, but she couldn't go through that again. She'd be a fool to give him another chance to hurt her.

"This isn't over," he warned her, but pivoted on his heel, picked up his discarded clothes, and left the room.

When she heard the door slam shut, she collapsed on the carpeted floor. "This is for the best," she told herself. Maybe if she said it enough times, she'd even believe it.

CHAPTER TWELVE

OUTRAGE, ANGER, AND A DEEP DESPAIR WERE ALL threatening to overwhelm Ransom as he let the door slam shut behind him. *Maybe I deserve it.* For leaving her. For letting her and Evan down.

He got dressed as he stomped down the hallway, determined to get away from her. His wolf protested loudly, snarling and growling at him. It wanted to go back. Back to their mate and their pup. He hadn't even had time to see Evan and hold him again.

Well what did you expect? Just because they had sex, everything was going to be fine? A happily ever after? Not after what he did. Sure, he would have left her again if it meant protecting her from that man, but had he known about Evan ...

He stopped in his tracks and then turned around, taking two steps back toward her apartment.

But no, he couldn't.

Not *yet*.

Taking a deep breath, he made a decision.

To let go and forget about revenge on Grant Anderson.

The decision was easier than he thought it would be. Despite the fact that years of his life had been consumed with pursuing revenge, now that Isabelle was within his reach, now that he had *Evan* to think about, it didn't feel like a waste at all. It was either this or never being with them.

The plan would have to be forgone. Sure, there was one hitch, one *person* that might not agree, but he'd take care of that, too.

Only Isabelle and Evan mattered now. And having them both back in his life—not in half measures like custody agreements to be debated on by lawyers and judges, but totally, completely his. As a family.

His wolf nodded. Finally, something they could agree on. "But how?" he wondered aloud.

Things were about to get messy. She would eventually have to tell her family and everything would be revealed, if they hadn't already guessed, if what Sabrina was saying was true. Her family would surely hate him and try to keep them apart. Grant Anderson would never let his precious girl be sullied by the likes of him. Plus, the fact that he left her in the first place wasn't going to help his cause either.

If only he could have her alone for a couple days. Just to get her away from her family's influence and—

An idea popped into his head. Isabelle wasn't going to like it, but she wasn't leaving him much choice. He was determined to win her and Evan at any cost, even if it meant playing dirty.

Slipping his hand into his pocket, he took out the gold coin he'd nearly forgotten was there. *Here we go.* "Cross?"

A few seconds passed and ... nothing. He tried again.

"Cross?" This time, the air shimmered with a familiar power, and the hybrid appeared beside him, dressed only in boxers and an annoyed look on his face.

"Sorry to call on you so late," he said. "Hope I wasn't interrupting anything."

"I take it things didn't go well?" Cross asked. "Or did they?"

"No," he groused. "But I'm hoping you can help me." And then he told Cross his plan.

"Absolutely not," Cross said vehemently. "Have you gone crazy?"

Yes, but that was the only plan he knew would work. "You owe me, remember? When I said I would come back here to help you with the mages. I'm calling that favor in now."

"You do know you could get arrested for that," the hybrid pointed out. "We both could. Not to mention, the Alpha—"

"We'll figure something out," he said. "Now, will you help me or not?"

Cross stared him down, but when Ransom didn't budge, he huffed out a breath. "God knows what you'll come up with if I didn't. We'll need to prepare a couple of things."

"We need to get it done soon."

"It's one o'clock in the morning," Cross reminded him. "And Sabrina's waiting for me."

"Then we need to get a move on, don't we?" Ransom was not going to wait a second more. He'd waited long enough for Isabelle, and he was not going to let this chance get away from him.

The preparations for his plan took much longer than Ransom wanted, but he supposed as long as they did it before Isabelle had a chance to see her family, then everything should all fall into place. Surprisingly, Sabrina had thought it was a great idea and even pitched in to help with the cover story.

"Are you crazy?" Cross had said. "You can't—"

"Call it hormones," she had replied with a shrug. "But I think it's romantic. Oh, don't you look at me like that, Cross Jonasson. May I remind you of *your* actions? Of the things you did, without asking me what I thought?"

It seemed the irony of what Ransom was asking Cross to do hadn't been lost on Sabrina either. "She got you there, buddy."

Now, they were ready to put this plan in motion. However, he couldn't help but feel apprehensive as they stood outside Isabelle's door. He was about to rethink this whole thing when his wolf howled its approval of the plan, and Ransom decided to follow his animal's instinct.

"Ready?" Cross asked.

He clutched the small vial in his hand tightly. "As I'll ever be."

Cross nodded and pressed up against the wall so Isabelle wouldn't be able to see him. Using his free hand, Ransom rapped on the door. It was nearly dawn, so she would have had a couple of hours sleep. A few moments later, he heard the sound of footsteps pounding on the floor, then the door flew open.

"What's going on? Is it the mages? Are they—" Isabelle's eyebrows wrinkled. "What are you doing here? I thought I told you to leave."

"I did," he said. "But now I'm back."

She crossed her arms under her breasts. "What do you want?" She tapped her foot impatiently when he didn't answer right way. "Well?"

"I'm sorry, Isabelle, but I have to do this."

"Do what?"

As Cross instructed, he opened the top of the vial and tossed the contents at her.

"What the—" Her eyes rolled back, and her body went limp.

Quickly, he caught her and lifted her up into his arms. "How long will she be out?"

"If I estimated her metabolism rate correctly, she'll be awake by noon."

"That's should be enough time."

Cross huffed out a breath. "I hope you know what you're doing. I'm still in trouble with the clan. I don't think kidnapping the Alpha's sister is going to help my cause."

"Don't worry," he assured the hybrid. "Everything will go according to plan." At least, he hoped so. Because he didn't know what he'd do if it didn't. A life without Isabelle and Evan wouldn't be worth living.

CHAPTER THIRTEEN

ISABELLE HAD NEVER SLEPT SO WELL IN HER LIFE. IT WAS a dreamless and deep sleep. Evan didn't even cry out for her, so he must have slept well, too.

Her lids, though, felt unusually heavy. But why would she want to get up? It was so nice and warm in this bed. Everything smelled amazing. Like rain and musk. And the flannel sheets were so soft and snuggly.

Flannel sheets?

She forced one eye open. The red, green, and black checkered pattern told her these were definitely flannel sheets. But she didn't own any sheets like these. For one thing, the colors were hideous. Though she gave up designer clothes long ago, she still enjoyed her thousand thread count Egyptian cotton bedsheets.

It was also unusually warm like she had her own personal electric blanket. As sleep began to leave her and her brain slowly became less foggy, she realized that was *not* an electric blanket. Rather, it was a heavy, muscled arm over her waist.

"Argh!" She scrambled to her knees and whipped

around. Ransom was in the unfamiliar bed with her, lying on his stomach. Rubbing her eyes, she glanced around at her surroundings.

Is this a ... log cabin? The dark, masculine furniture, minimal décor, and the view of mountains from the large window on one wall told her she was definitely not inside her apartment in The Enclave. *What the hell?* The last thing she remembered after he left was going to sleep, waking up to someone banging on her door and—

"Wake up!" She whacked Ransom on the head, making him start and jump from the bed, eyes glowing.

"What the—who's—" When his gaze landed on hers, his eyes returned to their normal green-gold color. "You're up."

"I'm up?" she said incredulously as she jumped off the bed. "That's all you have to say?" Running her hands down her body, she felt relief knowing she was fully dressed in the pajamas she had slept in. He, however, was shirtless and was only wearing his boxer briefs. "You knocked me out using some potion, and now I'm—Evan!" Dread creeped in, mixed with anger. "Evan's going to wake up, and I won't be there—"

"Princess, relax." He circled the bed and came to stand in front of her. "I wouldn't leave Evan alone, he's right here."

"Where?" Examining the rest of the room, she did not find any trace of her son.

"I mean, here, in my house."

"Your *house?*" she echoed. "What do you mean, your house?" Her sensitive ears perked up as she heard the distant sound of Evan's cry when he woke up first thing in the morning. "And where is my son?"

"He's in the other room," he said. "C'mon."

Ransom led her out of the bedroom and into the hallway.

The cabin was much larger than she thought, initially thinking it had been one of those one room cabins she'd seen in movies. There was a long hallway outside, also done in the same rustic, masculine log cabin style, but they only went as far as the bedroom next door. It was smaller, but clean, thankfully, and she saw Evan's crib in the corner by the window.

"Oh, baby," she lifted him out of the crib and held him close as he bawled. "I'm sorry, my love," she cooed. "I didn't know where you were. Mama's here." She walked over to his changing table and placed him down and took off his soiled diaper. Once she was finished cleaning and changing him, he finally stopped crying. "There's my good boy. You just needed a change and—" *Huh.* Upon a quick check of the room, she realized that his entire nursery had been transported here, from his crib to the rocker, and even the dresser with his clothes. His toys were piled in a heap in the corner.

"He okay?" Ransom stood in the doorway, looking apprehensive. "He sounded really upset."

"I usually change him at least once in the middle of the night," she explained. "But Ransom, what the heck are we doing here? Did you transport his entire nursery here?"

"I brought you here," he said. "Well, Cross did most of the work."

"What? We're not in New York?"

"No. You're in Kentucky."

"But ... but ..." she sputtered. "Why?"

"Because I wanted you here," he stated.

"You ... you ..." She placed an arm around Evan's ears. "Dick!" she hissed at him. "You kidnapped us!"

He didn't even have the decency to lie or look ashamed. "I did," he said. "It had to be done."

"Had to be done?" she repeated incredulously. "I told you, we could talk about visitation and maybe even custody when he's older!"

"I don't want that," he said in a low, menacing voice as he took a step toward them.

"Well you can't have him!" she growled, straightening her shoulders. "Over my dead body will I let you have him."

"That's not why I brought you guys here." He lifted a hand to her cheek. She wanted to shrug him away but couldn't. "I don't want just him. I want you. Both of you."

The declaration made her stomach flip-flop. But she couldn't go through this again. This time, she had Evan to think about. "You can't—"

"I was hoping you'd be up." Sabrina stood in the doorway. She looked at Isabelle sheepishly. "Everything ... okay?"

"You knew about this?" she asked accusingly.

"Not when we spoke," Sabrina answered, then nodded at Ransom. "It was all his idea, and he needed Cross, and so he told me. But the only way I was going to let him get away with it was if I could be here so you wouldn't be alone."

"Get away with this?" The earlier feelings of tenderness had dissipated. "You really think you can get away with it? I'm going to tell Lucas—"

"He already knows," Ransom stated.

"What?" She had raised her voice so loudly, Evan started in her arms. She shot him a glare and soothed her son. "How dare you tell Lucas you're Evan's father behind my back! You had no right—"

"Relax, princess," he said. "I didn't tell anyone."

She sighed in relief. "Well, when I tell them you kidnapped me, they'll come after—"

"They won't," Ransom said smugly. "After last night, I offered to shelter you, Evan, Sabrina, and a couple of your most vulnerable human clan members here," he said. "The Alpha thought it was a great idea. A couple of them are coming in the next few days once we get some of the rooms at the lodge ready."

"Lucas knows I'm here? And the rest of my family?"

"They know, even your sister," he said. "And they all agreed it was a good idea."

"You rotten bas—fink!" she spat. "I—" Evan let out a cry —one that she recognized as hunger. She glared at Ransom. "I don't suppose you thought to bring Evan's food, did you?"

"Huh?" He looked at her with a dumbstruck look on his face that said he did *not*.

"Then what is he supposed to eat?" Evan shoved a fist in his mouth and began to suck noisily as he continued to cry, which earned Ransom another irked scowl.

"It's a good thing these two geniuses told me their plan," Sabrina said wryly. "I called Cross this this morning to have him bring Evan's baby food and formula, plus a couple of your things, Isabelle. His food's down in the kitchen. I'll show you the way."

"You're a lifesaver, Sabrina." She glared at Ransom as they passed by and followed Sabrina out of the bedroom.

She had to admit, the log cabin house was much bigger and nicer than she'd imagined. Initially, she thought he didn't have a home and roamed around like her grandfather did. It was easy to picture Ransom living in here, among the dark, masculine decor and furniture.

The whole downstairs had an open-plan area, with a large living room and a big dining table separating it from the kitchen. Sabrina showed her the fridge, and Isabelle took out a jar of baby food and dug out a spoon from a nearby drawer.

"Let me help," Ransom offered, reaching out to take Evan.

"I can do it," she said. "I've been doing it by myself all this time, and I don't need you."

The hurt that flashed on his face made her chest twinge, but he quickly slipped on a stoic mask. She cleared her throat and nodded to the high chair folded in the corner. "Could you get that ready for him, please?"

Ransom immediately jumped into action, following her orders with careful precision like he was performing surgery and not just unfolding a child's high chair. "Is this all right?" he asked hopefully.

"It's good." She placed Evan in the chair and began to prepare his breakfast of mashed bananas and baby cereal on the kitchen table.

"As I live and breathe," came a voice from the other side of the room. "I thought Sabrina was pullin' my leg."

Isabelle stopped and looked up at the curvaceous redhead who had entered the kitchen area. She walked up to her, moving gracefully in her knee-high boots, jeans, and T-shirt. Isabelle thought she was one of the prettiest women she'd ever seen, with the only imperfection on her face being the faint scar on her cheek. *Human, definitely*, her senses told her.

"You must be Isabelle. I'm Silke Walker, Ransom's sister." She held her hand out. "I wish I could tell you Ransom talked about you all the time, but unfortunately, I just heard about you from Sabrina." Emerald green eyes snuck a reproachful look at Ransom.

"If it's any consolation, he didn't talk about you, either." She took the other woman's hand and shook it. Silke's grip was firm, but warm, much like her welcoming smile.

"Oh!" She covered her mouth with her hands as she dropped her gaze to Evan. "And you must be Evan! Oh, oh! You're a cutie patootie!" Bending down, she tickled Evan's cheeks. The baby laughed and slammed his little fists down on the table. "Hello, Evan, I'm your Aunty Silke. Hi there. Aren't you a cute boy?" Evan giggled as she made kissy faces at him. "He's so precious." Raising an auburn brow, she smiled wryly at Ransom. "Why, he looks exactly like you. Are you even sure she's the mom?"

Ransom scowled, but from the way he puffed out his chest, it was obvious he was proud that his sister saw the resemblance.

Sabrina cleared her throat. "Silke, I was wondering if I could talk to you about a couple of things."

"What? Oh. Right." She stole a glance at Ransom. "Sure. But, Ransom," she began. "I just wanted to let you know Joanie left a message."

Joanie? A hot twinge plucked in her chest, similar to last night at Muccino's when Jocelyn was flirting with him.

Ransom tensed. "Yeah?"

"She left for Mercer City yesterday. Won't be back for another day or so."

Isabelle wished she could look at him to judge his reaction, but Evan noisily let his hunger and displeasure known by banging his fists on the table. "Sorry, baby," she said as she fed him a spoonful of banana.

"Bring them to the lodge for lunch," Silke instructed. "No, don't give me that look, Ransom. She should meet everyone, and I can only guess what 'food' you have in here."

"Cross can get you anything you need," Sabrina said as she and Silke headed for the door. "Just let me know, and he'll get it for you. He'll be staying here in our cabin when he's not working."

"Thanks." When the two women left, she focused her attention on Evan and feeding him his breakfast until it was all done. She tried to ignore Ransom's presence, but it was hard as his stare was practically boring a hole into her back.

"All done?" he asked.

"Yeah." Putting the dish down on the table, she turned to face him and crossed her arms over her chest. "Ransom, last night—"

"Only proved we should be together," he finished. "You know it. Our wolves know it. We're supposed to be together."

Her wolf yipped happily. And she could see it, all of them together. Just like now. But this was all wrong. "No, Ransom—"

"Please." He cupped her jaw. "Give me a chance. I'll do anything. Let me prove to you this is how it's meant to be."

"I don't know."

"But you're not saying no," he said hopefully. "You don't have to say yes right away."

"I—" He was asking for a chance. And while she didn't want to give it to him, she didn't exactly have much of a choice now. Besides, maybe Lucas was right to have her stay here. Evan would be safe, and after what happened last night, that's the only thing she wanted. She and Ransom would have to find some kind of compromise. All she had to do was hold out and show him they were better apart. "I need something from you."

"Anything."

"I'll stay, but I'm moving into the room where Evan's staying. There's a twin bed in there and—"

"No," he growled.

"No?" *Was he crazy?* "What do you mean, no?"

"I have your things in my room," he said. "And beside, we've already—"

"Don't even think about it." But from the look on his face, he was thinking about it, and damn it, now she was too. "I need my own space. And Evan doesn't do well in new surroundings. He gets fussy and won't sleep whenever we stay somewhere new."

"Then he can stay with us."

"Absolutely not." This was one thing she wasn't going to compromise on. "You said you'd do anything. Besides I'm not ... I'm not sleeping with you anymore. I don't *want* to," she added for impact.

A dark look crossed his face, and he took a step forward. "Really, now?" The air around them turned thick with tension as he crowded her. "You don't want me?"

"I ..." She swallowed as his seductive scent tickled her nose. He was so close she could feel the intoxicating warmth of his body. When his hand came up to brush against her collarbone, she nearly melted.

Bending his head down, he nuzzled at her cheek. "So, I guess this isn't working at all?"

"N-n-no," she stammered, even as her nipples hardened to stiff points, and heat flooded her core. "Not at all." Her inner wolf, however, laughed at her. That *bitch*.

Abruptly, he pulled away. "All right then." He walked back toward the living room, but before he went out the door, he turned back to her. "I'll try harder next time." With a grin and a wink, he left.

"Whew." She wiped her brow with the back of her hand and leaned back on the kitchen table. *That was too close.*

Evan gurgled and waved his hands out to her, signaling he wanted out. "Just a second, baby, give Mama a minute."

Just resist him, until this is all over, she reminded herself. Protect her heart, and protect Evan. Those were the only things she had to focus on now. *Should be easy-peasy.*

CHAPTER FOURTEEN

RANSOM LEFT HIS HOUSE WITH A LITTLE SPRING IN HIS step. Proving Isabelle wanted him had been a good mood booster, and so was spending time with his son. His *son*. The words were alien to him, yet it felt right. Everything about this morning felt right—from the moment he woke up with Isabelle in his bed to helping take care of Evan. What did stick in his craw was the fact that she was still fighting him. Sure, she'd been outraged that he kidnapped and tricked her, but her arousal had been so potent before he left that he knew it wasn't wishful thinking.

Everything would soon fall into place. If only she could admit how perfect they were all together.

"My, my, don't you look like the cat that ate the canary."

He turned around. "Mornin', Bo."

"Wow, you *must* be in a good mood." The older Lycan quirked a white brow at him. "Does it have something to do with the chickee you got in your cabin?"

"Word travels fast around here," Ransom remarked. "Silke?"

"Yeah, she and Sabrina met Hawk on the way to the lodge and told him all about your girl. But you know gossip spreads like wildfire because of the men. So"—he rubbed his thumb and forefinger on his jaw—"anything you care to tell me, son?" As chaplain of the Savage Wolves MC and their most senior member, Bo's job was to counsel all the members and see to their mental health.

"No," he denied.

"Hmm ... it makes sense now," Bo began, "why you've been actin' the way you've been actin' the past year or so. Ever since Cross brought you back."

Not wanting to go where Bo was leading him, he quickly countered. "Is everyone at the clubhouse?"

"On their way, but a couple of us went ahead and got it all cleaned up," Bo replied, unruffled by the change of subject. "Was mighty surprised you wanted to use it again. You know if you need to talk—"

"I know where to find you."

He jogged a little faster, toward the Savage Wolves MC clubhouse, with Bo keeping up. Though the Seven Peaks Lodge and Cabins took up most of Silke's property, a portion was put aside for the use of the MC. All the members had their own cabins, plus acres and acres for their wolves to roam around in the Kentucky mountains. The clubhouse itself was set way back in a wooded area for maximum privacy and protection. However, ever since Pops died and Ransom became president, he'd been holding meetings in his cabin instead. But with Isabelle and Evan there, he knew it just wasn't going to be possible anymore.

He and Bo walked a few more minutes through a wooded path until they reached the clearing. The clubhouse itself was similar in construction to the other cabins, but it was single story with a larger footprint. Inside was a lounge area with big comfy sectionals, a bar, pool table, card table, plus two spare rooms in case members of other MCs they were allied with needed a place to crash.

And of course, there was the boardroom, where they had official meetings and where big issues were decided on. This was the first official meeting he'd called here as president since Pops died six months ago. The old man had been sick with some mysterious illness for a couple of weeks before he died. While Lycans could easily heal from wounds, for some reason they were still susceptible to some illnesses. The doctor had told them it might have been some form of internal cancer that quickly progressed.

As they entered the meeting room, Ransom's gaze fixed on the beat-up leather chair at the head of the table and he halted. It was an intimidating sight, and he never thought he'd be the one sitting there so soon. Pops was made for that chair—a natural born leader of their ragtag group.

Along with Bo, he had established the Savage Wolves MC a few years ago as a safe place where Lone Wolves could band together. The two of them had been part of another MC when they were younger and had long since retired, but when Ransom was growing up and had a few problems—not to mention, run-ins with the law—they decided it was time to introduce him to MC life to instill some discipline in him, and perhaps, a way to fulfill his wolf's need for a pack. Logan and Hardy had actually been in the same prison as him, where they had formed their little pack because they were the only Lycans in there. Once he got out, he tracked them down and recruited them to be part of Savage Wolves. Most of the other members of the MC just didn't fit into clan life or society in general for some reason or another, but even though they were forced to go through life alone, they all knew the truth: they were stronger together as a pack. However, unlike formal clans, they didn't have to answer to anyone as long as they didn't reveal their secret to humans, and they each still had a measure of independence.

Ransom would never know what his life would have been like if Pops didn't start the MC, but based on the trajectory it had been going on from the moment he was fifteen, he could have guessed. The old man had saved his life twice. He had big shoes to fill, and while he'd tried his best the last couple of months, he couldn't help but feel like he'd been coming up short.

"Go on," Bo urged from behind him. "He would have wanted you to have this. To sit in that chair."

He could feel the presence of all his wolves behind him, so he took a step forward. It got easier and easier as he drew closer until finally, he did sit down. The worn suspension on joints made the chair squeak, but he settled into the weathered leather upholstery with ease.

There was a somber note in the air as all six members filed in. Perhaps, much like him, they were all feeling the loss of Pops again. He was beloved by every single one of them, and once again, Ransom felt like he wasn't filling up those big shoes as he was supposed to.

"We all here?" Glancing around, everyone was here, even Logan, whom some of them didn't see for days, sometimes even weeks. The huge Lycan sat at the very end, arms over his chest and a constant scowl on his face, but those keen blue eyes were very much present and alert.

"Good, let's start." He reached for the wooden gavel on the table and slammed it on the sound block. "First, let's go around so everyone has a chance to put any business they need to address on the table."

Though most motorcycle clubs around the country had bad reputations because some were connected to criminal activities, because of their nature, the Savage Wolves MC stayed away from any illegal behavior that would bring too much attention to them. Sure, a couple of them—Ransom himself included—had done some time in juvie or prison in the past, but as far as anyone was concerned, the club itself had no ties to organized crime, drugs, or other unsavory enterprises. After all, they had their secret to protect and all the members just wanted to have peaceful lives. Mostly, they spent their days working for the lodge or Bucky's Garage in the nearby town. Once in a while, they did charity rides or helped with security for events, but otherwise, they kept to themselves.

"All right," he said once everyone had their say. "Let's get to some club business and why I've called you here."

"Is it because of your old lady?" Axle asked, his blue eyes twinkling.

There was hooting all around, and Ransom rolled his eyes. "All right, children, settle down." He knew he owed them at least an explanation about Isabelle and Evan. Trust was a key factor in keeping their bond strong. "I know you've all been gossiping like a bunch of old ladies at a knitting club, so let me give it to you straight since you're all going to be acquainted with them soon. Isabelle is my True Mate and the mother of my son, Evan."

All the men looked at him with varying expressions of shock and surprise.

"True Mate?" Hardy, his Vice President, said as his jaw dropped. "That's real?"

"Apparently so. She and I got together a while back in New York. And due to ... certain circumstances, I didn't know about him until yesterday. But you'll be seeing a lot more of them, so I hope you make them feel welcome and give them the respect they deserve."

"So, she *is* your old lady?" Axle repeated.

Ransom wasn't sure how to answer that. "We're working it out. You got a problem with that?"

"No, man." Axle waved his hands defensively. "I was just wonderin', 'cause, you know, now that you got your own woman, maybe we could at least be allowed to bring home our dates onto MC property. You might like livin' like a damned monk, but not all of us do. Besides, you've found the love of your life and all, we should be able to get the same chance."

A while back, Ransom had banned the guys from bringing home women or having parties on their property because of an untoward incident. While they complied because he was president and Silke was more than happy not to have strangers on her land, they were all ornery about the whole thing. He wasn't preventing them from hooking up with anyone, he only asked them not to bring it home.

"Somehow, I got the feelin' you ain't lookin' for love, Axe," Hardy quipped.

"Yeah, just needin' to get that dick stroked," Snake added with a laugh.

"Hey, love comes in all forms, fellas," Axle said

defensively. "'Sides, I still get plenty of action. But it would be nice to know I can bring a girl to a proper bed instead of banging her in the back of my truck or the alley behind—"

"All right, all right." Ransom massaged his temple. "I'll ... think about it. Now, next business. I told you all about Cross and New York coming to us for help. We're going to be taking in a few of their people, mostly elderly Lycans and humans, in the next couple of days. In turn, Cross is going to give us some protection from the mages." He cleared his throat and eyed Logan carefully. "In the form of magical barriers around the property. There's going to be a couple witches and warlocks from a nearby coven coming today to start—"

"What?" Logan growled. "No. Absolutely *not*."

"You don't have to be anywhere near them when they're here," Ransom said. "You can go into town with Silke—"

"Like hell I will." He stood up to full height. "I'm not lettin' those ... those people near me or my horses."

Ransom expected this, seeing as Logan hated witches, warlocks, or anything magical. "I don't expect you to be okay with this, but I do expect you to comply," he said in a serious tone. His own wolf did not like Logan's stance one bit as it raised its hackles and emanated dominant vibes across the table, making all of the others look nervous. "You have no idea what those mages can do." The things he'd witnessed in Central Park a couple of days ago, the evil, malevolent power he'd felt was nothing like he'd experienced before. "Witches and warlocks are nothing in comparison, and we won't stand a chance against the mages by ourselves. They're coming, and you can be assured they'll want every last one of us dead, Lone Wolf or not. They already tried to take Evan." He didn't even realize he'd been squeezing the gavel so hard until the wooden handle cracked.

"They tried to take your son?" Hardy slammed his fist down on the table. "Damned bastards! Logan," he barked. "Sit the fuck down. I don't care what you think. These assholes ain't gonna come here and try to take what's ours." Hardy himself was the father of a little girl. "Your girl and son are one of us," he declared, looking menacingly at everyone. "Anyone who doesn't want to protect them don't deserve to be sitting here."

"Didn't know they took your kid," Logan grumbled as he sat down. "I'll make myself scarce today."

"Good," he said. "And when it's time to fight—"

"We're behind you, boss," Hawk added, and everyone nodded in agreement, even Logan.

A few days ago, all Ransom wanted was for him and his crew to be left alone. But now, he was going to be knee-deep in trouble. Well, those damned mages made it all personal the moment they took Evan.

"All right then, if there's nothing else ..." Everyone shook their heads. "We're adjourned." He struck the gavel down to signify the end of their official meeting.

Bo glanced at him with a smile. "You did good," he whispered in a low voice.

Acknowledging the older man with a nod, he got up from the chair. It felt good, somehow. *If you're watching me from wherever you are, Pops,* he prayed silently, *I hope I don't disappoint you.*

———

After sorting out a few more things with the men, Ransom headed back to his cabin. It was nearly lunchtime, and he was pretty sure Silke would have his head if he didn't bring Isabelle and Evan to the lodge as she'd instructed. When he got inside his cabin, he was greeted with a sight that made his chest go all warm.

Isabelle had pushed the furniture aside and spread out some kind of play mat over the hardwood floor. She was sitting cross-legged, surrounded by toys as Evan held onto her hands and stood up, jumping up and down to a nursery rhyme she was singing. Sensing his presence, however, she glanced up at him and stopped singing, though Evan continued to bounce up and down.

"You're back," she said. "Sorry about the mess. The room upstairs is a little stuffy, so I thought it would be better to play with him down here."

"No! I mean, not at all." Padding toward them, he carefully got down on the mat. "Do you mind?"

"It's your house," she said with a shrug. "You can do what you want."

"Yeah but ..." Why the heck was he suddenly so tongue-tied around her? It was like he was afraid saying the wrong thing could make her and Evan disappear into thin air. "I want you to be comfortable while you're here. Feel free to go into any room or use my stuff. Anything you want or need, just ask." He'd give her and Evan the fucking world if they asked for it.

She sighed and eased Evan down to a sitting position, then gave him a toy. "You can't really mean for us to stay here?"

"Of course I do," he said.

"Won't Joanie mind?" There was an acrid hint in her tone, and her nostrils flared. "I wouldn't want to step on any toes."

"Joanie? Why—" Clarity flashed in his brain. "Wait, are you jealous?"

"What?" Her face scrunched up distastefully. "I don't know what you mean, and I don't care. But if you have a girlfriend—"

"Princess," he began. "Joanie is my mother."

"I didn't know you had a mother," she blurted out. "I mean, obviously you do. But why did Silke call her by her first name?"

"Because Joanie's not her biological mother," he explained. "Her father married Joanie when Silke was a baby and I was about eight years old. Pops brought us to live here with them."

"Oh. I see. And your dad? Your real one?"

"Pops *was* my real dad." In every way but one. Pops had rescued them, given them a home, cared for Ransom like he was his own. He could still remember what it had been like before they came here, and he quickly shut the painful memories away.

"I mean your biological dad," she clarified. "Where is he? Is he still around?"

"I don't talk about him," he growled.

Her mouth opened, and the fear that flashed across her face made him want to kick his own ass. Turning away, she busied herself with gathering the toys Evan had discarded, though the way she avoided his gaze made a pit in his stomach form. He didn't want to discuss his biological father with her. But he didn't want her scared of him either. "He's dead. Died in prison," he said.

Her head shot up, eyes filled with emotion. "Ransom ... I'm sorry. I didn't know."

"It's not your fault," he said automatically.

"I know, but ... I can't imagine ..."

How could he even begin to tell her what it was like, growing up the way he did? Always moving, never staying in one place, relying on handouts and being kicked out of various rundown motels and ramshackle apartments. All because of a bad turn of events that he had no control over. His childhood had been a nightmare, that was, until Pops found him and Joanie at the bus stop in town, hungry and homeless for what seemed like the hundredth time in his short life. "Pops ... he treated me like his own son," he said quietly. "Wish you'd met him. He'd spoil Evan so much."

"He sounded like a good man. I'm sorry for your loss."

"Thanks, I—" He stopped when he felt a pair of small hands grab at his. Somehow, Evan had crawled all the way to him. Mismatched blue and green eyes looked up at him expectantly.

"He wants you to help him up," she said. "I read that at this age, they're starting to develop their legs and it's good exercise to hold them up. Just let him hang on to you."

Following her instructions, he let Evan wrap his tiny fists around his forefingers and then lift himself up. "That's it," he encouraged. "So strong." He watched in fascination as Evan bounced up and down with his assistance. "I think he wants to go walk around."

"Let him lead you," she said. "You'll know what to do."

Getting up to his feet, Ransom pulled Evan up, much to

the boy's delight. He took a step forward, then another and another, until they had walked around most of the living room. When he tried to walk up the stairs, Isabelle swooped in and took him in her arms.

"We're not ready for that yet, baby," she said.

Ransom didn't want his time with Evan to end, but he understood that it cost Isabelle a lot just to leave them be for a few minutes. He'd take what he could and savor any time he would have with his son for now. "Um, it's almost lunchtime," he said. "Silke'll be expecting us."

"If you can grab his food, I'll run upstairs and get his diaper bag. Is it far?"

"Naw, but we'll take my truck."

Minutes later, they were on their way to the lodge. Ransom made a mental note to thank Cross for insisting on taking the car seat as now Evan was happily strapped in the back while Isabelle rode in the passenger seat. Soon, they pulled into the parking lot and were headed inside the lobby. Silke was already at the reception area with Sabrina and Arlene, who helped her run the lodge and also happened to be Bo's old lady.

"There you are!" Silke's face lit up as they drew nearer. "I was just telling Arlene all about you and Evan."

"I'm Arlene. It's lovely to meet you Isabelle," the older woman said. "Oh, and aren't you precious? Silke was right, you are Ransom's spitting image! Are you sure you gave birth to him?"

"That's what I said," Silke joked. "The resemblance ... it's startling."

"Isn't it?" Sabrina added. "I knew I'd seen that scowl somewhere."

Isabelle, to her credit, chuckled as she handed Evan over to Silke. The boy was reaching out for her, and the moment Silke took him, he grabbed fistfuls of her red locks. "Looks like you're all ready to pull on girls' pigtails in the playground," she said. "He's adorable."

"And those eyes!" Arlene slipped out from behind the reception table for a closer inspection. "They're so beautiful. Just like you, sugar," she said to Isabelle. "I can see why Ransom's had his panties in a twist for the last year or so."

Isabelle blushed prettily and said nothing but avoided his gaze.

"So, lunch?" he asked. "I'm starving."

"You always are," Silke said wryly. "But c'mon, let's go get some food."

They walked into the dining room just off the main lobby. The hostess sat them at a table in a corner, and Isabelle secured Evan in a high chair a member of the waitstaff had brought over.

"This is a lovely place," Isabelle said.

"That's what I thought," Sabrina said. "By the way, Silke, I have my paints and canvas ready. I'm going to get started on that painting of the lake for you today."

"That's wonderful, and sweet of you, sugar." Silke beamed. "Thank you." The Seven Peaks Lodge and Cabins were Silke's pride and joy, her true love, as she called it. "It was my mother's family's business, and she left it to me when she passed. I was a baby then, but Pops, Bo, and Arlene ran it while I was growing up."

"I can't imagine what it's like running this place with just you guys," Isabelle remarked. "My mother used to run our family restaurant in Jersey when her mother and grandmother passed."

Silke leaned forward. "Oh, so you're experienced in the restaurant business."

"She works as a hostess at a restaurant in New York," Ransom said.

"I also work as the manager. Well, almost the manager," she corrected, raising a brow at Ransom. "I've been doing it for a couple of months now."

"But the restaurant business is in your blood," Silke said. "Maybe you can give me some pointers? I mean, the lodge is profitable, but this place"—she glanced around surreptitiously—"I can't turn a profit. I mainly have it so I can serve breakfast, however, as you can see," she gestured to the mostly empty dining room, "no one wants to eat here."

"Hmm." Isabelle scratched her chin. "I'd like to see your operations and kitchens, but I'm not experienced enough to give you solid advice, so I might have to ask my Uncle Dante or Mama for help."

"Really?" Silke looked at her hopefully. "That would be amazing. Thank you."

"Hey, at least I'll have something to do and won't be bored out of my mind while in captivity," she said as she casually glanced at the menu.

"Captivity?" Silke asked.

"Yes." She smiled sweetly at Ransom. "Didn't you tell your sister that you kidnapped me? Dosed me with a sleeping potion and had me and Evan brought here without asking me?"

"Goodness!" the redhead exclaimed. "Is this true, Ransom? Did you kidnap them?"

"When you put it like that, it sounds really bad," he said. "I prefer to think of it as keeping them safe."

"Ransom," Silke warned.

"What?" he shrugged. "Someone tried to hurt my son last night. And I know they'll be safe here, where I can keep an eye on them."

His sister frowned at him. "I was under the impression you two were 'together' which was why you agreed to come here." She looked at Sabrina suspiciously, but the human suddenly found the paint job on the ceiling interesting.

"We aren't," Isabelle said quickly.

"Yet," he added saucily which earned him a scowl from Isabelle.

"Oh, my." Silke smirked at Arlene and Sabrina. "This is going to be interesting, isn't it?"

"Can we order? I'm hungry." He signaled for the waiter to come over, and he took their orders.

"I've decided something," Silke said. "I'm going to close the deck outside tonight so we can have a party."

"Another party?" Ransom asked. "Didn't you just have one when Sabrina came?"

"Yeah, but I'm going to be asking everyone to work harder the next couple of days just to get everything ready for our new guests," Silk reasoned. "It'll be a good way to thank them in advance. It's just burgers and drinks, nothing fancy."

"A party sounds nice," Sabrina said.

"Well, my party days are over," Isabelle said. "You guys have fun."

"But Isabelle, I want to throw this party for you too," Silke said.

"Silke, no," she protested. "Please."

"C'mon, it'll be fun, and you'll get to meet the rest of the guys," she said. "They're all dying to meet you, and that way, you won't be surprised if they decide to just pop up to get a look at you."

"They're worse than the town busybodies, unfortunately," Arlene said with a shake of her head.

"If Isabelle doesn't want to go, she won't," Ransom said. He did not like the idea of having her surrounded by other people, especially his guys. Not that he would think they'd poach or anything, but he certainly wasn't going to hear the end of it. "She and I will stay home with Evan."

Her gaze went laser-straight at him, narrowing down into slits. "Actually, Silke, I'd love to go. Evan, too, if you can make it early so I can get him to bed at eight."

"We can start at five." Silke clapped her hands excitedly. "I can't wait."

Ransom did not like this one bit. He was hoping to have some alone time with Isabelle tonight, maybe ask Silke to babysit, and he would take Isabelle out to dinner. A proper date, something they'd never done before. However, as Silke and Isabelle talked more about improvements on the lodge restaurant, he couldn't help but feel some relief that they were getting along, and her irritation at him had lessened as lunch wore on. In fact, she was so distracted that she simply handed him Evan when he was done eating and showed him how to burp him as she talked to Silke about supply management and decor.

Later, just as they were about to have coffee, his phone buzzed. Checking the message, he let out a soft curse. "Sorry," he said as he got up. "I got some business to attend to."

"Business?" Silke asked.

"The witches are here." He quickly explained to them about Cross's contacts. "They're out at the perimeter, I should go see to them. I'll see you later, ladies." Turning to Isabelle, he brushed his hand down her arm quickly before she could protest. "Have Silke call me if you need anything." He ruffled Evan's head and strode out toward the exit, hoping that this wouldn't take too long.

CHAPTER FIFTEEN

Isabelle had to admit, she was having a lot of fun. Before she had Evan, she went to a lot of parties and clubs, but frankly, she lost the desire to go out the moment she found out she was pregnant. She didn't miss it at all. Looking back, she realized how boring those parties were and how superficial those so-called friends had been. With the exception of Maxine, everyone wanted to be around her because she could get them into the hottest clubs, vacation spots, and restaurants, not because they liked her. And why should they have liked her? She'd been a nasty, vain person back then.

Out here, however, everything just seemed so ... genuine. Sure, they were drinking wine out of a box, and many of the guests probably wouldn't have been let into the most prestigious clubs in New York, but she would rather be here than anywhere else.

From the moment she stepped onto the outdoor deck, everyone wanted to meet her, especially all the members of the Savage Wolves MC. It was easy to tell who they were, not just because they were all Lycans, but by the leather vests they wore with the Savage Wolves logo—a roaring wolf head. Come to think of it, Ransom had been wearing the same thing this morning when he came back.

She did her best to remember their names as they introduced themselves to her. Hawk was the guy with the mohawk, so that was easy, and his brother was Snake. Ink was their "proby"—a probationary member, so his vest had a patch on front that proclaimed his status. Bo was the older man with the salt-and-pepper hair and also Arlene's "old man." Axle was the charming one with the pretty blue eyes and then there was Hardy, father to Annie, a precocious three-year-old who was fascinated by Evan. The little girl had begged to hold him, so Isabelle helped her sit down on a chair and placed him on her lap.

"Daddy, Daddy, look!" she cried out proudly, bouncing Evan on her lap.

"Good job, sweetie," Hardy said. "Keep him steady ... no sweetie, not like that, he's not a doll."

Annie looked down at Evan who seemed content to let her hold him. "Daddy, I want one."

Isabelle couldn't help burst out laughing as Hardy paled visibly.

"Uh, you might be a bit too young, Annie," he said.

"I know that, *Daddy*." She rolled her eyes in the most adorable way. "I want a baby brother or sister. Can I get one, please? I promise to be good. You don't even have to get me a Christmas present."

A vein throbbed on Hardy's head as he contemplated an answer. Wanting to spare the poor man, Isabelle spoke up.

"Annie, it's getting chilly." The sun was setting fast

behind the mountains. "Evan has a sweater with dinosaurs all over it. It's in his bag over there by the door. Would you be a sweetheart and get it for me?"

"Sure!" She let Isabelle take Evan off her lap, and the little girl bounded away.

"Thanks, you really saved my bacon there," Hardy said, smiling sheepishly.

"Don't worry, at least now I know I have about two years to think about what to say to Evan once he starts asking for a baby brother or sister."

Hardy laughed. "Well, Ransom'll want a big family, so maybe he doesn't need to ask."

It was on the tip of her tongue to tell him that there was no way she was going to have more children by Ransom, but she just couldn't, so instead she gave him a tight smile. The party was in full swing, the evening was lovely, and everyone was enjoying themselves, so why would she ruin it by flatly telling Hardy that there was no way in hell she and Ransom were going to be together?

"Isabelle, Isabelle, I found it!" Annie waved the sweater at her. "Can I help put it on, please?"

"Of course." She knelt down and instructed Annie on how to put the sweater on Evan.

"There's my handsome nephew," Silke exclaimed as she came up to them. "How are you, Evan? Oh look, he already knows Auntie Silke!" Evan babbled at the redhead, his hands reaching out. "Do you mind?"

"Not at all." She handed Evan over. The boy squealed in delight as he grabbed Silke's hair and gave a hard tug. "Evan!"

"It's all right." She peppered his face with kisses. "Evan can do what he wants."

"You're already spoiling him rotten," Hardy said.

"That's what aunties are for," she shot back.

"Since you already have him," Isabelle began. "Would you mind keeping him while I go get another glass of wine?"

"Not at all, go ahead, sugar." Silke turned back to Evan, who chortled with delight as she blew raspberries on his chubby cheeks. "Auntie Silke'll take good care of you. Leave him here as long as you need. Forever if you want."

Isabelle chuckled. It was very obvious Silke was in love with the boy. And after spending the day with her, Isabelle couldn't help but respect her. Not only was Silke a sharp businesswoman, but she also cared a lot about the land and her employees. It had been on the tip of her tongue to ask her about the faint scar that extended from her right lip to the tip of her cheekbone, but she refrained. There had to have been a painful story there, but she didn't want to pry.

"Thanks." Walking over to the refreshment table, she inhaled the cool mountain air. Despite the fact that she was enjoying herself, there was something missing. And she hated that feeling because she knew what was missing. Or *who*.

Where was he? It had been hours since Ransom left, and he still hadn't returned. She didn't have her phone with her, and she didn't want to bother Silke or anyone else just to ask where he was. If they weren't worried, then she shouldn't be. *How did the meeting with the witches go?* Hopefully, there were no problems.

As she was filling her glass from the box, the hairs at the back of her neck prickled. Her wolf flattened its ears as she felt a presence behind her. Slowly, she turned around.

"So, you're the one."

The question came out of nowhere and was so direct,

Isabelle didn't know what to say. The woman standing before her had her eyes narrowed and lips curled into a smirk. Her slim arms were crossed under suspiciously large and perky boobs barely covered in a pink tank top, while her spray-tanned legs were shown off thanks to jean shorts that rode high up her crotch.

"I'm sorry," she said. "Have we been introduced?"

"No, we haven't." The woman looked her up and down. "I just don't see it."

This was starting to get old. "If you'll excuse me—"

"I don't see what Ransom sees in you."

Now *that* got her attention. "Excuse me?"

"You know the saying, 'why go out for hamburgers, when you have steak at home'?" The woman's mouth twisted cruelly. "I don't know where you've been all this time, honey, but you can bet Ransom's been getting his steak."

Isabelle's wolf growled and pressed at her skin, wanting to take a swipe at this audacious bitch. However, seeing as she was human, Isabelle was not prepared to spend time in the Lycan Siberian Prison for revealing their secret, not for this fake-ass and her bags of silicone.

"Isabelle!" It was Silke, coming up behind the woman, Evan in her arms. "Did you get—" She stopped short. "*You.*" Her pretty face scrunched up. "What are *you* doing here?"

"Hello, Silke, honey," she drawled. "I seem to have misplaced my invitation to your little party."

"That's because I didn't invite you, Sue May," Silke shot back. "Or did you forget that time you got thrown off my property?"

"Tsk, tsk, that was months ago," Sue May waved her away and chuckled. "Surely that's water under the bridge now, right? See, when I heard through the grapevine—that is, my cousin who's the hostess at your restaurant—that you had a special *guest* from out of town, why I had to come and see her for myself."

Her eyes flickered over to Evan, and when her expression faltered for just a second, Isabelle couldn't help but feel smug.

Sue May composed herself and spoke in a sickly-sweet tone. "My, my, haven't you done well for yourself? Bless your heart."

Isabelle's patience was wearing thin. "Why don't you cut the bullshit? Whatever you have to say, say it to my face, *bitch*."

The other woman smiled smugly. "You're certainly something. You know, honey, where I'm from, a lady doesn't talk that way."

"Oh, really?" Isabelle planted her hands on her hips. While she may have grown up in Manhattan, she was Italian and from Jersey on her mother's side. "Well, *honey*, where I come from, we tell hoes like you to fuck off."

Silke burst out into laughter, as did Sabrina, Arlene, and all the other people who had started gathering around them.

Sue May's face turned fire-engine red as she let out a frustrated cry. "You slut—"

"What the hell is going on here?"

Isabelle's wolf started at the familiar voice. It, however, did not whine or cry out happily as it usually did when he was near. No, it was *furious*. As was Isabelle, but she would never admit it.

Ransom stopped short when he saw Sue May, his

expression suddenly turned stormy. "I told you never to come back here."

"But, Ransom," she whined. "We've always had so much fun together."

"Had," he said. "That was in the past. I told you a hundred times, it didn't mean anything."

Her face twisted up in fury. "You can't possibly want her over me!" Her head snapped back to Isabelle. "She's a fat, ugly cow."

"And you're the reason we have instructions on shampoo," Isabelle retorted, which made everyone howl with laughter.

Sue May blew out an outraged scream. "You baby-trapping whore!"

Isabelle saw Ransom's face turn furious, but she sent him a warning look not to interfere. This was woman's business, and she intended to finish it. "Listen here, Trailer Trash Barbie," she began. "No one wants you here, that's why you weren't invited. Why don't you turn around, take your fake tits and cheap blonde extensions, and *get the fuck out of here*."

Someone whooped in the background—probably Axle or Hawk—which only made Sue May turn redder with rage. "You'll regret this," she warned, fists curled tight at her sides. "He won't want to stay with you. You think you're so special? He's had dozens of girls—"

"All right, time to take out the garbage," Silke said as she handed Evan to Sabrina and dragged Sue May by the arm. "If I ever see you near my property again, I'm going to call the cops."

Isabelle didn't bother to watch or wait for anyone else to say anything. Spinning on her heel, she marched off, not caring where she went. From the tour Silke had given her earlier, she knew there was a large pool set in the back of the lodge. She followed the stone path until she saw the soft blue glow in the distance and followed it until it led her to the pool area. Staring into the water, she let out a sigh.

"Isabelle."

Ransom must have come up fast for him to sneak up on her like that. "If it's not obvious by now, I want to be alone."

"You need to let me explain. Please."

She whirled around. Her wolf was not very pleased with him, not after what that other female had said. It wanted to lash out at him and cut him into ribbons. "I'm not jealous, if that's what you're thinking. I know you've slept with other women before me and after, but they don't get to insult me or Evan—"

"I haven't."

Her temper flared at being interrupted. "Haven't what?"

"Haven't slept with anyone after you." He took a step forward, hand reaching out as if to touch her, but withdrew quickly when he sensed her wolf snap at him. "I swear, Isabelle, there's been no one but you."

The confession made her blink. "What? But it's been so long."

"I couldn't." The rough caress of his voice made her shiver. "Not with anyone else."

Flabbergasted was too mild a word for what she was feeling. She wanted to tell him, too, but held her tongue. "But Sue May said—"

"That was a long time ago, way before you." He rubbed a hand down his face. "I was young and stupid. Wasn't even president then, so she left me alone after. When I got promoted, well, she came sniffing around again, had her cap set on being my old lady. Snuck into my bed naked as a jaybird one night, while Axle was having a party at his place. Since then, I've banned the guys from having parties and overnight guests. Ask them yourself."

She did believe him. "She snuck in again."

"And you handled yourself well," Ransom said. "I wouldn't be surprised if you earned the respect of every single person out there."

The expression on his face was that of pride and made her stomach flip-flop. And the fact that he didn't even tease her or revel in the jealousy she displayed annoyed her—because it meant a lot to her. Her wolf, too, had been mollified. "We should head back. They'll be wondering where we are." *And why we're alone.*

Gold-green eyes bored into her as his expression turned serious. "Would it be so bad, Isabelle?"

"Would what be so bad?"

"You and me."

The ache in his voice, in his eyes, was so potent it made it hard to breathe. "Please, don't, Ransom. Not now." *Not yet,* a small voice echoed.

He nodded. "Let's head back, it's probably Evan's bedtime soon."

They walked in silence, just the sound of the wind and the chirps of the crickets accompanying them along the way. He motioned for her to walk up the steps heading to the lodge's outdoor deck first.

"There you two are," Silke said, looking hopefully at them. "You'll be happy to know I've taken the trash out. She won't be bothering you again," she said to Isabelle. "But I have a feeling you'll hold your own against her."

"Thanks, Silke," Ransom said.

"Where the heck were you, anyway?" His sister planted her hands on her hips. "I told you to be back by five."

"It's that old hag—er, witch," he grunted. "She was being particular about everything, and having her and her people place all the protection spells took longer than I thought. I'm just glad that pain in my ass is gone, and we should be good for a while."

"Well, I'm glad for that," Silke said.

"You won't be when that witch comes calling," Ransom said. "Despite her objections, she thought the lodge was stunning. Wants to talk to you about having some special event here."

"Where's Evan?" Isabelle asked.

"With Sabrina and Cross," Silke nodded toward the other side of the deck, where they were chatting with Arlene and Bo.

"He's ready for bed," she observed, seeing his little head nod off as Sabrina held him. "I should go get him. Goodnight, Silke, and thanks for the party."

"His seat's still in my truck," Ransom reminded her.

As if she could forget that she was staying with him. "I'll meet you out front."

After saying goodnight to Sabrina, Cross, and everyone else, Isabelle took Evan and headed to the parking lot. Ransom was already by his truck, the back seat open so she could put the drowsing baby into the car seat.

They drove in silence all the way back to his cabin, and it wasn't a surprise that Evan was already fast asleep. "The excitement tuckered him out," she said, just to break the tension in the air.

He didn't answer but helped her by opening the back door for her and she took Evan out. They walked into the cabin in silence and she made a beeline for the stairs. She was already on the first step when he called her name.

"Isabelle?"

Turning to him, she was momentarily stunned by the look of pure determination on his face. "Y-yeah?"

"What I said this morning? About trying harder?"

"What about it?"

"You better believe I ain't done yet."

She stared at him for a second, not sure what to say. "Goodnight, Ransom," she managed before looking away and began to ascend the stairs.

"Goodnight, Isabelle."

Even his goodnight sounded like a promise. Or a threat. She was surprised she made it all the way up the steps without her knees giving out. Her wolf very much liked what he said and the fact that he hadn't been with anyone else except her.

Would it be so bad, he had asked. And now she found herself asking the same question.

CHAPTER SIXTEEN

"THANKS SO MUCH, UNCLE DANTE, DOMINIC," ISABELLE said into the screen of Silke's laptop.

"Anytime, sweetheart," Uncle Dante replied. "You let me know how it goes."

"Thank you, sir," Silke added. "I already have a few ideas I can start implementing."

"It's my pleasure, Ms. Walker."

"I look forward to seeing any improvements," Dominic added. "And if you have any questions, just relay them to Isabelle, and we'll do our best to answer you."

After saying their goodbyes, Silke closed the laptop lid. "I can't believe your uncle is *the* Dante Muccino. He has, like, six restaurants all over the world, five cookbooks, plus that line of organic sauces and pasta." She shook her head. "I can't thank you enough, Isabelle."

"Don't thank me," she said. "My uncle and cousin are the chefs. I'm still figuring things out myself."

When she asked Uncle Dante for help with the lodge's restaurant situation, he had happily agreed, and since he was with Dominic—his other son who ran the French restaurant his wife owned—he put him on the call too so he could lend his expertise. Though Uncle Dante had asked about her and Evan's condition, Isabelle decided not to tell him or anyone in her family about Ransom yet. It was still a delicate situation, and with tensions running high back in New York, she figured it was one more thing they didn't have the bandwidth to handle.

"But without you, I wouldn't have gotten their expert advice." Silke drew her in for a quick hug. "You've already helped us. In more ways than you know."

"You're welcome."

Silke bit her lip and leaned in closer. "Now, I don't want to get into your business, and I promise I'll shut up if you tell me to. But ... have you given any more thought to you and Ransom?"

Did she have any thoughts? How could she think of anything else? "It's more complicated than you think. I'm just ..." How could she describe it? Apprehensive? Afraid? Worried? All three and more?

"You know, Ransom's never had a serious girlfriend. Sure, when he was growing up he was randy as any teen boy. But," she lowered her voice, "though he never tells me or anyone, from what I overhear from the guys, he's been living like a monk for the last couple of years."

Isabelle was floored once again and she didn't even want to think about that. "I don't know—"

"It's all right." Silke put a hand over hers. "Sorry for being nosy. I just ... I don't want you and Evan to live so far away if things don't work out. He's such a wonderful kid, and you're a wonderful mother. Thank you for taking care of him."

"I love him, I'd do anything for him." Her chest tightened at the thought of her son. "And someday, you'll be a mom, too, and have a baby of your own to love."

Silke's face faltered for a moment before she put on a tight smile. "Thanks, but that's not really in the cards for me."

"I'm sure that's not true. You're so young and—"

"No." She shook her head. "I can't. Have children, I mean. There was this ... incident." She swallowed. "Anyway, the doctor said it's impossible." The scar on her cheek deepened as pain crossed her face.

Isabelle stared at the other woman, unsure what to say. "I'm sorry, I didn't know."

"It's all right," she said. "I've ... accepted it. This place, the lodge, it's the only thing I have left of my own mom. So now it's my baby, my everything." An inscrutable look flashed across her face, but she quickly pasted a smile on her face. "Speaking of babies, why don't we go and get Evan back from Arlene? Her break's almost done."

They left Silke's office and made their way to the lobby. To their surprise, Arlene was already behind the front desk, but Evan was nowhere in sight.

"He's outside with Ransom," the older woman said as they approached, jerking a thumb at the doorway that led to the outside deck.

"I thought he wouldn't be back until later?" Isabelle asked.

That morning, Ransom had left early to go into town. He usually worked at a garage when Silke didn't need him at the lodge, and because he'd been gone a couple of days, his boss, Bucky, asked him to finish up some work he'd left undone.

"He just showed up," Arlene replied. "Said he was all done."

"I'll go find them." Isabelle made a beeline for the outdoor deck where they had the party yesterday. There, she found Ransom bent over, letting Evan hold onto his fingers as he helped him walk, encouraging him gently as he crossed the sunny deck. When they reached the end, Evan let out a squeal as Ransom hoisted him up in the air and caught him.

"Good job, Evan," he said triumphantly. "That's my boy."

Her heart flip-flopped at the sight of Ransom holding Evan. She found herself unable to move or speak, content to just watch them together, her son's face lit up in delight as he patted Ransom's face.

Feeling eyes on him, Ransom turned toward her. "Oh." A guilty look flashed across his face. "I uh, got back early, and Arlene was trying to eat her lunch in peace, so I offered to watch him for a bit."

"I ... that's nice." She strolled over to them, and when Evan realized she was there, clapped his hands and reached out to her.

"Mama!" he cried.

"I—Oh! Evan!" Tears formed at her eyes. "Yes, that's me, I'm your mama."

"He's never called you that before?"

"Never. He babbles a lot, but he hasn't said any real words yet."

"Mama! Mama!" He wiggled in Ransom's arms, so he handed him over to Isabelle.

"Hello, baby." She kissed his nose, breathing in his sweet scent. "Did you miss me? Did you have a good time with Daddy?" Ransom tensed, and she realized what she had accidentally said, those words that had remained unspoken until now. Finding her composure, she straightened her spine. "Thanks, um, for watching him."

"Of course."

The look on his face as he stared at Evan made her feel warm and fuzzy all over. "So, I don't want to keep you—"

"It's fine," he said, scratching the back of his head. "I mean, I'm done at the garage for the day. Silke has a checklist of things she wanted me to accomplish around the lodge and the property, but if there's anything you wanted to do—"

"I'm all good," she said awkwardly. "I mean, you should get a move on with that list."

"Would you and Evan want to come with me?" He rubbed the back of his head. "I ... could take you on a tour. I know Silke said she'd do it, but she's got her plate full because the lodge'll be at full capacity soon."

The hope in his tone made it hard to say no. "I guess that would be okay." Besides, it's not like she had much else to do. "I'm sure Evan could use the fresh air and sunshine. Except for the parks in New York, he doesn't get to go outdoors much."

And so, she and Evan accompanied him as he did errands around the lodge, driving around in his truck. First, they went to the one of the cabins to check if Hawk and Ink needed help in replacing the heater in the unit. Since they had everything in hand, they headed to the recreation area where Snake and Axle were doing some maintenance work with the lights in the tennis courts.

"I'd be done sooner if this guy didn't play with his phone every two minutes," Axle groused.

"This is serious work," Snake said. "Lizzie needs my code right away."

"Lizzie?" The other Lycan's eyebrows rose at the sound of the name. "You didn't tell me it was a girl. Well? Did you show her your code, yet?" He elbowed Snake.

"It's not like that," Snake replied.

"I bet it's not."

"Besides, she's already got a boyfriend ... I think."

"All right, ladies," Ransom scrubbed a hand down his face. "Show me what needs to be done so we can finish this before Evan goes off to college."

For the rest of the afternoon, Isabelle and Evan followed Ransom around as he checked off each item on Silke's checklist. She realized two things that day. First: It took an enormous amount of work to keep the lodge running, and second: Ransom cared about the place and the people as much as Silke did. He listened to every problem each member of the staff raised, giving his own input or promising to let Silke know about their concerns. It was obvious, too, that they looked up to him—not just the members of his MC, but all the employees. He was a natural born leader, very Alpha-like. Strangely, he reminded her a lot of her own parents while they were ruling Alphas of their respective clans.

They ended the evening at Bo and Arlene's cabin where the couple insisted that they stay for dinner. Silke and Sabrina joined them, too, and Isabelle had to admit, it was a good way to end a fun day. When things wound down and Evan began to get cranky, they reluctantly said their goodbyes and headed back to Ransom's cabin.

"Thanks," she said as he helped her out of the truck. He

had already taken the car seat out and carried it inside for her. When he handed her the seat, their fingers brushed together. Heat coiled inside her, along with a touch of disappointment because despite his proclamations yesterday, Ransom had not tried, well, anything at all. In fact, he was the perfect gentleman the entire day.

"Are you, uh, going to bed?" she inquired nonchalantly when he didn't follow her toward the stairs.

"I have to take care of some business with the club," he said. "But I'll be back soon, I won't stay out too late."

She bit her lip. "All right. I'll see you tomorrow, I guess."

"Goodnight, Isabelle." He glanced down at Evan. "'Night, Evan."

She stood rooted to the spot as he closed the door gently behind him. Her wolf cried out longingly at the loss of his presence. Yes, Ransom didn't try very hard today. But he didn't have to try at all, as just the thought of him made the butterflies in her stomach flutter.

———

Evan's cry in the middle of the night woke Isabelle up as it usually did. He'd been so tuckered out the last two days with all the excitement that he'd slept through the night both times, but she knew he was due for another late-night tantrum.

Rolling out of bed, she reached into the crib. "There, there, baby." She checked his diaper, and seeing as it was wet, changed it immediately. However, he continued to bawl, even as she rocked him back and forth.

"I'm sorry, sweetheart." She danced and swayed, but he

didn't stop crying. "I know, I know," she soothed as he continued to bawl.

"Isabelle? Is everything okay?"

Swinging around, she saw Ransom standing in the doorway. He was rubbing his eyes and was dressed in nothing but a pair of black boxer briefs. Evan's continuous crying, however, distracted her too much from appreciating his magnificent body or feeling self-conscious about the fact she was wearing the flimsiest sleep dress she owned and nothing else underneath. "I'm sorry," she said sheepishly. "Did he wake you up? I'm doing my best—"

"It's all right." He padded inside and cringed as Evan let out a particularly loud, outraged cry. "Whatsammatter, Evan?"

"He doesn't like new surroundings," she shouted over her son's screams of fury. "He was pretty tired last night so he slept through, but now ..." She winced when Evan's screams pitched higher. "He was like this when we went to Scotland for Keir's birth."

"Does he need changing? Food?"

"Done, but we can try his bottle," she said.

They headed down to the kitchen, and Ransom prepared the baby bottle as she gave him instructions. Still, Evan only took it for a few seconds before spitting it out and wailed like a banshee.

"I'm sorry for disturbing you," she said. "I can ... try to go outside if you need some sleep."

"You and Evan could never disturb me," he said. "But ... is he just going to keep crying until he conks himself out?"

"Pretty much," she sighed.

"Here, let me hold him, then." He reached out to her, and

she was just too tired to protest, so she let him take Evan. "It's all right," he soothed, rubbing a hand down his back. "Daddy's got you."

Her stomach flip-flopped at his words. Of course, she'd been the one to call him that first, but it had been an accident. *Oh God.* Now he was swaying side to side, doing a little dance to rock him to sleep, and her ovaries practically exploded. She knew her inner wolf, too, loved seeing them together like this. A warm feeling passed over her chest and the she-wolf let out a contented sigh. Her thoughts were bringing her into dangerous territory, but she was so exhausted right now, she didn't have the strength to fight it.

After a few more minutes, Evan finally started to wind down, his howls turning to hiccups. "Let's go take him back to his crib," she suggested, and they swiftly, but silently headed back to the room. However, as Ransom was bending over to lay him down on the crib, Evan started wailing again, so Ransom picked him up until he settled. The moment he got close to the crib, though, Evan fussed and protested angrily with a wail.

"Here, I can rock him to sleep," she suggested.

"You're about ready to fall over," Ransom said, keeping Evan close to his chest. "C'mon, I have an idea." Turning on his heel, he walked out of the room.

She followed him into the hallway, and down to the last room—his bedroom, as she recalled. "Ransom, what are you doing?"

He strode over to the edge of his bed, lay down and placed Evan on his chest, rubbing his back. Evan struggled and fought sleep, but eventually, his eyes closed.

Biting her lip, she stood in the doorway, unsure what to

do. On one hand, Evan was finally calmed and asleep so she didn't want to move him. But on the other, she'd never let him sleep alone whenever they weren't at her apartment.

"It's a big bed."

She started at his words. "W-what?"

"It's a king-sized bed." His eyes remained closed. "Just ... lay down next to me. To make sure I don't accidentally roll over and crush Evan."

Well, when he put it that way, she couldn't possibly say no. Padding over, she crept up on top of the bed and scooted closer to him. His scent was all over the sheets, and her core tightened at the thought of being surrounded by the fresh musk, leather, and rain smell.

Curling her arms under a pillow, she lay on her side, facing Ransom and Evan. He looked so relaxed and at ease, and so did Evan. It was as if he'd been doing this forever. The similarities between them were even more evident now; they even had the same resting expression as they slept.

She wanted to feel regret or guilt for letting things get too far and intimate with Ransom and not running away to protect herself and Evan, but she couldn't muster up any such emotions. Except maybe that she was tired—tired of fighting this thing between them that was much bigger than either of them. It was like a wave—no, a tsunami—and all she wanted was to be swept away.

Exhaustion left her, though she didn't move as she was content to watch father and son sleep peacefully, even as her own mind raced. Finally, she recognized the signs that Evan was deep in slumber. Carefully, she scooched over and slid her hand under Evan.

"Huh?" Ransom's eyes fluttered open. "Isabelle?" he whispered.

"Shh don't move ... he won't wake up for a while," she assured him and lifted Evan off his chest and held him close.

"I should—"

"No, stay," she said. "I'll take care of him." She padded out of his room and made the quick trip down the hall to the guest room. She lay him down in his crib, watching and waiting to see if he would wake up. When Evan's breath remained deep and steady, she turned around and headed back to Ransom's room.

"Isabelle?" His eyes went wide as she darted into the room and closed the door behind her, then crawled up onto the bed. "What's the matter? Is he all right?"

"I—yes. He'll sleep until morning, I think." She moved closer to him, tucking her legs under her.

That line between his brows appeared. "What is it?"

"Did you ... I mean, were you trying today? Like you said?"

His expression faltered. "I wasn't. There was too much to do and ... I really wanted to sweep you off your feet. Take you to dinner and—"

She silenced his words by pressing her lips to his. He froze initially, then relaxed under her mouth and curled an arm around her waist. Her heart fluttered madly, and heat swept across her body as she pressed her breasts against him, her nipples hardening instantly at the contact.

Ransom let out a groan and then rolled them over, his body flattening hers to the mattress. When he suddenly pulled away, she let out a whimper.

"What's wrong?" she panted.

"What does this mean, Isabelle?"

"Don't you want to—"

"Yes." He pressed a kiss to her lips. "But I want to know ... is this just sex? Or something else?"

She pushed her hips up at him, brushing against his growing erection. "Do we have to talk about this now?"

"Yes," he insisted. "I need to know."

Her brain told her that this was a bad idea, and she could very well get hurt. But other parts of her ... "It's not just sex," she said quietly. "I don't know what it is. But I don't want to fight it anymore." She paused, biting her lip. "A-and, there's been no one else since you."

His breath hitched. "It wouldn't have mattered to me. I would hate it, but I'd have no one to blame but myself." He kissed her lips. "Thank you for telling me."

"I—Oh!"

He rolled them over again so she was on top, straddling him. His large hands steadied her hips and then slid up to cup her breasts. "You always looked so good in white, princess."

She moaned when his fingers teased her stiff nipples under the fabric of her nightdress. "Why ... why do you call me that? Do you still think I'm a spoiled snob?"

"Is that what you think? Why I called you that in the first place?"

She arched into his hands as he cupped her breasts. "Isn't it?"

"Yes, but ... two years ago ... and even now ... you've always been far above me, out of my reach." Grabbing the bottom of her nightdress, he whipped it over her head, baring her heated skin. "I was never good enough for you. I'm still not."

"Stop." She bent down to cover his mouth. "Don't say that." Closing her eyes, she kissed him deeply.

He moaned as she reached between their bodies and pushed at his boxers to take his cock out. She squeezed his hardness and spread her thighs to give him better access to her entrance. Slowly, she sank down on him until he was fully inside her.

Bracing herself on his chest, she rocked back and forth, the pleasurable sensations rocking her very core. When she picked up her pace, he was switching between groaning, cursing, and encouraging her. Her body tensed as an orgasm ripped through her, but she was barely done when he rolled them over again, wrapped her legs around his waist and began to thrust into her.

There was something about this that was different from all the other times, but Isabelle couldn't put her finger on it. Sure, there was the urgency, that desperate need, but also, there was an aching tenderness from the way he cradled her body reverently and his lips covered every inch of skin it could find. Maybe, just maybe, this was what it was like when it was more than just sex.

"Isabelle," he groaned against her neck, then nipped at her ear. His hands cupped her bottom, pulling her up to meet his every thrust. When she finally reached that peak again and her body shook with pleasure, his movements turned erratic and he thrust in one last time, shuddering as he grunted in pleasure. His cock twitched inside her, flooding her with his come.

He pulled out and away from her, laying down on his back as he took deep breaths. After that, she needed to take a breather, too. Moments later, the bed shifted, and his arms came around her. Her eyes fluttered closed again, contentment spreading over her as her body came in contact with his but flew open when his hand slipped between her legs and parted her thighs.

"Ransom?"

"You said Evan won't be up for a while?"

She nodded, unable to speak or even think because of the sensations spreading out through her body as his thumb found her clit.

"Good." His breath was hot and warm against the back of her neck. "That might be enough time for what I have planned."

Oh Lord. And for the rest of the night, there wasn't much more talking or thinking.

CHAPTER SEVENTEEN

"Aren't you the happy camper this morning?" Silke remarked as Ransom entered the lodge's lobby.

As he held the door open, Isabelle followed and strode in with Evan in her arms. Their gazes met briefly, and she smiled as she walked past him.

His sister didn't miss the interaction. "And Isabelle ... don't you look all aglow."

"Sorry we're late," she said to Silke, who already had her arms out for Evan. "We got, uh, held up."

Silke eagerly took Evan and then flashed Ransom a wry smile. "I'm sure you did."

No matter how he tried to stop the grin, he just couldn't manage it. He and Isabelle had been up until dawn, and didn't finish until they were both exhausted. They woke up pretty late, only because Evan had begun wailing again. Together, they fed and cleaned him, and then made their way to the lodge for lunch.

"I'm starving," Isabelle declared. "Can we go eat now?"

"Of course," Silke said. "Are you coming, too, Ransom?"

"I need to go back to town to check on a couple of things, I'll grab something to eat along the way," he said. "I'll swing by later."

"All right," Isabelle said. "I'll—"

He cut her off with a swift kiss on the mouth. "I won't be long." Sliding a hand down her back, he squeezed her ass, making her yelp.

"Ransom!" Her cheeks went red, and Silke snorted behind her.

"I'll see you later, princess." He probably enjoyed seeing her embarrassed a little too much, but he couldn't help it. Isabelle was his, and he wanted the whole world to know.

After grabbing a quick bite at a nearby gas station, he headed to Bucky's Garage. Though he didn't really need the job there, he liked working with his hands and hanging around with the owner, Bucky Jameson. He'd been a friend of the MC since the days of its inception and had repaired or upgraded many of the members' bikes over the years. Though there wasn't much work to be done today, he did some of the more back-breaking chores since the old man was pushing seventy years of age.

If Bucky noticed anything different about Ransom, he didn't say anything, though he did raise an eyebrow when he started whistling as he finished up an oil change for Mrs. Carter's Buick. After a couple hours, the old man sent him home, and he headed straight for the lodge.

"Where's Isabelle?" he asked Silke, who was at the front desk, looking over the booking schedule with Arlene.

"Evan needed a nap," his sister said, not looking up from the computer screen. "I told her she can use room two-oh-four since it's empty."

"I'll go check on them." He took the stairs since it was only one flight up to the second floor, and headed to the room. The door was unlocked, so he padded in quietly.

Isabelle was on the bed watching over Evan as he slumbered. Sensing his presence, she looked up and smiled, then placed a pillow next to Evan as she slid off the bed.

"You're back," she whispered.

"And you're beautiful." He immediately wrapped an arm around her waist and pulled her close, breathing in her delicious, sweet scent. "How is he?"

"Good, just tuckered out after an exciting afternoon. I gave him a bottle, and he got milk drunk. It was so adorable; you should have seen it."

"Mm-hmm." He nuzzled her temple. "Is he sleeping soundly?"

"Yes, I—Ransom!"

He moved quickly, pulling her into the bathroom and closed the door behind them.

"What are you doing?" she asked, hands on her hips.

"I missed you," he stated.

"You were only gone four hours," she said.

"Uh-huh ..." He advanced toward her, maneuvering her right into the shower until her back hit the tiles. "So long ago ..." Lifting a hand, he caressed her cheek, moving his fingers lower, down her neck and collarbone, then cupped her breast through her dress.

She let out a gasp and closed her eyes as he rubbed her nipple through the fabric. "Ransom ..." The scent of her arousal mixed in with her sweet scent filled his nostrils. "Evan might wake up."

"Only if you're noisy." Moving even closer, he pressed his

hips to her, so she could feel his rapidly hardening cock. "Are you going to be noisy?"

She shook her head and arched into him.

"Good girl." Lifting the hem of her dress to her waist, he yanked down her panties and plunged a finger into her. As he suspected, she was already wet. "Hold onto me ... that's it," he praised when her hands clung to his shoulders. Unbuttoning his jeans, he pushed them and his boxers low on his hips and took his cock in one hand. Her hips lifted and a leg came around his waist as he slipped into her, smooth as a warm knife through butter. Bending his head down, he suckled at her neck, making her shiver.

"Ransom!" She moaned as he thrust into her. Her grip tightened around him, and he bit his lip to keep from coming right then and there. He wasn't going to last very long, but they didn't have much time. Anyone could walk in right then and there, though that added danger did bring a sweet edge to their fucking.

He slammed into her until she was panting with her orgasm. "One more time, princess," he urged as his free hand cupped her breast and he continued to suck on the soft skin of her neck. She babbled incoherently as he continued to fuck into her, his cock sliding in and out of her easily thanks to her slickness.

"I'm coming," she whimpered. "Oh God, Ransom, I'm coming!"

Her sweet pussy clamped around him so tight, he thought he was going to pass out, so he let go. His body shuddered with his orgasm, his balls draining until he felt fully spent and empty, groaning into her neck.

He held her up for a few more seconds until he slipped

out. Grabbing one of the towels hanging from the rack above them, he cleaned her up, then himself and tucked his softening cock away.

"Really, Ransom?" she said as she pulled up her panties, but he could see the smile she was trying to hide. "You couldn't wait until tonight?"

"Hmmm, why should I?" His eyes drew down to her plump ass and gave a squeeze, laughing as she yelped. "Besides, I needed you now. And from the way your pretty little pussy squeezed me so hard, you needed it too."

Another blush swept across her face. "W-we should go check on Evan."

Thankfully, he was still asleep when they stepped out into the room. Isabelle slipped back onto the bed next to him, and Ransom came to the other side, sitting on the edge of the mattress, content to look at his beautiful mate and pup. His wolf puffed up with pride, and he couldn't help but feel the same.

A soft knock from the outside shook him out of his thoughts. "I'll get it," he said before Isabelle could get up. Padding over to the door, he opened it slowly. "Silke?" The tight smile on his sister's face told him something had happened. "What's wrong."

"She's back. Joanie, I mean."

The mention of his mother always made Silke uneasy. Though he knew Joanie had never done anything bad to Silke, his mother never did anything to make her feel loved or at ease. He'd seen it all his life, and one time, he'd even talked to Pops about it. "Ransom," he had said. "Some people have a finite amount of love. And your mother is one of those people. She has you, and that's all she needs." He'd always felt guilty because he thought he was the reason Joanie never warmed up to Silke.

"Where is she?" he asked.

"Back in her cabin. Hawk called me, saw her car pull into the property a while ago." She paused and bit her lip. "What are you going to tell her?"

He met her emerald gaze head on. "The truth." Knowing Joanie, he had no doubt she already knew anyway. "I'll go over there and talk to her now."

Silke gave him a sympathetic look. "Good luck," she said before turning on her heel and walking away.

"Yeah." He was being a fool if he thought he was going to delay this particular confrontation. And he would have to prepare Isabelle for the worst. But could he tell her the truth? "I need to go out," he said to Isabelle as he approached her.

"To where?"

"My mother's back."

"Oh." She focused her attention back to Evan, who was still napping.

"I want to tell her in person. About you and Evan," he said. "That's the only reason she doesn't know."

"Okay."

"Okay?" he asked. "That's all you have to say?"

"You don't talk about her," she said. "I assume it's a sensitive topic, like your biological father. So, I don't know what I'm supposed to say."

That was fair, he supposed, but then why did it feel like she was pulling away from him? "I ... I'll come back and pick you up later." His wolf, which had been so agreeable minutes before, was now gnashing its teeth at him, not wanting to be away from their mate and pup. Ignoring it, he continued out of the room, down the stairs, all the way outside and got into his truck.

Minutes later, he pulled into the driveway outside Joanie's cabin. After Pops had died, she moved out of the main cabin, preferring to leave it to Ransom, now that he had taken over as president of the MC. As he hopped out of the truck, he saw Joanie sitting on the rocker on the porch, a glass of chilled rosé cradled in her hands.

"Hello, Mother."

Cool blue eyes turned to him. "Hello, Ransom. Is there something you want to tell me?"

His nerves frazzled, and his heart pounded in his chest. "Yes."

CHAPTER EIGHTEEN

Isabelle chewed on her lip as she listened to the door close behind Ransom. When she couldn't hear his footsteps anymore, she let out the breath she'd been holding.

What the heck happened? One moment, she and Ransom were basking in the afterglow, and the next, it was like an arctic wind crashed over them. The chill in his voice when he announced his mother had returned had made her uneasy. Maybe she should have waited longer before sleeping with him again. There were just so many things about his life before her that she didn't know about or understand. She chastised herself for being selfish and impulsive.

Evan twitched his hand as his eyes opened up. Blinking, he turned to face her and then smiled. "Hello, baby," she cooed. "Aren't you handsome?" Gathering him up in her arms, she cradled him close. "Oh, your smile always makes everything better."

She left the room and headed downstairs to the lobby. There was no sign of Silke, but Arlene was there, as was Hardy and little Annie. The girl squealed in delight when she saw Isabelle coming down the stairs with Evan in her arms.

"Evan! Evan!" she cried. "I wanna play."

"Sorry," Hardy said sheepishly. "I got some errands to run and I was dropping her off here so Arlene could watch her. I didn't know you'd be here too."

"It's all right." She smiled at Annie as she bent down so the little girl could see Evan. "I can watch Annie for a bit, if you want?"

"Really?" Hardy said. "That would be great. I know Arlene doesn't mind, but she's busy with other stuff. I'll be gone an hour, tops."

"No problem." She led Annie to the couches in the lobby. "We'll be right here. Evan needs his bottle and Annie can help."

That made the little girl light up, and Hardy's smile at his daughter's delight made Isabelle's heart melt. It was obvious he was a devoted dad, but she wondered what happened to the girl's mother. Though Annie's wolf would not manifest until she reached puberty, it was obvious from her scent—cool rain, vanilla, and mandarin oranges—that she was a Lycan. She wondered what would make a mother abandon her pup?

"You be good, sweetie." He leaned down and kissed her on the cheek.

"I will, Daddy." She turned to Isabelle. "Are we gonna feed him now?"

Isabelle got his bottle ready, placed Evan on Annie's lap, and showed her how to properly hold the bottle, praising her as she followed the instructions to a T. Once he was done, she burped Evan, and sat him down on the couch next to

Annie. The little girl insisted on telling him a story, which was a strange mash-up of Goldilocks, Cinderella, and Hansel and Gretel, which unintentionally made Isabelle chuckle.

As Annie continued on, she felt a prickle on the back of her neck. Turning around, she saw Ransom standing in the doorway, watching them with a grin on his face. She smiled back weakly, and he approached her.

Something in the way he walked seemed different—at least it wasn't like right before he had left to meet his mother. In fact, it was like nothing had ever happened. He sat down and listened patiently to Annie's story and placed a hand on the small of Isabelle's back.

"... and they lived happily ever after. The end!" Annie proclaimed with a flourish of her hand. Evan seemed to like the way she told the story as he let out an approving shriek.

"I think he liked it," Ransom proclaimed. "Annie, honey, why don't you go over to Arlene and see if she can get you a snack from the kitchen?" He caught the older woman's eye, who nodded back.

"Okay!" She bounded over toward the front desk.

"Everything all right?" she asked apprehensively.

"Of course," he said. "Joanie—that is, my mother—wants to have you and Evan over for dinner."

"When?"

"Now, actually," he said sheepishly.

"Oh." She worried her lip. "How did she react when you told her about me and Evan?"

"Surprisingly well," he replied. "She really wants to meet you, especially Evan."

"I guess that's okay." Why did something feel not quite right? *Oh, stop it*, she told herself. She'd never even met the woman. There was no reason to have any doubts. "I mean, should we go soon? I promised Hardy I'd look after Annie until he came back."

"That's fine," he said. "She's still getting dinner ready. We can leave as soon as he gets back."

It was only a few minutes later that Hardy strolled in the door. He thanked Isabelle and went off in search of Annie and Arlene. Ransom carried Evan out to his truck, strapped him into the car seat, and soon they were on their way.

His mother's cabin was located further away from the MC's group of cabins, all the way on the other side of the property. A white Lexus was parked outside the two-story cabin, and Ransom pulled up beside it. Carrying Evan in her arms, he led her up the porch steps, then opened the door so they could go in.

Isabelle stepped inside, looking around the surprisingly plush surroundings. While Ransom's cabin had been masculine and functional, this cabin was utterly feminine and luxuriously tasteful. Pure white couches sectioned off the living area from the rest of the space. Art books lay artfully on the glass and metal coffee table, and a chandelier hung overhead. From what she could tell, everything had that sheen of newness, including the car outside.

"Welcome," a feminine voice said.

She turned her head toward the staircase, where a woman dressed in white linen pants and a cream-colored shirt slowly made her way down. Her honey blonde hair was arranged carefully in a twist, and her ballet slippers barely made any sound as she walked toward them.

"You must be Isabelle." Her voice was crisp, like freshly-fallen snow. Though her words were friendly, the smile she had on her face didn't quite reach her cool blue eyes. "And this must be Evan." She acknowledged the baby in her arms. "I'm glad to meet you. I'm Joanie."

"Nice to meet you, too, Joanie." Though she attempted to sound warm and friendly, her wolf was wary, as it cautiously eyed the other Lycan.

"Can I offer you a drink?" Joanie padded over to the glass cabinet in the corner of the dining area. "Wine? How about some rosé? Or something harder, maybe a martini?"

"Um ..." She was still reeling from the fact that this was Ransom's *mother*. Why, this woman looked more like she belonged in a country club in Long Island, not married to a Lone Wolf biker in the Kentucky Mountains. "Actually, I'm good with water, if you have it." However, upon closer inspection, she could sense something ... not quite right. Joanie was classically beautiful, but there was a hard, flinty quality in her eyes that said she had seen many things and been through a lot.

A blonde brow rose. "Of course. Ransom, will you be a dear and help me get the food out?" Pivoting daintily on her heels, she headed for the kitchen.

"Why don't you and Evan sit down." He motioned to the sleek white dining table that had been set so lavishly. "I'll be out in a bit."

Though she still felt like she was in a bizarre, alternate universe, Isabelle managed to sit down. Since they hadn't thought to swing by for Evan's high chair, she placed him on her lap. "Isn't this a strange place?" she whispered to Evan. He didn't seem to pay her any mind as he reached for one of the crystal glasses on the table. "No, baby!" She snatched it away just in time before for his small fist caught it.

"Everything all right?" Joanie came out, a salad bowl in her hand, Ransom following behind her with a casserole dish.

"It's fine." She looked over to Ransom. "That smells good."

"Oh, it's just something I had in the freezer," she laughed. "I was caught by surprise. By your visit, I mean."

It rankled her, the way Joanie had said 'visit', but Isabelle knew she couldn't complain. She and Ransom hadn't talked about what was going to happen after all this business with the mages was done. "It was a surprise for us all," she managed to say.

Joanie set the salad bowl down, and Ransom followed suit, then sat down next to her. "Now, let's eat," she began as she offered the salad to Isabelle. Since she had her hands full with Evan, Ransom served her some salad before taking some for himself.

"So, Ransom," Joanie began. "I need to tell you about this new restaurant that just opened in Mercer. They have the best...."

Joanie's words washed around her. The casserole felt like ash in her mouth, but she was starving, so she ate it to feed her growling stomach, while feeding bits of vegetables to Evan. Joanie continued talking about her mini vacation at a spa in Mercer City, or rather, she talked about it to Ransom. While she wasn't mean or outright nasty to Isabelle, it was like there wasn't anyone else in the room. Once in a while, Ransom would include her by asking a question, but ultimately, Joanie would find a way to refocus the conversation to things and people only she and Ransom knew about. For someone who 'really wanted to meet' her and

Evan, Joanie seemed distinctly uninterested in getting to know them.

"Dessert?" Joanie asked sweetly. "It's just ice cream."

"Thank you," she said. "That would be nice."

"Ransom, dear?"

He immediately got up. "Of course, let me get it."

An uncomfortable silence filled the room once they were alone. "How old is he?" Joanie asked, finally acknowledging Evan's presence.

"Ten months," she answered.

"How ... nice." She reached into the pocket of her linen pants and took out a gold cigarette case and a lighter. "You don't mind, do you?"

She did, but it was Joanie's home. "Not at all."

"So," she lit up the cigarette she had taken out of the case, "Ransom tells me you're from New York."

"Yes," she said. "Have you been?"

"No." She took a deep drag and blew the smoke out. "Not in a long time," she added, as if she'd changed her mind.

Just then, Ransom walked in with the ice cream and bowls. "Mother," he said disapprovingly at the lit cigarette in her hand. "Please don't smoke around my son."

"What?" She waved it around, smoke billowing around her. "Isabelle says it's okay. And I smoked around you all the time, remember? We didn't always have the luxury of multiple rooms or outdoor decks. I've made so many *sacrifices* for you, and yet, you won't let me smoke in my own home?"

His expression turned dark, and he sat down.

Isabelle stared at him, dumbfounded. She wasn't shocked that he hadn't pressed on the smoking around Evan, but only that he backed down so quickly. It made her instincts flare up; something was not quite right here, or at least, not right with Joanie. Her wolf agreed, raising its hackles.

Isabelle cleared her throat. "I need to change Evan." His diaper was totally dry, but she needed an excuse to get out of here. "Oh, and I used my last diaper in his bag just before we came here. I have more back at the cabin."

Ransom quickly stood up. "We should head back, then."

Joanie's mouth pulled back into a tight line. "Surely you don't have to go *now*." But she was looking straight at Ransom. "The boy can wait a bit, can't he?"

"I'm afraid not, Mother."

"If you must," she said dramatically, then stood up. "Isabelle, it was nice to meet you and your son." Her gaze once again flittered to Evan. "Let me walk you out."

"No need," Ransom said curtly.

"I'll see you tomorrow," Joanie said with a wave of her hand. "I'll stop by around noon."

"We'll probably be at the lodge," Isabelle added.

Joanie's lips pursed. "I'll have to make a visit there, then."

"Let's go, Isabelle," Ransom said.

She got up and followed him out the door. He seemed like he couldn't get out of there fast enough as he grabbed Evan from her and put him in his seat, then pulled out of the driveway. When they got back to the cabin, he stopped the truck and cut off the engine.

"Wait," she said before he could open the door. "Are we going to talk about this?"

His grip on the wheel was so tight, his knuckles went white. "What do you mean?"

"Your mother." The atmosphere grew thicker in the confined space. "I just ... what happened back there?"

His brows snapped together. "What do you mean?"

"Something's not right with her," she blurted out. But she had to follow her instinct and it was screaming at her now. "I don't want her around Evan." The thought made her skin prickle.

"She's my mother," he said in a deadly voice.

"Then why did it seem like you couldn't get away from there fast enough?" she shot back. "I'm telling you—"

"You don't understand!" He slammed his palms down on the wheel. "You grew up with everything you could possibly want and need. Meanwhile, everyone she knew turned their backs on her because of something that wasn't her fault. She ... she raised me all by herself, even when she had nothing and we kept getting tossed out of every rat and roach infested motel or apartment we lived in when she couldn't make rent. The things she h-had to do to make sure I didn't starve and had a place to sleep ... I could never repay ..." He closed his eyes, his lips trembling. "I owe her everything. I owe her my life."

"Ransom." The pain in his voice made her heart ache. The thought of Ransom as a kid ... the things he must have seen and heard, living like that and what Joanie had gone through ... she briefly glanced back at Evan, and thought that there was nothing she *wouldn't* do for him. "I don't want to fight over this."

"I ... I don't either." He took a deep breath.

"Ransom, I'm sorry." Placing a hand over his, she gave it a squeeze. "Lock those memories away for now, so they can't hurt you. We'll make new ones, you and me and Evan. And someday, when you're ready to unpack everything and air it all out, we'll do it." She sucked in a breath. "Together."

He turned to her and gathered her hands into his. "Isabelle, I love you."

The confession made her head spin. "W-what?"

"I love you." He kissed her hands. "I love you so goddamned much, you could fill the entire ocean and it wouldn't even be half of what I feel for you. Or stack up bricks to reach the moon and it wouldn't measure how much I love you. I love you and Evan so much I can't breathe and—"

She stopped him by leaning over and pressing her mouth to his. He stopped, surprised at first, and then fully melted into her, kissing her back like his life depended on it. His tongue flicked out, urging her lips open to deepen the kiss and his strong, masculine taste and warmth burst into her mouth. It was only when Evan let out a soft cry that they pulled their lips from each other.

Ransom pressed his forehead to hers and sighed. "Let's get him to bed." He gave her a quick kiss before slipping out of the door.

She sat there, stunned for a moment. Ransom loved her. Did she love him? She thought she was in love with him back in New York a year and half ago, but now ...

"Coming?" he asked from the backseat as he unbuckled Evan.

"Yeah," she replied. Opening the door, she hopped out and followed him into their cabin. Watching Ransom holding Evan so tenderly made her heart burst in happiness. There was so much they still needed to say and do before everything could well and truly be settled, but she supposed for now, she could just enjoy this moment.

The thought of Joanie still niggled in her mind, how she

had acted around Isabelle, but worst of all, how she seemed to have a stranglehold on Ransom. It was manipulative, the way she was able to shut him down when he didn't agree with her. But, Joanie had her own issues too. Her wolf was telling her not to let her guard down around the other Lycan, but Isabelle supposed she could at least try to be understanding of what the poor woman had gone through, and be thankful for everything she had done for Ransom.

CHAPTER NINETEEN

Neither of them spoke of the dinner or Joanie again. In fact, it was as if that evening hadn't happened. His mother not showing up at the lodge or his cabin made it easier. It was like Joanie had just disappeared. Still, Isabelle couldn't quite put her finger on why Ransom's mother made her uncomfortable. Her manipulative behavior should have been enough, but there was still something else that bothered Isabelle. In any case, the farther that woman stayed away from her and Evan, the better.

Indeed, the last two days had been heavenly. She spent them with Silke and Sabrina, helping with improvements in the lodge's dining room and preparations for the New York clan members who were going to arrive in the next few days. In the evenings, after putting Evan to bed, she and Ransom made love until they were both exhausted, exploring and getting to know each other's bodies again. Both times, when Evan woke up in the middle of night, Ransom told her to go back to sleep, and instead took care of their son.

Though he had not repeated the words he had told her the other night, he hadn't asked her at all how she felt. But, being around him, seeing him taking care of Evan and proudly showing him off, how could she not fall in love with him? Or maybe she'd always loved him deep in her heart. But how to tell him? *Maybe tonight.* After Evan went to bed, she'd tell him before they made love.

"Isabelle? Isabelle, did you hear what I said?"

Jolted out of her thoughts, she blinked at Sabrina. "What?"

"Hmm, what could possibly have you distracted?" Silke chuckled and shook her head. "If he wasn't my brother, I'd ask for details."

She turned red, and Sabrina, thank goodness, pointed to the paint samples on the table. "What do you think of this color, Isabelle?"

"I think the coral is great." She shot Sabrina a grateful look, then grabbed a muffin from the plate on the table and stuffed it into her mouth. "Wow, I'm really hungry this morning." Hopefully, that would stop her from having to give them any more details.

They were in the dining room, selecting new color palettes for the dining room's interiors. One of Uncle Dante's suggestions was to make the place cozier with a fresh paint job, to make it more inviting and encourage people to stay. The dull, almost sterile walls of the room did make it seem more like a hospital than a restaurant. Silke had taken a look at her budget and decided she could at least look into a fresh paint job.

"Coral it is," Silke declared.

Isabelle got up from her chair and stretched her arms over

her head. "I'm gonna go check on Evan." She had left him napping in his car seat at the reception desk while Arlene watched over him. Ransom was out in his truck, checking on some damage on the docks by the lake so he didn't want to take him. He said he would come back later this afternoon, but he could come earlier if he finished sooner.

Walking out to the lobby, she spotted Arlene coming out of the ladies' room. "Hey, Arlene," she greeted. Glancing around, she didn't see Evan's car seat. "Where's Evan?"

She pointed to the couches. "Why he's just—" The older woman frowned. "They were just there, right before I went into the ladies' room."

"They? Was Ransom here?"

"Oh, no. Joanie sauntered in and saw Evan. Started fussing over him." She lifted a brow. "I ain't never seen that woman give a lick for anyone but herself or Ransom, but I think Evan charmed her."

"But where are they?"

"I asked Joanie if she could watch him for a second while I went to the facilities," Arlene shrugged. "I wasn't gone longer than five minutes."

Isabelle's heart began to drum against her rib cage. *Calm down*, she told herself. There was an explanation for this. Her inner wolf, however, began to pace uneasily. "Maybe they went outside."

She jogged out of the main entrance, but there was no sign of them. Dashing back into the lobby, she headed for the outdoor deck, but it was empty save for a few guests lingering outside, sunning themselves. Her stomach was tied in knots now, and she wanted to throw up. Call it maternal instinct, but she just *knew* something was wrong.

"Isabelle?" Silke asked as she walked back into the lobby. The redhead was standing by the front desk with Arlene and Sabrina. "What's wrong?"

"I ..." Her voice shook so bad, she feared she might croak. "I think ... oh God." She buried her face in her hands. "I don't know if I'm overreacting. Maybe I'm wrong." *Please let me be wrong.* Her wolf growled at her, so certain in its suspicions.

Silke gently removed her hands from her face. "What is it? Tell me?"

"This is silly ... but Evan's gone—not here, and I-I think Joanie took him."

Her dark auburn brows drew together, and her lips pursed. "I'll call Ransom." She turned to Arlene. "Call Bo, and ask him to check if Joanie's car is in her driveway, then send out a message to everyone to let me know if they've seen Joanie or Evan anywhere."

"I'm being silly, right?" Isabelle forced a laugh. "They're probably just somewhere around here."

"Isabelle," Silke began, her emerald green gaze boring straight into her. "Do you believe Joanie might have taken Evan? And that she could harm him?"

"I ... I don't know," she cried. "She's Ransom's mother. Evan's her grandson."

"What does your instinct tell you?" Silke gripped her wrists tight. "And don't sugarcoat it."

God, she didn't want to believe what her gut and wolf were telling her. Everything had been fine, until now. Ransom loved her, and she loved him back. She was going to tell him tonight. They were going to be a family.

"Isabelle!" Silke shook her.

"She took him!" The words burst out of her mouth. "Joanie took him."

Silke's eyes narrowed. "I'll call Ransom right away."

"Oh, Isabelle." Sabrina drew her into a tight hug. "Do you really think she could have done it?"

She didn't answer, but instead let Sabrina's comforting arms soothe her. The knots in her stomach became tighter as the seconds ticked by. "I just need to see my baby and know he's all right," she whispered.

"You'll get him back," Sabrina assured her.

"Hey, Silke, I finished—What's going on?"

Isabelle's head snapped up, and she met Ransom's gold-green gaze. His brows pressed together into a scowl, and his body went entirely still. "What happened?"

Her mouth went as dry as the Sahara, but thankfully, Silke spoke up. "Evan's missing. Joanie took him."

"What?" He turned back to Isabelle. "Are you sure?"

"I ..." Her wolf protested, seething at him that he could even doubt her.

"I'm sorry, Ransom," Arlene said, tears pooling in her eyes. "I just left them alone for a minute and—"

"It's not your fault, Arlene," Isabelle said. "I—"

The front desk phone rang, and the older woman started, then picked up the receiver. "Seven Peaks—Bo! What did you find out? Her car's not there? But ... gotcha. You're the best, hon." She turned to them. "Her car's not at her cabin, but Axle said he saw her driving down the main road, on the way out to the property gates."

Ransom's entire body tensed, fingers curling into fists. "Send out a call to everyone to stop her if they see her." Turning on his heel, he jogged out toward the exit.

"Ransom? Wait!" She chased after him. "Where are you going?"

"I'm going after her," he said tersely as he continued toward his truck. When she made a grab for the passenger side door, he yelled, "What are you—stay here, Isabelle."

"No!" She yanked the door open. "I'm coming with you."

"I need to deal with her myself," he said. "Stay here and—"

"He's my son," she snarled. "If you want me to stay here, then you better be prepared to drag me out of this truck kicking and screaming!"

Scrubbing a hand down his face, he let out a frustrated growl, then slid into the driver's seat. "If—when we find her, let me talk to her," he said. "You stay in here."

There was no way in hell she was going to sit by while that ... that woman had Evan, so she didn't say anything. Instead, she strapped on her seatbelt and held on to the grab handles as Ransom sped out of the driveway.

The tension in the small space was thick enough to cut with a knife. A million questions raced in her head, but she couldn't say them out loud. Why would Joanie take Evan? Did she have emotional problems? What was she planning to do?

He drove like a madman, racing down the road that led out to the main gate. She spotted something in the distance— a white car. Ransom pushed the truck harder, swerving off the road to circle the Lexus then suddenly hit the brakes.

Gears screeched loudly, hurting her sensitive ears. Her brain rattled in her head from the sudden jolt, but she recovered quickly. But Ransom was faster, and he was already sliding out of the driver's side. Her hands shook so hard it took her two tries to unbuckle her seatbelt, but she finally did, and bolted out of the passenger seat.

"... let him go, Mother," Ransom said.

Isabelle's stomach dropped when she saw Joanie had stepped out of the car, Evan in her arms. He was facing away from them, babbling quietly, but she had a small knife pressed to his side.

"You bitch!" she screamed and lunged for Joanie. Her wolf, too, was pressing up at her skin begging to be let out so it could tear her apart. Unfortunately, she didn't make it far as Ransom hooked his arm around her waist and pulled her back.

"Don't even think about it." Joanie's face was eerily calm, though there was an unnerving glint in her eye. "Not if you want to keep your precious Evan in one piece."

"What do you want with my son?" Isabelle cried. "Please ... I'll give you anything." She took a deep breath. "Is it money? I can give you anything you want. My family—"

"Is the reason we're here in the first place. But," she smiled down at Evan, "I'll be getting what I want soon enough."

Her family? "What do you mean?" she asked.

There was a dark glint in Joanie's cool blue eyes. "Such a gorgeous boy you have here. Who knew our genes mixing would produce such a beautiful pup? I'm sure your father would find this as ironic as I do." Joanie's face twisted in hate.

"What the hell are you talking about?" Her patience was running thin. "Let my son go or—"

"Ransom, should I tell her? Or do *you* want to?"

Isabelle swallowed hard as her gut wrenched. Slowly, she looked up at Ransom. "What is she saying?"

His face was inscrutable. "Isabelle, please, I—"

Wrenching away from him, she straightened herself and went toe to toe with him. "What's going on?"

"Tell her!" Joanie barked. "I think it's better she hears it from you."

His Adam's apple bobbed as he swallowed hard. "Isabelle, I swear ... I didn't mean for this to go this far. When I found out about Evan, I'd already decided I wasn't going to go through with it."

"Go through with what?"

When he didn't answer, his mother did. "Revenge, dear," Joanie scoffed. "On your father."

"My f-father?" Her head whipped back to Ransom. "What is she saying?"

He glared at Joanie, before turning to her, green-gold eyes filled with emotion. "My father ... my biological father, I mean, was an Alpha." He swallowed hard. "His name was Grayson Charles."

Was she supposed to know who that was? "And?"

"He was the Alpha of Connecticut," Ransom continued. "*Was*, until the council had him sent to the Lycan Siberian Prison."

There was something familiar about this story. She racked her brain, trying to recall the things she's learned and heard about from the first war with the mages. "Why?"

"Because of Grant Anderson," he said. "Grayson went to Grant for help so they could warn the council about the mages. But your father ignored him. He fought Grant because he wanted to save everyone."

"That's not true!" Her heart felt like it was breaking in half.

She'd never heard of this story before. Sure, there were skeptics at first who didn't believe the mages had come back then, but her father had been one of the first ones to sound the alarm.

"It is. Then Grant had him labeled a traitor and the council sent him to Siberia, where he died a few months later." he insisted. "I was a baby back then, and my mother and I ..."

Her throat burned, recalling the things he had mentioned before. "W-what happened?"

"What do you think happened?" Joanie's voice was dripping with venom. "We were taken to a safe house at first, to a family in a neighboring clan. But they found out about ... about Grayson's imprisonment and then they kicked us out. I went to all my old 'friends', but each and every one of them turned their backs on us."

Ransom's face was hard as granite, but it was obvious he was struggling with the memories again, as he had the other night.

"I'm sorry for what you went through," she said. "But my father wouldn't do that."

"Lies," he said. "Mother, you lived through it all. She'll realize that Grant Anderson's been lying to her."

Joanie smirked. "Does it matter, Ransom? What he did and how we suffered, that was the real crime."

Realization passed across his face. "What are you saying?" Ransom growled.

"My boy," she began. "Your father and I had a complicated relationship. Our marriage was arranged by our parents, but I was happy because he was able to keep me in the lifestyle I was accustomed to." Her teeth bared. "But he played a dangerous game. Wanted to hedge his bets. Play on both sides to see who came out on top."

Ransom went visibly pale. "No."

"I'm sorry, dear," she said. "Your Anderson whore is right. Your father was a traitor. But he didn't deserve to die in prison alone. *We* didn't deserve what happened to us! To be treated like garbage because of your father's sins."

"You lied to me."

"I did it to protect you," she said. "I couldn't tell you the real reason why we kept moving from place to place. Why other Lycans shunned us and threw us out of their homes when they found out who we really were. And why we were forced to become Lone Wolves." Her eyes darkened.

"You told me it was Grant Anderson who was the bad one," he said. "That's why we needed to get our revenge."

Isabelle's heart dropped. "That's what this was all about, wasn't it?"

His head whipped over to her. "Isabelle, it's not what you think."

But she couldn't reply. Her mouth had turned to dust and her throat burned. The implications of Joanie's words were too much. When he tried to reach out to her, she swatted his hands away.

"Stop this," Ransom said to his mother. "There's no need for revenge. You have a grandson now—"

"No need for revenge?" Joanie screamed. "Have you forgotten what it was like for us? Out in the streets, fending for ourselves? The things I did to make sure you never went without?" Evan began to wail and wiggled in her arms. "Stupid brat! Shut up!"

Isabelle gasped. "Joanie, please—"

"Don't call me that!" she hissed. "My name is Caroline Joanna Charles, rightful Lupa of Connecticut." Turning to Ransom, her voice softened. "You should have been Alpha. You would have been Alpha now if Grant Anderson's actions hadn't sent your father to prison!"

"Can't you hear what you're saying?" Ransom said. "Have you gone insane? He betrayed us, our kind! He would have let the mages take over and kill Lycans—"

"Why do you think he sided with them? Mages are so efficient at killing rivals."

"Please, Mother," he begged. "It's all in the past. We have a good life here. Pops—he did us good—"

"Don't look at me like that, Ransom. He wasn't much different from the men who came before him," she scoffed. "The only difference was he was stupid enough to fall in love with me. The only good thing that man did was die and leave me his insurance money. But then again, belladonna will do that to you."

"Shut up!" he growled.

Isabelle couldn't process what the hell was happening. However, she did notice something strange. "Where are you going, Joanie?" she asked.

"I told you not to call me that, you little slut." She tightened her hold on Evan, who was now full-on bawling. "I'm going where neither of you will find me."

Maybe Joanie didn't think they'd notice, but Isabelle did. During their lengthy conversation, she had been inching her way toward the gate, farther and farther away from them. She had been stalling, but for what? "Why are you slowly walking away?"

"You think you're so smart, huh?" She glanced toward the

edge of the property. "It doesn't matter, I suppose. My new friends will be here in—ah, here they are."

Right outside the gates, the air shimmered, and a crackle of electricity in the atmosphere made Isabelle shiver. A large red blur appeared, and when it came into focus, her skin crawled. *Mages.* A group of them stood there, at the edge of the property line.

"Bastard!" Ransom growled. "I should have stuck the dagger into *your* gut!"

One of the red-robed figures stepped forward, lips turned up into a smile, but his eyes were cold as ice. "I was surprised by your actions, boy. I didn't think you'd be the martyr type. While I hated leaving the dagger behind, it made for very good optics."

"What's going on?" He looked at his mother. "What is he saying?"

"Who do you think has been helping us?" she said nonchalantly.

"No!" he shouted. "That's not ..." He looked at Isabelle. "I didn't know, I swear it."

She didn't know what to believe anymore. Her chest was so tight, she feared it might implode.

"They came to me a few years ago," Joanie began. "And told me they could help me get revenge on Grant Anderson. I jumped on the chance of course." Her eyes narrowed at Ransom, her voice dropping low so only they could hear her. "And you were supposed to help me."

"Do you think it was easy for me to conceal what you did to your contact in New York? If they find out you killed one of them, we'd face a fate worse than death, but I did it anyway because I love you, and you're my son." Her face twisted with hate and fury. "Yet you betrayed me by spawning with his whore daughter!"

"Stop the dramatics, woman!" The head mage said. "And bring me the child."

Isabelle screamed. "No! Don't take him, please!" Her wolf snarled, pushing at her skin, begging to be let out so it could rescue their pup.

Ransom surged forward, but it was too late. Joanie crossed through the gate and reached out to the mage. Ransom was thrown back by a powerful sonic wave that also sent Isabelle flying a few feet into the air. She landed on the ground with a hard thud, the back of her head bouncing off the gravel. "Evan!" She struggled to get up. "Oh God ..." A hand curled around her wrist and pulled her to her feet. "I—" When she realized who it was, she slapped him away. "Get away from me!"

"Isabelle—"

"You did this!" she screamed at Ransom. "You were in on it all along!" Her wolf snapped its gigantic teeth, claws ripping out.

"I wasn't! I didn't know she was working with the mages."

"I don't believe you, you bastard!" Tears pooled in her eyes, but she was too angry to stop them. "You wanted revenge on my father? Is that why you went after me? Was screwing his daughter part of your plot?" Oh God, she felt disgusting and dirty. She let him—

"No! Isabelle, please, listen to me!" He raked his fingers through his hair. "I didn't even know who they were, only that my mother had found them somehow and wanted revenge on Grant Anderson as much as I did." He sucked in a deep breath. "You have to believe me. I love—"

"Don't! Don't you dare say those words." *Lies. All lies.* And she had been a fool to believe them. Well, no more. "I hate you, and I never want to see you again. I hope you rot in hell!"

"Isabelle? Ransom? What happened? Sabrina called and said you might need my help."

Whirling around, she saw Cross had appeared a few feet behind her. "Cross!" She ran to him and clung to his arm. "Get me out of here, please!"

"What happened?"

"They took Evan." She swallowed gulps of air. "The mages." She turned hateful eyes at Ransom. "And he was in on it, all this time. Working with them."

"No," Ransom denied. "Cross, you have to believe me—"

"I saw it with my own eyes!" she cried. "They came and took Evan. His mother helped. Please, Cross," she begged. "Let's go back to New York *now*. Lucas will find a way to get him back."

Cross's blue-green eyes turned stormy. "I'll deal with you later," he growled at Ransom.

As a cold sensation wrapped around her, she tucked her face into Cross's side. She thought she heard Ransom scream her name, but it faded away as she felt the ground under her feet disappear. Moments later, they landed on solid footing. Looking up, she saw they were back in the lodge's lobby.

"Sabrina!" Cross barked. "We have to go now."

She was standing by the front desk with Silke and Arlene. "What? What's happening?"

Cross disappeared and popped up beside her. "We need to leave."

"What's going on?" Silke asked. "Where's Ransom?"

The hybrid gripped Sabrina's waist. Isabelle was already running toward them, her arm stretched out to Cross's offered hand. As soon as their fingers touched, that coldness wrapped around her again. She allowed her mind to get lost, in that brief moment when she was between time and space, because reality would soon hit her hard

CHAPTER TWENTY

"Fuck!" Ransom slammed his fist into the side of his truck, the metal denting under his fists. *What a fucking mess.* No, it was more than that. His whole world was flushed down the shitter. "Goddammit!" He punched the door with his other hand, the pain brief but soothing. He deserved it. No, he deserved more than that.

Isabelle's look of betrayal and hate made his stomach curdle. And he couldn't blame her. Keeping her in the dark about his past and the plan against her father had been for her own good. But deep inside, he knew he had been selfish, not wanting to lose her if she found out. And now, he had anyway.

Yanking the door open, he got back into his truck and started the engine. He had to get his son back from those bastards. Those mages were going to regret taking what belonged to him.

The plan formed in his head as he drove back to the lodge. Maybe it wasn't a well-thought-out plan, and he could end up getting himself killed, but he didn't care. His life was worthless without Isabelle and Evan. But before he could put his plan into motion, there was one thing he needed to do.

As soon as he reached the lodge, he stopped his truck in the driveway and headed into the lobby. Aside from Silke and Arlene, Bo, Hardy, Axle, and Snake were also gathered around the front desk. When he met his sister's gaze, she sprang forward.

"Ransom!" Silke crashed into him with such force he nearly fell over. "What in heaven's name happened?" Her nails dug into his forearms. "Cross came here with Isabelle, grabbed Sabrina, then they all took off without an explanation. Isabelle wouldn't even look at me."

Worry crossed his sister's face. She always did have a good instinct.

"I need to tell you something." There wasn't much time, but he owed her the truth. Lying was what got him here in the first place.

"What is it?"

Those caring green eyes looked up at him with so much love that his throat tightened. He remembered the first day Pops had brought him here, and he saw Silke in her crib. He vowed to always protect her and be the big brother she would need. With a deep breath, he confessed everything. About his childhood before he came here, Joanie's plan, and her involvement with the mages and how they had conspired to kidnap Evan.

"Oh, Ransom." She hugged him fiercely. "I'm so sorry."

"There's something else, Silke. And—and I'll understand if you won't be able to stand me after this." Joanie's words had been clear. Belladonna was a substance that was deadly to Lycans. It could kill one of their kind if the dose was strong enough. Small doses over time, however, could keep one of them ill. "I think ... I think Joanie may have poisoned Pops."

Her face went white as a sheet. "What?"

"She didn't say it outright, but that's what she implied. I'm sor—"

A heart-wrenching sob escaped her mouth as she pulled away from him. "I ... I can't ... I'm sorry." Spinning around, she darted out of the lobby, and through the glass doors that led to the outdoor deck.

The pain in his chest was crippling, and all he wanted to do was break something. How the fuck did he end up hurting the two women he loved most in the same day?

"Ransom." A hand landed on his shoulder. Bo looked up at him sympathetically. "I'm sorry, son."

"It's all my fault," he said through gritted teeth. "I shouldn't have ... I should have told Isabelle right away. And Silke ..."

"Listen here, Ransom." Bo's voice turned serious. "You are not your father. Or your mother. You can't pay for their sins, and you can only do so much with what information you have."

"But—"

"No buts," he said sternly. "The past is past. You can't change it. The question is, what are you going to do now?"

His fingernails dug into his palms tight. "I'm going to get Evan back." That was the first thing on his list. Then he would beg both Isabelle and Silke for forgiveness. "Hardy," he called.

"Yeah, man?" Hardy stepped forward. "What do you need?"

"Take care of things here for me," he said. "I need to go get ready."

"Get ready for what?"

"A very long trip."

"What?" Hardy asked, flabbergasted.

"I'm going to New York," he said. "I don't know how long I'll be gone, but I trust you'll keep things going around here." The implication of his words weighed heavily between the two men, but Ransom quickly strode out to his truck.

There wasn't really anything he needed to prep. The only thing he needed was to get his bike. It was going to be a long ride, but with minimal stops, he could make it to New York in ten hours.

He was near the gate that led out of the property when he heard the roars of engines behind him. Checking his mirror, he saw six motorcycles coming up from behind. It seemed all of them had come out to chase after him. He slowed down and swerved his bike around, cutting the engine off. The six bikes slowed to a halt in front of him.

"What the hell are you doing here?" he groused. "I told you to take care of things for me, Hardy."

"No way, man," Hardy said. "We're a club. And we stick together."

"We may be Lone Wolves," Snake began. "But we're a pack. Stronger together than apart."

He rubbed his hand down his face. "I can't ask you to do this for me. Those mages are dangerous."

"You would do this for every single one of us." Surprisingly, it was Logan who spoke. "And so, we sure as hell are gonna do this for you."

"We owe you and Pops," Axle said, his expression serious for once.

Ransom blew out an impatient breath. "There's nothing I can do to stop you from coming with me?"

"We'll chase you all the way to New York if we have to," Hawk added.

The look of determination on their faces told him they were ready to do just that. "All right," he relented. "I don't have much time, so we need to coordinate this."

In the end, he was able to negotiate two members—Bo and Hawk—to stay behind to protect the lodge. "I think the witches did their job protecting the property," he told them. That was the reason Joanie was trying to make it past the gate and the mages appeared right outside. "But that doesn't mean they won't send their human goons in."

"We'll be ready," Bo assured him.

They were about to hit the road when an insistent blasting of a horn made Ransom pause and turn his head. A truck was headed their way, kicking up dust as it zoomed down the gravel path. It stopped a few feet away, and Silke jumped out and dashed over to him.

"Silke?" he asked incredulously. "What—"

Her arms came around him in a tight hug. "I couldn't just let you leave like that," she whispered. "I want you to know, it's not your fault what happened to Pops. Just ... be safe, and bring back my nephew, okay?"

As she released him, he looked down at her face. "I will."

Her face lit up in a smile. "Love you, bro."

"Love ya back, sis." He gave her one last hug before turning to the rest of them. "Let's move out."

The trip took a little longer than Ransom wanted, but they somehow made it to New York just before midnight. He knew Isabelle would probably be at The Enclave, so that's where he went first.

"Wait out here," he said to the guys as they stopped in front of the building that served as The Enclave's entrance.

The man at the front desk looked up as he burst through the door. He must have recognized Ransom, because he immediately shot to his feet. "I can't let you in here."

"I just need to talk to Ms. Anderson."

"You're not authorized to be here, Lone Wolf." His tone was anything but polite, and Ransom could feel the other man's wolf becoming agitated.

"I don't need permission to be in New York since I'm a Lone Wolf," he pointed out.

"You can come and go into the city as you please, but this is private property. Now," he straightened his shoulders. "You need to leave, or I'll call security."

"You're going to call them anyway," he said confidently. "I'll wait."

The man looked dumbfounded when Ransom shrugged and crossed his arms over his chest. Slowly, he reached for the phone, picked it up and murmured into the receiver, nodding as he listened to whatever the other person on the line said.

It only took about two minutes before the elevator dinged and the door opened. Ransom definitely expected the two burly Lycan meatheads in suits who marched out the door menacingly. But he did not expect the third man who stepped in from behind them.

"What do you want?"

Dark green eyes pierced right into him. Even though he was no longer Alpha, there was no doubt of Grant Anderson's power and authority.

"I want to talk to Isabelle."

"Do you have any idea what you've done to her?" His voice was menacing and would have sent a less dominant Lycan cowering. But Ransom was Alpha, too, even if he didn't hold the ruling status of one. "I'm not just talking about letting the mages kidnap Evan," he added. "But also leaving her pregnant and alone!"

The words made Ransom flinch internally, but he couldn't show fear now. "I realize that, sir. And I don't deserve her or to even see her right now. So, could you please just tell her I said goodbye."

That stunned Anderson into silence for about five seconds. "Goodbye?"

"I'm going to do whatever it takes to get my son back," he stated. "Even if I have to tear the entire world apart. Even if I have to die trying." Turning on his heel, he strode out the door. He wasn't sure what to do now, exactly, but he had a few ideas.

"Wait."

Ransom froze, pivoting slowly. He watched as Grant Anderson stepped out of the building and slowly advanced toward him. "What do you want?"

"Your mother," the former Alpha began, "wasn't being truthful to you. I know you've spent your life believing her, but I wasn't the one who sent Grayson Charles to prison. He was conspiring with the mages, and he was caught red-handed."

His chest tightened. "I know that, now. My mother said as much." It stung that she had lied to him all this time. He would have preferred the truth, even at a young age, so at least he could have understood better why everyone seemed to hate them.

Anderson's dark brows drew together. "For what it's worth, I was told you and your mother were taken to a safe house and that you would be provided for. Your father's Beta, who became Alpha after he went to Siberia, said as much. If I was at fault for anything, it was believing him. I'm sorry for what you and Caroline had to go through."

Ransom's lips tightened, then relaxed. "Then you have to believe me: I didn't know she was working with the mages. I want to help defeat them." He looked back at the rest of the MC. "We want to help." They all nodded in agreement.

Anderson sized him up, those piercing eyes looking him up and down. "All right. If you want to help, then wait here." He strode back inside. Moments later, he came back out. "I hope you guys are ready."

Before he could ask what it was they should be ready for, the air shimmered around them, and the hairs on his arm stood on end. Daric Jonasson appeared a few feet away.

"Thanks for coming, now let's go to HQ," Anderson said to the warlock. "Ready?" he asked Ransom and his men.

"All right."

Daric instructed them all to stay close together and make sure they were all linked by holding their hands. Moments later, they were in the garage of the Guardian Initiative's headquarters in the Brooklyn Bridge.

"Oh God." Axle doubled over, dry-heaving.

"You'll get used to it," Snake said sympathetically.

They all filed into the elevator, and Daric pressed the button for their destination. Ransom already knew where they were headed—the top floor. But tonight, the Guardian Initiative's command center looked nothing like it did when he first came here. The energy was more frenetic, and the whole place was buzzing with activity.

Anderson nodded to the conference room in the corner. Indistinct figures moved from behind the frosted glass. "Looks like not everyone's here yet, which is what I was hoping for."

They crossed the room, and it was so busy that no one paid them any mind. Before they entered, Anderson turned to Ransom. "I'm no longer Alpha here. Lucas is in charge, and you can bet he's going to have objections to having you join us. I do, too, but as a father, I know you'll do everything in your power to get Evan back. But I'll stand by my son's decision, since he's in charge."

He nodded. "You guys stay out here first," he told Hardy and the others. "I don't want any blowback on you."

"Whatever you say when you enter that room will matter," Anderson advised. "Choose your words carefully." With that, the former Alpha entered the room, and he followed him inside.

"Papa." Lucas looked somber. "There's something you need to know. The mages—" The air in the conference room turned cold and thick as molasses. "What are *you* doing here?" Mismatched eyes flashed like fire.

"Alpha, I came here to—"

"Ransom?"

His heart slammed into his chest. He had expected everyone else in the room to be here—the Alpha, Cross,

Julianna, Duncan, Frankie Muccino, Mika Westbrooke, and people he assumed were members of her team, but *not* Isabelle. His mouth dried up all of a sudden. "Isabelle." Had it only been hours since he'd seen her? It felt like a million years. But there she was, looking so achingly beautiful, even with her eyebrows slashing downwards and her nostrils flaring.

Her palms slammed down on the conference table as she stood up. "How the hell did you get in here? I told you, I don't ever want to see you again."

"You asshole! Motherfucker!" Julianna shot out of her chair and went flying at him. Her husband, fortunately, managed to grab her by the waist.

"You know I want to eviscerate him as much as you do, darlin'." Duncan shot a dirty look at Ransom. "But we can do that later, once we defeat the mages."

"Goddamned bastard," she hissed at him, mismatched eyes full of fury. "I'm going to kick your ass when this is all over."

"Get him out of here," Lucas said to Cross. "Send him to the Fenrir basement holding center. We can deal with him when this is all over."

"Wait," Anderson held a hand up. "He wants to help."

"He—hold on." Lucas's dark brows knit together. "You brought him here?"

"He came to me," his father answered. "And he wants to help. I think you should consider it."

"Consider it?" Lucas asked incredulously. "After what he did to Isabelle? And the fact that he was working with the mages to kill you?"

"I wasn't." Ransom insisted. "Isabelle, you heard what Joanie said. She kept me in the dark."

"Isabelle?" Lucas turned to his sister.

"How could I believe him?" she said, lower lip trembling. "After everything. They took *my son* right in front of me!"

"I swear to you, on Pops's grave," he begged. "I didn't know they were mages. But," he took a deep breath. "You're right. I was here in New York to get my revenge on your father. I didn't know who you were at first. Yes, I was here to scope out your clan. That night, when you told me who your dad was, I felt like a bastard. I couldn't go through with it, but they—the mages—they found out about us. They wanted me to bring you to them, but I wouldn't. And ... and I killed one of them. That's how I ended up in the Hudson." He glanced over at Cross surreptitiously, but the hybrid's face was inscrutable. "And I vowed to stay away from you to protect you. I didn't even know about Evan. Or that you were my True Mate. But I swear to you, I'll get Evan back. No matter what it takes."

"Well you better have a plan then," Lucas said. "Because the mages have sent us a message. They want the dagger in exchange for Evan. We're supposed to meet them at the top of Fenrir building at two o'clock."

"Goddammit!" he cursed. So that's why his mother kidnapped Evan. "If I can talk to Joanie, I can convince her to let Evan go. Or at least get close enough so I can grab him."

"Are you prepared to do anything to get him back?" Lucas challenged. "Even if it means choosing between Evan and your mother?"

"I lost my mother to the mages a long time ago," he said sadly. "I just didn't know it. If that time comes, I know what choice I'll make." He looked at Isabelle. "I love you and Evan, even if you don't believe it now."

Before Isabelle could react, the door to the conference room came crashing open. "This is bad, guys, it's *really* bad!" Lizzie exclaimed as she dashed into the room, computer tablet in hand. Snake had followed in behind her.

"What's wrong now?" Lucas said.

"We're getting reports that Lycans have been disappearing all over the world."

"What?" Frankie gasped.

"It started about an hour ago," Lizzie said. "According to our witnesses, the mages have been popping up and snatching Lycans, using their transporting spell. And get this: They've only been showing up in places they had already attacked in the last year."

Lucas met Ransom's gaze. "You were right. They've been testing their defenses. Lizzie, do we know where they're being taken?"

She flipped her tablet to face them. "Snake and I have been working on this software that tracks cellphone tower pings." There was a map on the screen, with orange blinking dots popping up every few seconds. "Using what data we have, including those from phones from our contacts who've disappeared, we were able to track a large amount of pings coming from this town in Upstate New York. It's called Lake Hope, right at the border of Connecticut." Her brows drew together.

"There's more, isn't there?" Lucas asked.

"It's not just Lycans we're seeing pop up there." She bit her lip. "Humans, too."

"How many?" Cross asked.

"We're getting more and more pings, see?" The orange dots had already multiplied since she'd shown it to them. "Right now, I'm guessing one hundred and fifty and growing." She zoomed out of the screen. Although the orange dots were concentrating on one area, even more blinking lights surrounded them. "And those are the human soldiers around them."

Cross and Daric looked at each other. "Three hundred Lycans and three hundred humans," Cross said. "That's been their plan all along. They're going to use them in some sort of ritual."

"Kidnapping three hundred Lycans and humans over time would have attracted too much attention, plus there's the problem of keeping them alive until they completed their numbers," Daric added. "Coordinating it and doing it in one swoop would ensure we were caught off guard."

"But what do they need them for?" Ransom asked.

"We're not sure yet," Cross said, then his face lit up in realization.

"What is it?" Lucas asked.

"It's a risky move, taking all those people. You know it has to be something big—their end game."

"Go big or go home," Lizzie said, her face draining of blood.

Cross's jaw hardened. "The three artifacts contain Magus Aurelius's power. He was about to perform this ritual that would bring the world under his power when the Lycans, magical beings, and humans banded together to stop him just in time. What if ... what if he knew he would be defeated that day, and so, instead of continuing the ritual, he distilled his powers in the artifacts? And left instructions for his followers on how to revive him through his writings?"

"The double Alpha blood," Grant Anderson said. "We need to secure you and Adrianna," he said to Lucas.

A grave expression passed over the Alpha's face. "That's what I was trying to tell you when you came in. They already have it."

"Adrianna?" Anderson's eyes glowed.

"No. It's Reed Wakefield. Elise said he was taken about an hour ago."

Cross spoke in a somber voice. "I think ... I think I know what they're planning to do." His ocean-colored eyes turned stormy. "They're going to revive Magus Aurelius and restore his power using the dagger, the ring, and the necklace. Then, he'll continue whatever ritual he had planned with the Lycan and human sacrifices all those centuries ago."

"There's no time to waste," Lucas said. "We need to move in on the mages."

"We've already run through several plans and drills," Mika added. "Including one with hostages, but just not this many. But we can certainly modify our plans."

"Good. We'll have to figure out a way to free the sacrifices and stall the exchange of the dagger. We're not letting them complete the artifacts," Lucas said. "If Cross's theory is right, then they still need the dagger to execute their final plan."

"What about Evan?" Isabelle piped up.

"We'll get him back, Isabelle," Ransom said. "Even if I have to rip every one of those mages apart."

"So, what's the plan?" Duncan asked.

"The mages want us to exchange the dagger for Evan," Lucas said. "We have," he checked his watch, "an hour and thirty minutes." His mismatched eyes turned hard as steel. "And they want Isabelle to make the exchange."

"Fuck no!" Ransom objected. "You can't be serious. No way. You're not going to—"

"Of course I'm going to do it!" Isabelle countered. "He's my son."

"And mine too!" he growled. "I'm not going to lose either of you. Alpha, why is Isabelle even here? She should be at The Enclave, where it's safe."

Lucas's expression remained impassive. "I know. She's my sister. Do you think I want her in danger any more than you do? Or my mother?" He nodded at Frankie. "But this is the end of the world as we know it, Ransom. It's all hands on deck."

"She'll be fine," Julianna said. "She's—"

"I need to do it." She sent what looked like a warning glare at her sister. "The mages were clear on their instructions. They want me. And they warned us if Cross or Daric was anywhere near there or attempted to steal the dagger or Evan away, there would be consequences."

"But what's the plan then?" Ransom asked.

"We'll need her to stall as long as possible," Mika said. "We'll create a diversion to draw out the human troops. They have the numbers, but we do have two big guns on our side, plus our forces and those of our alliances." She looked at Daric and Cross. "They're ready when you are."

"We'll start moving them into position now." Father and son nodded at each other, and then disappeared.

"I'm still not letting you do this alone," Ransom said.

"There's no more time for debate, we're running out of time," Isabelle retorted.

His chest tightened. She was not facing those mages alone. "You'll need me there."

"Oh yeah? Why?"

"Because I'm the only one Joanie will listen to."

"You don't even know if she'll be there," she reminded him. "It could just be the mages."

"Of course she'll be there," Ransom said. "Why do you think you're the one to make the exchange? She wants to see you suffer."

She opened her mouth, then closed it again. "You're not wrong there," she conceded.

"There's only one thing my mother wants out of this," Ransom began. "You." He looked at Grant Anderson. "Specifically, your death. If we give her what she wants—"

"No!" Frankie cried. "You can't—"

"Sweetheart," Anderson began. "He's ... he's right. If anything, we can use this to our advantage."

"I'm not losing you," she said.

He smiled at her. "And you won't. The mages couldn't stop me from spending the rest of my life with you, what makes you think that's any different now?"

"I have an idea," Julianna said. "But we'll need some extra help from our other secret weapons." She looked at Mika meaningfully.

"The clock's ticking," Lucas said. "Let's get ready. Tonight, we end this war."

Ransom clenched his fists. He agreed with Lucas on one thing. One way or another, it would all end.

CHAPTER TWENTY-ONE

As she stood just outside the stairwell that led to the Fenrir Corporation building rooftop, Isabelle held Magus Aurelius's dagger in her hand. *Definitely heavier than it looked,* she mused.

The long, silver weapon was about the size of her forearm and had a large green jewel in its pommel. A shudder went through her, knowing how it was made and what it was capable of. Everything weighed on this one object—Evan, and the fate of the world—and her actions tonight.

Years ago, she never would have thought she would be in this position. She was the party girl, the one with the pretty face and nice clothes and not much else beneath the surface. Everything had changed since Evan. Since meeting Ransom.

"Really, Belle?" Julianna whispered. "Him?" She nodded at Ransom, who was deep in thought, hands in his pockets and leaning against the wall. "I always thought preppy boys were more your type. Not tattooed bikers."

Her sister was trying to help her lighten up, and it was working. She couldn't help the bubble of laughter that rose from her throat. "He's my True Mate, how was I supposed to resist him, Jules?" Elbowing her sister, she nodded at Duncan. "And you? A Scottish laird? I thought you hated those trashy bodice-ripper novels."

"Duncan's not a laird. He's a viscount." Julianne rolled her eyes. "But that doesn't matter because I'm still going to rip Ransom a new asshole when this is all done."

"Jules ..."

"What?" her sister asked innocently. "Not everyone's here yet, which is what I was hoping for. You're going to get Evan back, we're going to win against the mages, and then I'm gonna go kick your mate's ass for leaving you alone and pregnant and plotting to murder our father."

"You don't have to remind me." Her wolf yowled sadly. It had been so excited to see him enter the conference room. And there was a tiny part of her that soared with hope and joy. Even now, he was doing what he said he would—get Evan back. But the betrayal was still weighing heavily on her.

"Are you gonna tell him?"

"About what?"

Julianna gave her that 'don't-look-innocently-at-me' look. "You know—"

"Bad news." It was their father. "Daric did a surveillance of the area in Lake Hope where the mages are. They have some sort of red glass dome over the hostages."

Julianna's eyes widened. "Just like the one in Central Park. That means no one will be able to get in or out."

"It'll be tricky, but Daric and some of our witch and warlock allies are working on a way to break the spell." He turned to Isabelle. "Almost ready, sweetheart?"

"As I'll ever be. Dad—"

"You can do this." He kissed the top of her head. "You're the daughter of two Alphas. Now, go get my goose."

"I will, Papa." She took a deep breath and grabbed the door handle. *I can do this. I have to, for Evan's sake.*

"Isabelle."

That voice never failed to make her knees weak. She didn't turn to Ransom or acknowledge him, though her hand did not turn the door handle.

"For what it's worth, I want you to be safe. And I love—"

"Thanks." No, she couldn't bear to hear those words. *Not now.* Her aching heart wouldn't be able to take it, and *damn it,* she needed to keep her head clear.

"I'll see you on the other side, Belle." Julianna said before flashing a dirty look at Ransom.

"See you, Jules." Turning the handle, she opened the door and walked into the stairwell. It was about three flights up to the roof. When she stepped out, the cool night air hit her face instantly, drying the tears pooling in her eyes.

She moved forward until she reached the helipad in the middle of the roof. Her watch said it had just turned two. So, where were they?

The air was suddenly filled with a salty, metallic tang. Her wolf went on full alert and raised its hackles, while every bit of hair on her arms and the back of her neck stood on end.

"Good evening, my dear."

She turned around. Behind her was a group of mages, all clad in their usual red robes. One of them, the same one who had kidnapped Evan in Kentucky this morning, stepped forward.

"I'm glad to see your Alpha has followed my

instructions." His red eyes grew wide as he greedily stared at the dagger in her hands. "Give it to me."

"Where's my son?" Her fingers curled tighter around the dagger. "You're not getting this until I have him. I want to see him first."

"As you wish." The mage waved his hand at his followers, who parted like the Red Sea. Ransom was right. Joanie stepped out from behind the mages, Evan in her arms.

"Evan!" Her rage began to bubble when she realized he was totally limp, his head lolling back as Joanie walked closer. "What did you do to him?"

"Your little brat wouldn't stop screaming his head off," she complained. "Don't worry, a little sleeping potion never hurt anyone."

"I'm going to kill—"

"Shut up, both of you," the main mage said.

"But, Krogan—"

"Let's stop the theatrics." Krogan turned back to Isabelle. "There's your precious boy. Now, hand over the dagger."

"No, I want him first."

"I can kill him with the snap of my fingers." Krogan's voice was cold and emotionless. "Do you think I care for this child? I have no other use for him."

Isabelle gritted her teeth. "But you need the dagger. Once your plan succeeds, you'll kill him, and all of us, anyway. Just let me have this last night with my son." Her own words made her want to vomit, but this was part of their plan. And the cue for the next part.

"Mother!"

They all turned to the doorway that led to the stairwell.

Ransom stepped out, his arm around her father, a knife to his throat.

"Ransom?" Joanie's voice shook. "Is that you?"

"Yes, it's me." He dragged Grant with him as he shuffled forward. "I have him, Mother. See? Grant Anderson. He's here."

Joanie's expression turned from shock to disbelief, until finally, her lips curled up. "Oh, Ransom! I knew you wouldn't betray me. Darling boy, come here."

He moved closer, keeping the knife pointed at his hostage's throat. Isabelle could see the sick pleasure on Joanie's face, and it made her stomach curdle.

"What the hell are you doing, woman?" Krogan groused. "We're supposed to get the dagger! You can have your stupid revenge later!"

"When?" Joanie cried. "I've waited thirty goddamn years for revenge. You had so much power, and yet this one thing you couldn't do for me. You kept me waiting, dangling Grant Anderson in front of me like a carrot on a stick. Well, no more. I don't care about your stupid dagger!"

"Woman ..." The mage warned. His followers moved forward, but he held them back. "Be reasonable, Caroline. Soon, they'll all be dead, even Anderson."

"Dead? Ha! Death would be too good for him." Her teeth bared. "I want him to suffer. For every humiliation and indignity I've had to go through because of him!"

"That's right, Mother," Ransom said. "We'll make him suffer. For what he did. Now, why don't you hand Evan over to Isabelle, and we can get our revenge?"

Joanie laughed. "Oh no, Ransom! Can't you see how perfect this is? How we can make him *really* pay for what he did?" Her eyes widened as she stared at Isabelle. "What better way to make Grant Anderson suffer than to hurt his precious baby girl and grandson, right in front of his very eyes while he can't do anything to help them."

The bile rising from her stomach made Isabelle's throat burn. "You're insane."

"Shut up, you whore!" Joanie pointed the knife at her. "You'll pay for your father's sins."

"Insolent bitch!" Krogan screamed at Joanie. "You're ruining plans that were set in motion centuries ago for your petty revenge?" Hateful red eyes turned to Isabelle. "I'll kill every last one of you here until you *give me the dagger!*" He advanced toward her. "I'll—" He stopped short. "What's going on?"

Isabelle's heart pounded in her chest. Shadows began to creep around them like dark curling waves, filling every crack of light. Then, one by one, they appeared—Marc Delacroix and two of his relatives, plus Julianna, Duncan, Astrid, Zac, and Cross.

"You damned dirty dogs!" Krogan screamed. "Kill the child now, you bitch!"

Ransom let go of her father, and together, they lunged at Joanie. She screamed and tossed Evan in the air.

"Evan!" Isabelle shouted as she watched her son fly up in an arc toward the edge of the building. "No!"

It all happened so fast. Her wolf ripped out of her body, leaping forward. It sailed over Grant and Ransom as they landed on Joanie, hurtling toward the edge of the building. But they were still too far. Too slow. Isabelle screamed as she watched her son nearing the edge of the building and—

Poof.

A female figure appeared out of nowhere, arms outstretched as she caught Evan like a linebacker intercepting a football. But her son's momentum made her teeter back, so Isabelle's wolf stretched forward as far as it could, jaw opening up and teeth snagging on the woman's shirt and pulled, sending them rolling backward.

Isabelle blinked. *What the hell happened?*

"Isabelle, you're crushing me," a pained groan said from somewhere underneath her.

The wolf rolled to its side, a sleeping Evan protected against the chest of the woman and the cage of her arms. It blinked at the woman who had been pinned under them.

"Phew!" Astrid stood up and glanced down at Evan with a tender smile. "Glad I caught this one right on time."

Oh God. She had almost forgotten Astrid was a hybrid and had similar powers to Cross, albeit a limited range. She must have seen Evan flying off and transported herself just in time to catch him.

Isabelle quickly transformed back, and the first thing she did was embrace Astrid. "Thank you," she sobbed. "Thank you for saving him."

Astrid smiled at her. "Thank *you* for catching me. But, we're not done yet."

"I—Oh no! The dagger!" She must have dropped it when she shifted. But where was it?

It was pure chaos all around them. Wolves and witches were battling the mages. She saw Delacroix deftly weave in and out of the shadows as he dodged a mage who could throw balls of lightning. One of his witch cousins was using the shadows around them to contain a mage in a dark fog, while Julianna's wolf was ripping into another's throat.

"Get him to safety," she told Astrid, then retraced her steps. *There it was!* The dagger was on the ground, the green jewel glinting even in the darkness. She dashed toward it, practically diving at it, but it was too late. A gray, ashen hand snatched it seconds before her.

"Finally!" Krogan held the dagger up in triumph. "Now we can fully revive the master!" He took something out of his pocket and smashed his hand onto the dagger. It dripped with something sticky and red, then he disappeared.

"No!" Isabelle scrambled forward, but he was gone. "Goddammit!" Her chest tightened, and tears clung between her lashes.

"Isabelle?"

She turned around. "Papa!" Flinging herself at him, she cried into his chest. "Papa, I'm sorry. I dropped the dagger when I went after Evan and—"

"Shh ... shh, sweetheart, you did good."

"But the dagger—"

"Evan is safe," he said. "That's all that matters. We always knew there was a possibility that they would get the dagger, and Evan's life would always come first."

"But what about the mages? And Magus Aurelius?"

"We'll get them." There was pure determination in his eyes. "I know it."

"Isabelle."

Her father's arms loosened and fell to his sides before she turned. Ransom was staring at her, white as a sheet. "Evan's fine. He's—"

He snatched her to him, wrapping his arms around her. "I thought I'd lost you. Lost you both."

God, his scent was so comforting right now, so she let him hold her. "I'm fine."

Cross came up to them from behind Ransom. "We have to get a move on. I—" The hybrid's eyes bulged as he realized she was naked. Glancing briefly at her, he waved his hands, and a shirt and loose pants appeared on her body. Clearing his throat, he continued. "Krogan must have had some of Reed's blood, which allowed him to teleport using the dagger. He's probably back at Lake Hope."

"What's the situation there?" her father asked.

"According to Dad, not so great." His dark blond brows snapped together. "There's no counter spell for the dome, and unless someone from the inside can stop the mages powering it like we did in Central Park, we can't get rid of it. But," he paused for a breath. "Seems they haven't quite completed the required number of Lycans and humans yet, so they keep switching it on and off as they're gathering more sacrifices. Dad's waiting for an opening so he can slip in with a small group and turn it off."

"We can't just sit around and wait, though," Grant said. "But also, the plan was to stage a full-scale attack should the mages get their hands on the dagger." It was risky, but they knew it would have to be done.

"It's all my fault," Isabelle said. "I—"

"No one's blaming you, sweetheart," Grant assured her. "Besides, they would have done anything to get the dagger, and Evan might have been killed."

"Let's go get those bastards," Ransom growled. "We can't let them win."

"Gather everyone," Cross instructed. "I'll be back in a sec." He turned to Isabelle. "Your grandfather Noah, Gunnar and my Uncle Jackson and his wolves are ready to be transported to Lake Hope. I can bring Evan to their home in West Virginia, and Lily can take care of him. It's safe and has all the protections."

"Yes, please do. Where—"

"Here you go!" Astrid had already come up to them, Evan in her arms.

"Oh, baby," she cried as she took him. She kissed his forehead. "I love you. Stay safe." Her heart was wrenching as she handed him over to Cross, but she knew it was the right choice. The hybrid took him and disappeared.

"He'll be fine," Astrid whispered. "We sent Annaliese there too. Lily will take good care of them."

She knew that, but she couldn't help the tightness curling in her chest. "We need to stop these mages."

Her father went off to see to everyone. They had some mage prisoners and dead bodies to take care of, plus a few minor injuries on their side, not to mention, Joanie. One of the members of the Lycan Security Force had taken her away in cuffs, strangely silent as she kept her head down and refused to look at anyone.

Isabelle watched Ransom as he stared after his mother. God, the expression of anguish on his face made her want to reach out and comfort him, but she was too scared. Instead, she stood next to him. Both remained silent, the tension between them stretched tight like a rubber band.

"Ready?" Cross reappeared moments later. Everyone was assembled around the helipad. "Hold hands, everyone."

Her father took her left hand. On her right, Ransom cautiously took the other one.

"He said to hold hands," he murmured.

She nodded, but kept her lips shut tight as she tried her hardest to ignore the rough, warm texture of his large hand around hers. The coldness of Cross's magic wrapped around her, and she closed her eyes. Half a second later, the asphalt that was under her bare feet was now replaced with grass. When she opened her eyes, her Lycan senses adjusted to the darkness.

"It's just over there," Cross said, pointing to the ridge on their left. He touched his ear and winced. "Okay, gotcha, Lizzie," he said into the communicator. Lizzie and the rest of her IT team were sitting in a van somewhere nearby, forwarding orders from Lucas and Mika and giving intel. "Dad's already in. The dome is being dismantled as we speak."

"Let's move out," her father ordered, and they all marched to follow him over the hill, trudging up until they reached the top and were able to look down.

"Jesus H. Christ on a bicycle!" Julianna burst out. "What the hell—"

Isabelle could see why her sister looked astounded. Up ahead of them, a humungous red dome made of pure light was stretched over a massive field. However, it was slowly shrinking, revealing hundreds of people under it. They all stood in neat rows, unmoving, like they were hypnotized.

"It's the necklace," Astrid explained. "They must have used Reed's blood to supercharge it so they could control the humans *and* Lycans."

Thunder broke through the silence in the air. But it wasn't thunder. No, it was Lycans—hundreds of them—racing into the field from the east side.

"We need to go now." The muscles under her father's

cheeks were already shifting, and his eyes glowed with his wolf. "They'll need our help."

"You know the plan," Astrid reminded them. "I'll remain in human form and work as support to coordinate the fight and take anyone injured to safety." She turned to Zac. "I love you, baby. Go get 'em!"

"Love you back." With a savage growl, Zac shifted into his brown-blond wolf.

"You better get back to me in one piece, MacDougal," Julianna said to Duncan as she was ripping off her shirt.

"*Och*, darlin', don't I always?" Her brother-in-law laughed and kissed his mate full on the mouth.

Her and Ransom's gazes crashed, but she quickly turned away. There were more important things now, and they would have to save whatever it was that needed to be said for later. Quickly, she shifted into her wolf. While she was in tune with her Lycan side, she hadn't really shifted this much since she was a teenager and learning to control her wolf. It was kind of freeing in a way. Her wolf was gorgeous, with glossy black fur and brown patches on its legs and belly. She told herself when this was all over, she would spend more time shifting. Her wolf liked the sound of that.

Fully transformed, she dashed into the fray with her companions. Up ahead, she could see that the red dome was gone and replaced with a dark, shadowy fog. Moving over five hundred people was simply not feasible, even with Daric and Cross working non-stop, not to mention, if any of the humans were to escape before they were doused with a forgetting potion, they could reveal their secrets. So they had decided to keep them where they were and put a protective shadow barrier around them, care of another of Delacroix's witch relatives, so the mages would not be able to reach them for whatever ritual Magus Aurelius planned.

The Lycan forces were still outnumbered based on the surveillance they had conducted. The mages and their human troop numbers combined were over two thousand, while the Lycans and the witches and warlocks were three to four hundred. However, the idea was to draw the enemies into two different spots away from the hostages so they could put the next stage of their plan into action.

Isabelle had little experience fighting, but she did have the advantage of being a wolf, plus her super speed. Her wolf ran head on toward a group of humans, growling at them and dodging the bullets they shot at her. She could sense Ransom's wolf beside her, following in her steps, then overtook her as he leapt at the group. Her wolf was miffed that it didn't get there first, but nevertheless jumped right in, ripping and tearing at everything it could get its teeth and claws on.

A buzzing, piercing sound made her flinch. But neither the mages nor the humans noticed because it was set at a frequency only wolves could hear. *That was the signal.*

The wolves and their allies spread out into two groups, then began to retreat in separate directions. The humans and mages, seemingly energized by their enemies' retreat, pressed on, not realizing that they were moving farther and farther away from their main encampment.

There was another buzzing sound—three short bursts instead of a long one this time, and Isabelle knew that was the signal to disperse. The wolves scattered away, as the humans and mages remained clumped together.

There was silence for about two seconds, which was

broken with a loud, high-pitched screech, followed by a second one. The wind picked up around them, and then whipped furiously as the screeches became louder.

Isabelle looked up and gasped. Though she'd seen Sebastian Creed's dragon once or twice while growing up, she'd never seen it quite like this. It looked menacing as it soared overhead, its giant golden wings flapping rhythmically to keep it afloat. Even more frightening was the sight of a second dragon—King Karim of Zhobghadi. His dragon was silver, but just as terrifying as Creed's. The two colossal creatures swung in arcs around each other, then separated, heading toward the two groups of humans and mages. The humungous claws and gigantic mouths razed through the crowds, crushing through the mass of enemies. Many escaped, but the Lycans and witches were able to easily pick off the stragglers.

Isabelle was about to join in when she saw something in the distance. Near the shadow dome, a beam of yellow light burst out, shooting straight up into the sky. The atmosphere grew thick and crackled with electricity as a metallic tang wafted into her wolf's nose. What the hell was that?

A hand touched her wolf's flank. A human hand. For a second, she thought it was Cross, but it wasn't. This man had cropped blond hair and a shorter, leaner build. Amber eyes gazed into hers.

"Remember me, Isabelle?" He smiled at her weakly. "We used to play at your house in Long Island when we were kids. I'm Gunnar."

Gunnar Jonasson. Cross's younger brother. But what was he doing here?

"You should come with me. Now." He stretched his neck

as his limbs began to grow, and white fur sprouted on his body. Red eyes bored into her, and the albino wolf swung its head, signaling for Isabelle to follow him.

What is going on? Still, she trotted after him, her gut instinct telling her this was right. Moments later, she realized they were running in the direction of the yellow light. It had grown even brighter now, and as they drew closer to the source, she gasped. A group of mages were gathered, the yellow beam shooting out from their circle. Immense power rippled from them, making the air smell thick, like smoke.

The albino wolf yowled to catch her attention and motioned with its head again. About twenty feet away from the circle of mages was a white table where a naked, dark-haired man lay prone on top, bloody and bruised. A large glass bowl was next to the table, catching the blood slowly dripping from the man's neck. Three mages stood guard over him.

Gunnar had transformed back to his human form. Isabelle followed suit, pushing her wolf away until she gained control of their body. "Is he—"

"He's not dead. They need Reed alive, to keep draining his blood."

"What are they—" She gasped, then turned to the circle of mages. "Magus Aurelius."

He nodded. "Reed's blood is reviving him."

"We have to stop them!"

"Isabelle!"

She turned around and saw Ransom running toward them. His face was drawn into a scowl as he glared at Gunnar. "Who the hell are you?"

"We don't have time for this." She pointed to the group of mages. "They're reviving Magus Aurelius."

"Fuck," Ransom rubbed his hand down his face. "I'll stop them." He was about to march toward them when Gunnar held his hand up.

"We all will," he said. "But first, you and Isabelle get Reed to safety. I'll distract them."

"What about the artifacts?" Isabelle asked.

"Cross will come with Dad soon," he said. "They just need to help with the critically injured first."

"Go back, Isabelle." Ransom caught her hand. "It's too dangerous."

"No way!" she shouted. "I'm not wasting any more time." She yanked her hand away. "I'm going with or without you." Once again, she shifted into wolf form.

He let out a growl and then nodded. Together, they dashed over to the table. The mages guarding took defensive stances, ready to protect their victim. One of them raised his hands, and the earth began to shake underneath them and split open.

Steady! Isabelle directed her wolf to leap to the right as the ground opened up. Ransom followed her, while Gunnar went the other direction. Pushing her wolf as much as she could, she surged forward. Ransom was way ahead of her and landed on the powered mage, so she directed herself at the other one on the right, swiping a claw at him before he could toss a bottle of potion at her. The mage screamed as blood spurted out from his neck and hit the wolf's face, though it continued to hold the mage down until his body stopped struggling and twisting. Glancing over at the other side of the table, she saw Gunnar had made quick work of the third mage as well.

Shifting to human form, she walked over to the white table. She touched Reed's back, relief pouring through her as she felt the rise and fall of his breath. Ransom, who had also shifted back, turned him over and removed a small blade embedded in his neck that kept the wound open and the blood flowing without killing him outright. The thought of the mages using Reed as some kind of never-ending blood bag made her stomach heave.

"It'll heal in no time." Ransom hefted Reed onto his shoulders in a fireman's carry. "Let's go."

As they walked away, Isabelle felt something ... wrong. *Where the heck was Daric and Cross?* Surely, they had the power to stop the mages? Ransom was a few feet away from her when she turned her head. *Oh no!*

The albino wolf was heading in the direction of the circle of mages. It let out a long howl and leapt toward them, but it froze in midair. The wolf's limp body remained floating in the air as a mage stretched his arms over him. The mages were still chanting surrounding that yellow light, which had not diminished but now grew so bright, it was like daylight around them.

Adrenaline mixed with fear pumped through her, and she knew what she had to do. If she didn't, then this whole thing was pointless. She had to do this. For Evan. For Ransom.

He must have sensed that she'd stopped following him, because he turned around. "Isabelle? What's wrong?"

"Ransom ... I ... I love you!" she blurted out. "I always have." Her lungs squeezed tight.

"Isabelle?" Gold-green eyes grew large. "Isabelle ... no!"

Spinning on her heel, she sprinted away from him. He screamed her name again, but she kept pushing herself until she reached the group of mages.

"Our master is nearly here!"

Her wolf burst out of her and then lunged at the first mage it could reach, breaking the circle and sending them tumbling forward.

"Bitch!" Krogan screamed. "You're too late." He cackled with glee, raising his hands up, dagger in one hand. In the middle of the broken circle was what looked like a translucent figure, its features not quite fully formed, but it was obviously human. It reminded Isabelle of those anatomy mannequins that showed what the inside of the body looked like.

The she-wolf scrambled to its feet. *Oh no,* she cried. Before their eyes, the figure was materializing into solid flesh. The man who stood before them was tall and imposing, and surprisingly, young and healthy-looking, except for his ashen gray skin.

Magus Aurelius opened his eyes—they were pure red and filled with hate—and zeroed in on Isabelle. "You've done well, my followers." The voice made her blood freeze in her veins. "Bring me that dirty dog."

A large gray wolf suddenly burst in from behind Krogen, tackling the mage to the ground. *Ransom!* The dagger skittered across the ground, landing at Magus Aurelius's feet.

"Ah, my old friend," he said, picking it up. "I can't wait to be reunited with the powers you contain. But first ..." He strode toward Ransom's wolf, whose back was turned as he continued to maul Krogen, and raised the dagger.

Isabelle's wolf burst forward, and reached the master mage before it plunged the dagger into the wolf's head. They tumbled together in a heap of limbs and fur.

"No!" Magus Aurelius cried. His grip on the dagger didn't loosen, and he plunged it straight into the wolf's neck.

Pain shot through her, but her wolf didn't relent. Its large jaw opened up and went for the jugular, sharp teeth piercing through skin, flesh, and bone. Sticky, warm blood flooded its mouth, and it bit harder as Magus Aurelius screamed in agony.

When lightheadedness was setting in, the she-wolf finally let go and then rolled over on the ground, shifting back to human form. *It's all right*, she told her wolf. *Rest now. You did good. We'll be okay.* Her wolf yipped gratefully and nodded in thanks.

Unfortunately, the master mage was still breathing and got up to his knees, a smile on his blood-stained face, his hand clutching at the gaping hole in his shoulder. "Damn dog ..." he gurgled. "You'll have to do better than that."

A black blur leapt from behind him and tackled the mage down, its massive claws raking down Magus Aurelius's back, sending him to the ground as he howled in pain. Raising its head, the wolf chomped down on the master mage's head. Isabelle recognized the markings on the wolf's body—black with brown patches, just like her own. It was her mother.

"No, no, no, no!" It was Ransom's voice she heard as she felt her head being cradled on his lap.

His scent—oh his wonderful scent—dispelled the chill from her body.

"Isabelle." Tears were running down his cheeks. "Why ... please ... don't die."

She laughed, but it came out in a gurgle. "No ... Ransom ... I won't." Oh, it was so warm everywhere. She knew that sensation, so familiar with it. But Ransom didn't know yet. She hadn't told him.

"You can't! I won't let you die, not now," he shouted. "Not now when you love me."

"I've always loved you," she said. "I ... help me get this damn thing out." She reached for the dagger stuck in her neck.

"Don't touch it," he said. "It'll make it worse."

"But it's starting to itch."

"Shh ... that's the blood loss talking. Conserve your energy until—"

"Oh, for Christ's sake!" Gritting her teeth through the pain, she sat up, yanked the dagger out of her neck, and threw it aside. "I'm fine, you dense idiot!" The wound immediately sealed up. "You got me pregnant. Again."

Ransom's expression was one of pure disbelief. "Y-you're okay. And you're *pregnant*?"

"I'm your True Mate, of course I'm okay," she said, exasperated.

"Then why the hell did you tell me you loved me?" he shouted.

"Because *I love you*?" she screamed back.

"Are you guys mad at each other or in love?" It was Julianna, who had come up from behind them.

"Both," they said at the same time.

Rolling her eyes, she walked over to the black and brown wolf, who was still standing guard over its victim. Or what was left of him. "I'm gonna go check on Mama."

Isabelle turned back to Ransom. "By the way, I told you

to go and take Reed to safety! Why—Oomph!" Suddenly, she was pressed against his hard, muscled chest.

"I love you," he whispered against her temple, his voice croaking. "I don't know what I would have done if something happened to you. Forgive me, please. For not telling you the truth."

"I understand," she said. "It can't have been easy for you growing up. And Joanie ..."

"She's going away," he said, resigned. "To Siberia."

"We'll ... we'll get through this," she said. "Together. That is ... if you still want to be with me."

"Do I want to be with you?" He pulled away from her, cupped her face in his hands, and stared into her eyes. "Isabelle, nothing in the world could stop me from being in your life. I love you, and if you had died today, I would have followed you because I couldn't live without you." He paused. "Well ... I probably could, but I would stay because of Evan, but I would wait out the rest of my life until we could be together again. So, do I want to be with you? You're damned right I do."

"Then kiss me."

And he did.

―――

With the battle now ended and the mages defeated, Isabelle and Ransom held each other and watched the sun rise over the valley. Sometime later, they managed to retrieve their clothes, then made their way back to where the Lycans and their allies were lingering about, tending to the injured and resting from the major battle. Their forces were looking the worse for wear, but overall, they seemed in good spirits. Of course, Isabelle was not naive enough that she didn't think there weren't any casualties, but she knew there would be time enough to mourn the dead. For now, it really was a true victory, as they stopped Magus Aurelius from taking over the world.

"I need to check on my guys," Ransom said in a tight voice.

She squeezed his hands. "Look," she pointed to two figures a few feet away. "I see Mika and Delacroix. She should know where Hardy and the rest are."

They trudged over to the couple, who were overseeing the medical team with their treatment of those who were not so critically injured and thus didn't need to be transported back to The Enclave.

"*Cher*, sit down, take a breather," Delacroix urged. "We've won. You and our baby can rest now."

"I'm the head of the Guardian Initiative," Mika retorted. "I'll rest when everyone is taken care of. And I'm not even tired."

"The captain doesn't always have to go down with the ship, or in this case, be the last one to leave." He placed a hand over her pregnant belly. "Please? At least have a bite of food. You must be starving."

"I'm not—oh, hey, Isabelle." A dark brow shot up as her gaze dropped to their linked hands. "Ransom."

Being her cousin, Isabelle knew Mika probably knew everything. "Hey, Mika."

She eyed Ransom warily. "I heard you got Reed back for us. Thank you."

"*Merci*," the Cajun added.

"Have you seen my guys?" Ransom asked quickly.

"I last saw them—oh, I see one of them over there." She pointed to a grassy patch, where Hardy was sitting down, chatting on the phone.

"Thanks, Mika," she said.

"We'll talk later," Mika replied, eyeing Ransom again.

They trotted over to where Hardy was sitting. He looked exhausted, bloody, and bruised, but the VP managed a smile as they approached. "You shoulda seen the other guy," he joked as he tried to open his left eye, which was swollen shut.

"Where's everyone?" Ransom asked.

"They're fine. Snake got hit with some kind of spell that encased his arm in ice, so they took him back to the Medical Wing to get checked out. Axle's already, you know, being Axle." He jerked his thumb at said Lycan, who was chatting with a couple of witches.

"And Logan?"

Hardy's lips pulled back into a grim line. "Pretty bad shape. He refused any help from the witch healers, but you know that bastard's tough. Found him limping away somewhere."

Ransom grunted. "Right." A look passed between the two men, a silent communication only they understood.

Isabelle tugged on Ransom's arm. "Would you mind if I went off to check on my family?" She wasn't worried about them, because surely, if any of them had been hurt seriously, Mika would have said so. "You can stay here with Hardy, if you want."

"We're cool, right?" Ransom asked Hardy, who nodded. "Let's go. We should find Cross and see if he can take us to Evan."

They continued their walk along the battlefield, and as if by silent agreement, chose to walk around the areas where their forces were cleaning up the bodies of the fallen. It was a somber sight, and Isabelle made silent prayers for all of them—even their human and mage enemies. Death, after all, was not something to celebrate. She knew Lucas, and anyone in his position, would have preferred a bloodless war, but he also had to protect their kind and the rest of the world, and that came with a devastating cost.

As they moved farther away, Ransom's grip on her hand loosened—she hadn't even realized that they were clinging to each other as if their lives depended on it. They reached the edge of the field, near the dirt road that wound around the valley, where more people were gathering in groups.

"You stupid asshat! What were you thinking?" It was Lizzie Martin, wailing at what looked like a man who was unconscious on the ground. "You didn't have to go tearing into half a dozen armed men just because they took our van hostage."

"There, there, dear," an older woman, who was sitting on the ground with the unconscious man's head in her lap, said. "My son's going to be fine. The bullet holes are already sealing up." It was Wyatt Creed. His face looked terribly pale, and his chest was covered in blood, but the wounds looked like they were already days old.

"Do you think he'll wake up soon?" Lizzie asked. "He lost a lot of blood. Why would he do that?"

Jade Creed looked at the young woman knowingly, the corners of her lips tugging up. "I really couldn't say. Here, why don't you take my place for a bit, that's it ..." Lifting

Wyatt's head up, she slid out from under him, and Lizzie took her place.

"Mom! Are you okay? What happened to Wyatt?" Jade's only daughter, Deedee Creed—or rather, Queen Desiree of Zhobghadi now—came up to them, her face in shock as she knelt down next to her brother.

"This idiot was supposed to stay with Cliff and his team," Lizzie explained. "My team and I were in the surveillance van when we got boarded by those scumbag guns for hire. He must have heard it over the comms and rushed back to help us. He managed to take down about six of them, but the rest shot him down. They were distracted enough though and my team and I took them down. Then I dug the bullets out of his chest."

"And look, he's already healing thanks to you," Jade said. "Your Majesty," she nodded to Deedee's husband, King Karim, who was right behind her. "How was everything?"

"Easy as pie, as you Americans say," he scoffed as he helped his wife up.

"Is that guy the dragon?" Ransom whispered to her.

"Yeah," she confirmed. "The silver one. The other one is Jade's husband."

"Oh, forgive my rudeness," Jade said. "Your Majesty, this is Isabelle Anderson, sister to our Alpha, Lucas Anderson. And her ..." Light green eyes squinted at Ransom.

"My mate, Ransom," Isabelle finished.

Jade's eyes lit up. "Oh."

"Mate?" Deedee asked. "As in, True Mate?"

"Yes."

"Congratulations, Isabelle," she replied, pulling her into a quick hug.

"Thank you, Your Majesty."

The other Lycan laughed. "Please. Just Deedee when it's us."

"Ransom and Isabelle were the ones who rescued Reed," Jade explained.

"Then we are in your debt," King Karim said with a slight nod of his head.

"I should go find my husband." Jade raised the bag slung over her shoulder. "I told him this time I was going to bring him his own clothes. Will you be all right, Lizzie?"

"I'll be okay, Mrs. Creed. I'll watch over him until the medics can get here." But, as soon as Jade was out of earshot, she leaned down and whispered into Wyatt's ear. "If you die today, I'm going to hack into your credit card and order ball gags and gimp suits and have them sent to your office. Or your parents' house."

"Er, we should go over there," Isabelle said. "I think I see Julianna and Adrianna there by those trees. You haven't met her yet. Your Majesties, please excuse us."

"Of course. We'll see you around, Isabelle," Deedee said.

They walked to her sisters, who were also with their respective mates.

"Isabelle!" Adrianna cried as she enveloped her in a hug. "It's been so long." Adrianna was Lupa of New Jersey which was why she didn't live in Manhattan, but also, since the mages had been after both her and Lucas, they had to stay separated at all times to reduce the risk of them being kidnapped together. "I've missed you."

"I've missed you too, sis. This is Ransom."

Adrianna placed her hands on her hips and raised a brow. "So, you're Ransom. I've heard a lot about you." Her mate,

Darius, stood behind her, silent as usual, but his expression was just as foreboding.

"Lupa," he bowed his head in respect. "It's nice to meet you."

"Huh." Her oldest sister's eyes narrowed at Ransom. "You're not what I expected."

While Adrianna could be the sweetest person in the world, she was also very intimidating as well as protective of her family. "Adrianna," Isabelle began. "He's my True Mate. And father to Evan and"—she slid her hand down to her belly—"Evan's baby brother or sister."

Adrianna's jaw nearly dropped to the ground. "Really?" She wrapped Isabelle up in another tight hug. "Oh, that's wonderful."

"My congratulations," Darius offered curtly. "It is a blessing to have an addition to our family."

"Ransom, this is my mate, Darius. And don't worry, his face is always like that," Adrianna joked. "He's just envious because he's been trying to get *me* knocked up for months."

"Diana will need a sibling soon," Darius explained matter-of-factly.

"What's your secret, Ransom?" Duncan piped in. "Asking for a friend."

"Don't even think about it, MacDougal. I'm definitely not having your litter any time soon." Julianna smacked him on the arm, then turned to Isabelle. "So, you finally told him?"

"It was pretty obvious," she retorted.

"Isabelle?"

Turning around, she saw her mother and father standing behind them. "Oh, my baby." Frankie reached out and pulled her into her arms. "Did I hear right? Are you really pregnant again?"

She nodded. "And by the way, thanks for the save, Mama."

"You know I'd do anything for you," Frankie said, tears in her eyes.

"Pregnant?" Grant rubbed the bridge of his nose with his thumb and forefinger, then let out a sigh. "I supposed that means only one thing." He reached his hand out. "Congratulations, son. I'm looking forward to seeing more of you."

Isabelle felt tears burning at her eyes when her father and Ransom shook hands sincerely. She knew there would be a lot of healing to be done, but it was a good start.

"We should go get Evan," Ransom said. "I think I see Daric over there."

After promising they'd return once they got their son back, they strode over to where the tall Viking-like warlock stood. But before they could reach him, a man and woman approached them.

"Isabelle, it's me, Elise. From San Francisco." Elise's electric blue eyes were shiny with tears. "I heard what you did for Reed, thank you."

The tall, dark-haired man beside her smiled at Isabelle and Ransom. "I can't thank you enough for saving my life," he said, his English accent posh and crisp. "I would have died without you."

"You're welcome," she said. "Ransom was the one who carried you out," she explained. "He's my True Mate."

"Splendid," Reed exclaimed, reaching his hand out and shaking hands with Ransom. "I owe you one."

"You're welcome in San Francisco, anytime," Elise said. "Now, if you excuse us, I have to go find my mom and dad."

They said their goodbyes and proceeded onward until they reached Daric, who was with his wife Meredith, as well as Astrid, Zac, and Gunnar.

"Stop hogging her!" Meredith groused at her husband, who held their granddaughter, Annaliese in his arms.

"You have had your turn," the warlock retorted. "And she prefers me."

"She does not," his mate replied. "Tell him, Astrid."

Astrid slapped a hand to her forehead and then took the child from Daric. "I'm her favorite, now stop it you two."

The young girl, who was probably over a year old, started wiggling in her mother's arms and clapped her hands together. "Unca Gaga! Unca Gaga!" She was reaching out to Gunnar.

"Well, call me a monkey's uncle." Relinquishing her hold on her daughter, Astrid let her youngest brother take her.

Gunnar took the child gingerly in his arms. "Hey, pumpkin."

"Unca Gaga!"

"She won't even say Mama, but she can call your name?" Astrid moaned. "Sometimes, I swear she annoys me on purpose."

"Gee, I wonder why," Meredith said with a smirk, which earned her a glare from her daughter.

"Sorry to barge in," Isabelle began. "But Cross said he took Evan to West Virginia with Annaliese."

"I saw your son there when I went to pick up my granddaughter," Daric said. "I didn't take him as I wasn't sure what your arrangement with Cross was."

"I'll call him and ask him—oh! There he is."

Walking toward them were Cross and Sabrina; Evan in Sabrina's arms. Excitement, worry, and pure joy all rushed through Isabelle as she sprinted toward them. "Evan!" Tears blinded her eyes, but she didn't care. "Oh, Evan." Sabrina relinquished her hold on Evan, and Isabelle held him tight, breathing in his scent. "My baby."

"Mama! Mama!" he shrieked enthusiastically as Isabelle kissed his cheeks. Ransom had caught up to her and wrapped his arms around them both, pressing a kiss to Evan's forehead and then hers.

"Th-Thank you," she said to Cross. "Is he all right? Did the sleeping potion have any effects?"

"Lily said he was dehydrated and in need of a changing, that's all," Cross said. "The potion should have no long-lasting effects."

Her shoulders relaxed, tension draining out of them. "Thank goodness."

Ransom's grip tightened on them. "I love you both so damned much," he whispered. "You're my heart. Both of you."

Ransom and Evan were her heart, too, and so was the new life growing inside her. While it felt like the time they had spent apart, the time Evan spent without his father, seemed like a waste, fate had brought them together again. And she would never take any moment for granted from now on.

"I love you," she murmured against his chest as she breathed in his scent.

"I—"

"What the fuck is that?" Meredith interrupted.

There was a loud mechanical noise overheard. It was rhythmic, like the rapid beating of a heart, going *chuf-chuf-chuf-chuf-chuf* at an accelerated pace.

As Isabelle looked up, the sun blinded her briefly, but something very large swayed to the side, and she realized what it was. "It's a helicopter."

"Did Lucas send for a chopper?" Astrid asked.

"That doesn't look like the Fenrir chopper," Isabelle said. "That's a—"

"News copter," Cross finished.

"Oh my," Sabrina gasped.

The chopper closing in on them had the bright blue logo of the local New York news station.

"Jesus fucking tangerine penguins!" Meredith cursed. "And—fucknuts, they're everywhere!"

Two more choppers had joined in, from the rival stations, plus about several news vans were racing toward them in the distance.

"Oh God, the human hostages." Astrid slapped her hand on her forehead. "They were all still under control of the necklace, and since we didn't have enough forgetting potion, we've been leaving them under its influence. One of them must have snapped out of it and called the cops."

"Or posted on their social media," Isabelle said.

"This is a nightmare," Astrid groaned. "We'll never be able to clean this up."

"We need to start transporting people out of here, son," Daric said to Cross. "Before this becomes an even bigger circus. Take Annaliese with you."

Cross turned to Ransom and Isabelle. "Come on, you can hitch with me and Sabrina."

Exhaustion was taking over her body, and frankly, Isabelle didn't really give a flying fig if the entire world knew about them right now. She had everything she wanted and needed, after all. "All right." She held onto Ransom tighter. "Let's go home."

"Which home?" Ransom asked. "Manhattan or Kentucky?"

"Don't forget," Gunnar added. "You're also the rightful Alpha of Connecticut."

"Hmm." Ransom rubbed his chin. "What do you think, Isabelle?"

"It doesn't matter," she rested her cheek on his chest and cuddled Evan closer. He reached up and patted Ransom on the cheek. "As long as we're all together."

EPILOGUE

TWO MONTHS LATER ...

RANSOM POURED HIMSELF A CUP OF COFFEE FROM THE pot and then walked over to the living area and sat down on the large leather couch facing the television. As the commercial faded to black, the screen lit up with the local morning show's bumpers before the anchor's face filled the screen.

"*Welcome back. And now,*" she began, "*we bring you news from Washington DC where the Senate hearings on the so-called 'Supernatural Beings' have come to their conclusion after three days of testimonies. Live from Capitol Hill, we have Dave Green. Dave?*"

"*Thanks, Shauna,*" the remote reporter greeted as he stood on the steps of the Capitol. "*Today marks the fourth and final day of the Senate subcommittee hearings on Supernatural Beings. If you recall, about two months ago, it was revealed the so-called Supernaturals—werewolves, dragons, and witches—have been living among humankind when videos surfaced of these creatures during a battle with their enemy forces now known as the 'mages.'*" The images turned into various wobbly cell phone videos from the battle —Lycans jumping on top of mages, witches throwing potions, and two large dragons flying overhead. *"Most of these videos came from the Three Hundred—a group of three hundred humans who were kidnapped by the mages—who had witnessed the entire incident."*

"So, Dave," Shauna interrupted. *"In the past three days, we've heard from several witnesses during the inquiries, including medical experts and representatives of some newly-formed anti-Supernatural groups, but also from the Supernaturals themselves, including Sebastian Creed, CEO of Creed Security, one of the largest privately-held security companies in the world, who also was revealed to be a shapeshifting dragon. Mr. Creed came to the hearing with his lawyers after he was served a subpoena, and questioned for over five hours."*

"Yes, Shauna. That was the highlight of the second day's hearings. Mr. Creed answered all of the committee's questions, though mostly they seemed to focus on his previous military contracts here in the US and abroad and if he has ever used his abilities while on contract, and not so much on his life as a dragon shifter. Some people have speculated that the committee did not ask him about this because of his past as a member of the US Marine Corps, though it's most likely that his lawyers were able to strike a deal with the committee beforehand to limit the questions."

"What about the news from the previous day about his resignation as CEO?" Shauna asked.

"Yes, the news that Sebastian Creed was retiring as CEO and appointing his son, Wyatt Creed in his stead, did certainly add more buzz to his upcoming testimony, with many analysts

speculating that he was collapsing under pressure and even predicting he might tear up the capitol. But after holding up under five hours of questioning and never once faltering or buckling, it seems Mr. Creed has not only proven that he was untroubled by the inquiry, but had now spawned the term 'cool as a dragon under fire.'"

The corners of Shauna's mouth turned up in a half smile. *"And we've all seen the memes. Speaking of dragons, it has also come out that Creed's son-in-law, King Karim of Zhobghadi, who made headlines last year when he married Dr. Desiree Creed, is also a dragon shapeshifter. Queen Desiree, as she is now known, is a supernatural being herself, a werewolf or 'Lycan' as they preferred to be called."*

"Well, King Karim was also invited by the subcommittee to testify, but he has politely declined." The screen changed to a graphic of a document with the royal seal of Zhobghadi on top. *"Instead, the government sent an official letter to the committee reminding them that '... Zhobghadi is a sovereign nation, and His Majesty is head of both the parliament and military. Any attempts to impose on our independence shall not be tolerated and will be met with equal force.' It remains to be seen if the Senate or POTUS will reply to the letter."*

"Now," Shauna continued. *"Lucas Anderson, CEO of Fenrir Corporation, the largest privately-held company in the world, also testified before the committee yesterday."*

"That's right, Shauna, and what a testimony it was. Anderson, the so-called Alpha of New York, did finish his testimony yesterday afternoon, right before the committee convened."

The screen changed to a view of one of the internal chambers in the capitol, before zooming in on the face of a man with graying hair and glasses, dressed in a dark suit, his face drawn into a grave expression. The nameplate in front of him read "Senator Greg Houseman."

"*Now, Mr. Anderson,*" the senator began. "*Let me ask you the question that everyone seems to be tiptoeing around: Are you and your kind a threat to the rest of humanity?*"

The camera focused on Lucas, who looked calm and collected, his hands folded in front of him. "*Let me put it this way, Senator,*" he said into the microphone. "*If we were, we wouldn't be here having this conversation now.*"

"*Wha-what do you mean?*" Houseman blustered.

Lucas unfolded his hands and leaned back in his chair. "*Think about it: We're faster, stronger, and we can heal from injuries, plus we have not one, but two dragons. Yet, we choose to live among humans in peace, and even count many of you as ours—whether as our True Mates or natural born human children. We prefer to live quiet lives, and in the history of Lycans, we have never sought to take over the rule of humans or acted as aggressors in war. Humans have always had the numbers, perhaps it's to keep the balance in nature, yet in the last hundred years or so, humankind has never been a more destructive force, overruling this planet with pollution, wars, sickness, greed, and lust of power and wealth. So maybe, the question isn't if we are a threat to humanity, but if humanity is a threat to us?*"

Senator Houseman's face turned red, while the rest of the committee, and the entire room, were stunned into silence.

When no one else spoke, Lucas continued. "*The only thing I can say is that if anyone wants to mess with us, they better be prepared.*"

"Are you watching that again?"

Ransom looked up from where he sat on the couch in front of the TV. Isabelle was coming down the stairs, Evan on her hip. "I can't help it," he said. "I just love watching Lucas wipe the floor with those assholes in the Senate. And he didn't even lift a fucking finger." He already had respect for the Alpha, but now, it had grown even more, especially with what had been happening in the last couple of weeks.

It had been a nightmare, being exposed to the world like that, and as always, his number one priority was his people. Isabelle and Evan had gone back home with him to Kentucky to escape the madness in New York with the paparazzi and the protests, but he knew he couldn't hide out forever. Silke was disheartened by the people who cancelled their reservations at the lodge that first month. But once it was known that she had Lycans living with her—and that she herself was a human child of a Lycan—people all over the country and the world were calling up for reservations, hoping to get a glimpse of the Supernatural beings. They were booked up for months in advance now. The rest of the MC, except for maybe Logan, seemed to be enjoying the attention, especially since the town had come to their support because of all the good they did for the community.

"God, I was so nervous I couldn't watch it without wanting to throw up," she declared.

"Are you okay?" He rushed to her side and placed a hand over her belly. "Maybe you should lie down. And you shouldn't be carrying Evan anymore, he's growing too big."

"Dada! Dada!" Evan cried, reaching up to Ransom. It never failed to make his chest puff up with pride, and frankly, he had teared up the first time he said it days ago.

"I'm fine," she grumbled, shifting Evan to her other hip

before he could take him. "There's still no bump, Ransom," she said as he possessively caressed her belly. "There won't be for a while."

Unable to stop himself, he knelt down. "I can't help it." He smoothed down the white linen of her sundress, and pressed a kiss to her stomach. "I missed it the first time with Evan, and I'm gonna enjoy every minute of this." He was looking forward to watching her belly grow with his child.

"You mean, every minute I'm fat?" She sighed unhappily. "You might change your tune a few months from now when we get to the gross parts of pregnancy."

"Never." How could she even think that? She was the most beautiful woman in the world. The white linen sundress she wore clung to her gorgeous body, the sun shining behind it just right to show off her curves.

She laughed as he kissed his way up from her belly to her lips as he stood up. "C'mon, let's go. Silke's already called three times." Turning to Evan, she nuzzled his cheek. "We can't let the birthday boy be late to his own party."

"Right." It seemed impossible that Evan was a year old. He'd missed so much of his life, and Ransom vowed he'd be there for his son and all his kids for as long as he could. "Let's go."

They got into his truck, with Evan strapped safely in the back, and made their way to the lodge. It was a beautiful summer day in the Kentucky mountains. The grass seemed greener and the air sweeter, though Ransom knew it was probably because for the first time in his life, he truly was happy.

"It's so gorgeous out here." Isabelle said, as if echoing his thoughts.

"So, you're not regretting moving out here with me?"

Her smile was even brighter than the sun. "Of course not. I'd move to Timbuktu if you wanted me to. But how about you? Do you regret not taking over as Alpha of Connecticut?"

He looked up at the road ahead. "No, not at all. That place ... I was born there, but I have no other connection there. I don't know the people or the territory. They're better off under Cooper."

Adam Cooper, the current Alpha, had taken over a few years ago when his uncle Logan had died. Cooper had apologized on behalf of his clan for what happened to them, but Ransom recognized that neither he nor his father was to blame. It had been chaos when Grayson Charles had been imprisoned and they suddenly scrambled to keep their clan intact. While it was sad, the truth was, it was mere oversight. But the past was past, and Ransom had let go long ago, the moment he decided to live for his mate and children.

"Have you thought about the council's offer?" Isabelle asked.

"I have, actually." Though he had declined the Connecticut territory, the Lycan High Council had offered to incorporate the Southeast Kentucky territory as a clan, with him as Alpha. This was a first in a very long time the Council offered to make a new clan and Alpha, and certainly the first ever for a Lone Wolf to be offered such a position. His first instinct, of course, was to decline.

"And?" she pressed.

"And I'm seriously considering it. Your father advised me to do it."

"Hold on." She held a hand up. "*My* father? You've been talking to my father?"

"Mm-hmm." He guided the vehicle onto the road that led to the lodge.

Grant and Frankie had visited several times over the past couple of weeks to help Isabelle and Evan settle in. He had taken the opportunity to ask the former Alpha his thoughts on the offer. "He says I should do it in case things get sticky with the humans. The national government is close to recognizing the High Council as an official organization that represents the Lycans, so it would at least show the local authorities that everything's above board and keep the heat off us, plus take off any Lone Wolf stigma."

Grant had also said that the members of the MC obviously already considered him their Alpha anyway, plus with an Alpha status and a formal territory, he could offer other Lone Wolves protection. That was probably the part that enticed him the most as he knew it was something Pops would have done if he could.

She raised a dark brow. "Anything else you guys talked about behind my back?"

There was *one* more thing, but he didn't want to ruin the surprise. "Wow," he said as they neared the lodge. "You and Silke really went all out, huh?"

The entire front of the lodge was decorated with balloons, streamers, and banners, in all shades of blue. There were big blue and white letters on the front lawn that spelled out 'Evan', plus a small petting zoo, a bouncy castle, and even a carousel.

"It was mostly Silke," Isabelle laughed. "I think she had more fun than me."

As if on cue, his sister bounded out of the lodge to meet

them. "There you are!" she greeted. "Where's the birthday boy?"

Ransom was already unstrapping Evan out of his seat when Silke practically threw him aside to get him out. "Oooh, Evan, I missed you."

"You were just at our place last night," Ransom pointed out.

She covered his face with kisses. "Didja miss me, baby?"

Evan laughed and grabbed fistfuls of her red locks, tugging at it like he always did.

"Is everyone here?" Isabelle asked.

"Almost," Silke said. "Cross and Daric are running transport for your guests who aren't staying the night." Isabelle's family arrived earlier in the day and had settled into their cabins as they were going to be there for the weekend. "Oh, my God, I still can't believe I have *actual* royalty and dragons here in the lodge! The king is *sooooooo* hot and the queen is really sweet. Have you seen their son, the prince? Absolutely gorgeous, but," she kissed Evan again. "Not as handsome as my Evan."

Isabelle laughed. "Let's go say hi to them."

"Give me a sec," Ransom said. "I need to talk to Silke for a bit."

She nodded at him and then proceeded into the lodge.

"Are you okay with having him for the night?" Ransom asked Silke.

"Am I?" she asked. "Of course I am. Evan and I are going to have so much fun, aren't we?"

He had no doubt that Silke was the best person to leave Evan with for the evening, as it was obvious his sister loved him. Of course, he couldn't help feel that twinge of sadness, because he knew how much Silke wanted a child of her own and was robbed of that opportunity. It was a sensitive topic, and they never talked about it, but he knew how much it hurt her. Maybe someday, Silke could adopt, or maybe even find a husband of her own who would love her enough to get past all the walls she'd put up around herself. For now, he would do his best to protect her and ensure her happiness.

"Are you nervous?" she asked, giddy.

"Me? Naw." Of course, his palms started sweating, but he pretended he was brushing some lint off his jeans as they strode into the lodge. The inside of the lobby was just as excessively decorated as the outside, and four huge tables were heaving with food, courtesy of the new chef Silke had hired upon the recommendation of Dante Muccino.

"Ransom!" Isabelle called from where she was talking with Lucas, Sofia, and Alessandro by the fireplace.

"Alpha," Ransom greeted, but took the offered hand. "I saw you on TV yesterday."

"Who hasn't?" Sofia quipped. "It's all over the news. They play it all the time, even at the station. Everyone cheers when they show the senators look like they're shitting their pants."

Lucas rolled his eyes. "Hey, they asked, I answered."

"Isabelle, there you are!" Maxine Muccino sauntered up to them, her smile bright as she embraced her cousin. "I've been looking all over for you." She went up to Evan and kissed him on the cheek. "There's my godson! How are you, Evan? Happy Birthday!"

The younger Lycan reminded Ransom a lot of his mate the first time they met, with her designer clothes and glossy hair. Isabelle said they had been very similar in the past, but had drifted apart. He was glad to see the two cousins and best friends had mended their relationship.

"Hey, Maxine, are you enjoying the lodge?" Ransom asked.

"Yeah, but I had to change into my flats," she nodded at her shoes. "My heels keep sinking in the ground. There's so much soil here. Anyway, I just wanted to say hi. Axle says he's going to take me for a ride on his bike."

Ransom groaned. "Just be careful, okay?"

But Maxine had already trotted off, presumably to go on a ride with Axle.

"Her and Axle?" Isabelle shook her head. "I just can't see it."

"Hey, stranger things have happened," he said meaningfully. "But don't worry, he'll tread carefully." Maxine, after all, was family, and Axle knew better. He was a flirt, but he wouldn't encroach on *that* territory. Besides, he didn't know if there was any girl who could make the charmer change his ways.

"C'mon, I'm starving!" Isabelle declared. "Let's eat."

The rest of the party proceeded with much eating, drinking, and merriment. Everyone in New York and their allies had been invited and the clan came out in full force. Even Jared and John were there, along with their three adopted children. Annie was thrilled with all the babies around her and begged her father for a baby sister or brother, much to Hardy's chagrin.

As the day turned to evening, things started to wind down, though there was still much food and cake left, so people lingered about. Ransom was exhausted, but happy, though the night wasn't done yet, at least not for him and

Isabelle. With Evan in his arms, he handed him off to Silke and murmured his thanks before going in search of his mate. He found her chatting with Julianna and Duncan near the bouncy castle.

"Can I steal you for a second?" he asked.

Julianna eyed him warily. "Before you do, let me just tell you one thing."

He knew Julianna was very protective of Isabelle. "All right. What is it?"

Mismatched blue-green eyes flashed at him. "I've told Isabelle over and over that she can always change her mind, and if she does, she and Evan have a place with us." Duncan nodded in agreement.

He wanted to shout, *over my dead body*, but controlled himself. "I know the two of you have been her support throughout her pregnancy and after Evan was born. For that, I'll never be able to repay you. But from now on, I'll be the one taking care of her and Evan, and all of our future pups." Julianna open her mouth to say something but he held up a hand to stop her. "If I ever hurt her or Evan, you don't have to kick my ass. I'll do it myself first."

Julianna stared at him. "All right." She patted him on the arm. "Glad we're in agreement."

"Let's go to the bouncy castle, darlin'," Duncan said. "I don't see any kids in there, anymore."

"Just what are you planning, MacDougal?"

"Och, just you wait and see." Suddenly, Duncan hoisted her up over his shoulder, fireman-style. Julianna shrieked, but let out a laugh as her mate smacked her behind and carried her off.

Isabelle shook her head. "Those two. Anyway, did you need something, Ransom? Is it Evan?"

"No, princess. Don't worry, everything is fine. I wanted to show you something." He tugged at her hand. "Come with me?"

"Of course." She followed him as he led her around the outside of the lodge, where he had left his bike parked this morning. "You're showing me your bike?" she asked, a confused look on her face.

He straddled the bike and turned to her. "Why don't you ask me for a ride, princess?" he said, hoping to jog her memory of that first night they met.

She must have remembered, because her face lit up. "Give me a ride?"

He held his hand out, and when she took it, pulled her to him. "Oh, I'm going to give you a ride, all right." She giggled. "You're still not dressed for riding."

"Is this better?" She hiked her skirt up, flashing him those shapely thighs he'd been dreaming about all day.

His cock twitched in anticipation. "Much. Hop on."

When she settled in behind him and wrapped her arms around his waist, he zoomed off. His vision immediately adjusted to the darkness as he drove on a worn path that headed straight into the hills.

The bike climbed higher, until they reached the flat clearing on top of a crest. It was almost completely dark out here, with only the full moon and stars to light them.

"Where are we?" Isabelle asked.

"I used to come out here with Silke and Pops when I was younger to watch the stars. Sometimes ... Joanie would join us too." He swallowed the lump growing in his throat.

She soothed a hand down his arm but said nothing. Not that she needed to.

Joanie, as he predicted, was sent to the Lycan prison in Siberia, as his father had. However, both Grant and Isabelle had spoken during her hearing and asked for clemency. The Council considered their testimonies, and instead of giving her a life sentence, had it reduced to ten years. He hadn't spoken to her at all, even though he attended the hearing, and Joanie hadn't answered his letters or request to see her. He just hoped his mother needed time, and maybe someday, they could at least talk.

"Ransom?"

He cleared his throat. "Sorry." He took her hand and dragged her toward the center of the ridge, where a picnic basket and a blanket were already laid out.

"Did you plan this?" she asked, her eyes widening.

"Mm-hmm." He tugged her onto the blanket. "Finally," he whispered. "I have you alone."

"Ransom," she purred as he nuzzled her neck and reached for the straps of her dress to push it down. "Oh ..."

He made love to her slowly, yet eagerly until she was crying out in pleasure. When he was spent and done, he rolled onto his back and held her close, looking up at the blanket of summer stars above them shining so bright without any light pollution to dim their glow.

"Should we get back soon?" She was tracing patterns on his chest. "Evan—"

"Is in Silke's safe hands," he finished, grabbing her hand to kiss her fingers. "She knows we'll be out here for a while."

"For a while, huh?" She raised a brow at him. "What else did you have planned?"

"Actually ..." He quickly got to his feet and pulled her up with him, then reached over into the picnic basket, feeling around for the box he'd placed in there before he took off his clothes. Finding it, he took it out.

She gasped when he got down on one knee and presented her with the diamond ring. "Ransom ..."

"I know you're already my True Mate," he began. "And I'll be forever grateful to fate for bringing you to me. But I want you to be mine and for me to be yours in every way possible. I'd marry you every day for the rest of my life if that would prove how much I love you, but just once would make me happy. So, whaddaya say, princess?"

"I ... of course! I mean, yes." She let out a small squeal when he put the ring on.

"Do ... do you like it?" He'd ask Frankie for advice on rings after he'd come to her and Grant for their blessing. She said to pick whatever he thought would suit her, so of course, it was a princess cut diamond.

"It's perfect," she said breathlessly. "And I love you."

"I love you more." When he tugged her back down on the blanket, she let out a squeal. "You're my heart, Isabelle." He placed her hand on his chest so she could feel the steady beating.

"And you're mine." She kissed him on the lips and cuddled up to him.

His wolf sighed, content at last with their mate. Fate, he thought, was a funny thing. But it seemed to know what it was doing, so who was he to question it?

The stars above them twinkled in agreement.

———

Thank you so much for going on this journey with me. It's been a privilege to tell these stories.

I love hearing from readers! Drop me a line at alicia@alicia-montgomeryauthor.com anytime.

I have some extra HOT bonus scenes for you that weren't featured in this book - just join my newsletter here to get access:

http://aliciamontgomeryauthor.com/mailing-list/

You'll get access to ALL the bonus materials from all my books and my **FREE** novella **The Last Blackstone Dragon.**

Thanks so much for reading!

All my love,

Alicia

ABOUT THE AUTHOR

Alicia Montgomery has always dreamed of becoming a romance novel writer. She started writing down her stories in now long-forgotten diaries and notebooks, never thinking that her dream would come true. After taking the well-worn path to a stable career, she is now plunging into the world of self-publishing.

facebook.com/aliciamontgomeryauthor

twitter.com/amontromance

bookbub.com/authors/alicia-montgomery